ARLENE HUNT

WHILE SHE SLEEPS

HACHETTE
BOOKS
IRELAND

First published in Ireland in 2022 by HACHETTE BOOKS IRELAND

1

Cataloguing in Publication Data is available from the British Library

Trade paperback ISBN 978 1 47369 952 6
Ebook ISBN 978 1 47369 955 7

Typeset in Georgia by Bookends Publishing Services, Dublin
Printed and bound in Great Britain by Clays Ltd, Elcograf, S.p.A.

Hachette Books Ireland policy is to use papers that are natural, renewable
and recyclable products and made from wood grown in sustainable forests.
The logging and manufacturing processes are expected to conform to the
environmental regulations of the country of origin.

Hachette Books Ireland
8 Castlecourt Centre
Castleknock
Dublin 15, Ireland

A division of Hachette UK Ltd
Carmelite House, 50 Victoria Embankment, EC4Y 0DZ

www.hachettebooksireland.ie

WHILE SHE SLEEPS

To Jennie Ridyard

1

November

Jody Kavanagh sat on the edge of her bathtub, staring at her bare feet. She was studying her toes, concentrating on their shape. She had nice feet and took care of them. Even now, despite everything that had gone on throughout the year, she made sure she took the time to have a pedicure once a month.

As always, appearance was everything.

The dog, Cooper, stood in the doorway watching her, his head tilted ever so slightly. Jody had never owned a dog before Cooper, had never realised how intelligent dogs could be, how empathetic. He seemed to understand her in a way most people did not.

It was a little alarming, if she was honest. Being so transparent to an animal.

She looked at him now. 'What?'

He made a soft huffing sound in the back of his throat and backed up two steps.

Jody sighed. 'All right.'

Together they went downstairs. Jody put the kettle on and let him out into the back garden while it boiled. She watched him patrol the perimeter, sniffing, cocking his leg here and there, watched him check the back gate.

He was thorough.

Worth every penny.

To keep her mind busy, she put the radio on, made a cup of breakfast tea and drank it standing at the island, staring into the middle distance. Her mobile phone vibrated twice in the charger: she ignored it.

She drained the last of her tea, let Cooper back in and they went upstairs.

The pregnancy test was where she had left it, resting on the edge of the sink, like a foreign artefact.

Slowly, as though approaching danger, she sidled towards it. Before she read it, she closed the door on Cooper, mouthing 'Sorry'.

This was a private moment.

She opened her palm and stared.

Two clear lines.

Two lines that changed everything.

She stood up abruptly and tossed the test into the bin by the sink. Outside, the morning traffic was building. People going about their day, oblivious to this rip in the fabric of the universe.

Jody stared at her reflection, allowed her mind wander in search of an emotion that could adequately cover this occasion. She found precisely what she was searching for. A fresh, exciting sensation, coupled with one word.

Mine.

2

Fiona Hynes felt her husband get out of bed, and she lay as still as possible. She heard him get dressed, heard the morning sounds he made, sounds that used to make her laugh but no longer did. Heard his heavy tread as he made his way from their bed to the bedroom door, heard him open it and close it without bothering to be quiet. Heard the creak of the loose floorboard on the landing, and then when she was certain he was gone, she turned onto her back and allowed herself to breathe normally.

Things between them had been strained since the last miscarriage. Malcolm had initially been supportive, though she sensed his anger, his disappointment. Now it was time, he said, to try again, time to refill the vessel.

The night before he had taken her, even as she protested, pleading exhaustion. He had forced her legs apart and lay on top of her. When he was finished, he kissed her hard on the mouth – too hard – rolled over and fell asleep, his work done, his seed spent.

Fiona forced her fist against her teeth and bit her knuckles, savouring the pain. Maybe she deserved pain for what she had done.

Monstrous.

Evil.

God should strike her down.

Not that anyone at the homestead seemed to care how she felt, she thought bitterly. Judith, Malcolm's mother, seemed to take a malicious delight in what she saw as Fiona's failing as a woman. Malcolm's three sisters, big blousy woman who toiled day and night under the guise of cheerfulness, paid little heed to her at the best of times, and less when she was fretful. To them, pregnancy and childbirth came under the catch-all umbrella of 'God's will'. They never thought to question it nor wonder about any deviations. Miscarriage was sad, but it was part of the Divine plan.

They bore up. They filled the quivers with God's arrows.

Fiona allowed herself to drift. The children would be awake soon and so would begin the day proper: hours of food and fights, of washing and scrubbing, of arguments and temper tantrums, of weepy apologies, of cuddles, making food, more food, drinks, energy draining, energy she had little to spare, until night fell and she could escape them, escape them all until he came home, looking for a final scrap of what she had left.

Better to be dead, she thought, staring into the darkness. Better for everyone.

Better for her.

A sin.

Guilt weighed heavily on her mind, pressing down like an anvil. She would never be free of it, never be able to walk a day in the sun without it trailing her like a stray dog. Guilt and regret, two sides of the great spiritual coin.

Under the covers she pressed her hand against her stomach. Flat. The seed was still travelling to find haven, to create life anew. How that must feel, she thought, to have no tarnish, to have no past; new and fresh, potential made form, made flesh as God intended.

She heard a child cry out.

Time to move.

The covers were heavy and casting them aside brought the familiar shock of cold. The farmhouse was old and dilapidated with no central heating. Malcolm's father had bought it back in the sixties, declaring it an oasis in a sea of sin. Enoch Hynes had a vision. He would raise his children under the only law he recognised: God's Law. Men provided, women submitted, children were the blessing.

The farmhouse stood now, all angles and draughts, dark corners that never welcomed the sun. Fiona had thought it was charming the first time she'd laid eyes on it – it had been summer, and warmth and climbing roses were admirable stage dressing. Winter revealed the truth, paring existence back to the bare bones and bitter cold.

Marriage had proven much the same.

Sometimes, Fiona watched for the lights of her husband's truck and felt an overwhelming urge to take down the shotgun that rested on top of the highest press, load both barrels and wait with her finger poised on the trigger for him to enter the back door. She imagined his dark head ducking under the low stone mantel. She imagined telling him she was leaving, her and the children, that she had tried but she had not signed up for this life. Oh, he would be surprised and dismissive. But she would persist. And in the end, her demeanour of certain, quiet determination would make him understand that she meant business.

Well, that and the gun.

In those daydream thoughts, Fiona's voice did not shake, nor her body quake. She would pack the children into the rust bucket and drive ...

Where?

Anywhere but here.

Jody would help, wouldn't she? Jody understood the way of the world. She could guide Fiona to a new path, a new destiny.

Save her.

A creak outside the door: a child's hesitation.

'What is it?' she called.

'Rachel got sick.'

Fiona put on her robe, walked to the door and opened it.

Sarah stood in her pyjamas, bare foot, hair mussed, button nosed and pretty. She had turned ten in September, a bright child but quiet for her age, watchful even. Fiona worried about her.

A lot.

She took Sarah's hand and together they walked across the landing to the bedroom she shared with her sisters – Eve who was nine, Leah who was seven and Rachel who was eighteen months old. Their six-year-old brother had a box room next door all to himself, and when Fiona checked, Joshua was still asleep, flat on his back, blissfully unaware of the unfolding drama. A tiny part of Fiona's brain, a sliver, a whisper, thought, *Well, of course, uncaring like his father*. A sick child was women's work.

Menial.

She chased the thought away, threw mental stones at it. The boy was a child, there was still time.

Rachel was sitting up in her cot, forlorn. When she saw Fiona, her little face crumpled with despair. Only a year and a half and already an old soul. Fiona's mini-me.

'I sick on my baby,' she said, holding the vomit-covered doll aloft.

'It's okay,' Fiona said. 'It's okay.'

She reached in and lifted Rachel into her arms, carried her and her 'baby' to the bathroom at the end of the hall, where she put the doll in the sink and sat on the toilet with Rachel on her lap. The child's forehead felt hot to the touch and her pyjamas were damp with sweat.

'Do you feel sick?'

Rachel nodded, put her thumb in her mouth and leaned against her. Fiona hugged the child and rocked her gently. Sarah stood at the bathroom door, watching.

'All right,' Fiona said after a moment. 'Sarah, go wake your brother and help the girls get dressed. I'm going to drop you to Gamma's house—'

Sarah's face fell.

'It's only for a little while.'

'I can watch them.'

'Do as I say.'

Twenty minutes later they crossed the yard to her mother-in-law's home, a converted barn. It was far warmer and nicer than the main house – not that it mattered to Judith, who complained endlessly about living there. She opened the door wearing a sour expression that increased as Fiona explained the situation.

'Doctor? She doesn't need a doctor.' She peered at the toddler. 'Give her a nip of prune juice, grind some ginger and add—'

'I'm taking her to the doctor. She keeps getting sick.'

'Probably all that muck you let her drink, full of e-numbers and chemicals.'

'I'll be back as soon as I can,' Fiona said, shooing the children inside.

Fiona put Rachel in her car seat and reversed out of the yard without waving. It was all she could do not to give her mother-in-law the finger, and sure what good would that do anyway? Why give her any more ammunition?

The GP's office was in town and wouldn't be open until nine. Dr Sullivan was a lovely man, but Fiona dreaded going to see him, dreaded the small talk, the questions, the terrifying receptionist who seemed to think Fiona had a learning difficulty and needed things to be explained in a slow and condescending voice.

Fiona drove without thinking. She put the radio on, glanced in the rear-view mirror and saw Rachel was asleep, one pudgy hand clenched tight around her hastily washed doll.

At last, some time to herself.

She left the motorway and drove along the coast road, pulling in to a rocky outcrop overlooking the sea. She got out and stood with her face to the wind, her hair blowing wild, the gulls wheeling overhead, riding the currents with effortless grace.

She could end it right now, take a few steps, nothing to it. The drop was enough, the rocks sharp enough, the sea wild enough.

All of it, enough.

All she need do, her end of the bargain, was take the steps.

Fly.

But when she closed her eyes, she saw Sarah's face and knew she would not walk further that day. She would go home, clean, scrub, wash clothes, make food.

Endure.

She would endure.

For now.

3

Monday

It was the fall that did it: the simple stupid accident that had irrevocably undermined his authority with the zeal of a slashing machete. One minute Elliot Ryan was an independent man, sober, upright – all right, a widower, but not a tragic one. He owned a semi-D in Castleknock; drove a decent car; had a full head of hair and a job with a title that still garnered respect, though even that was waning thanks in no part to an endless 'ACAB' narrative whipped up by cretins on social media, the same spineless twerps who'd shit their pants if they had to deal with a fraction of the things he'd endured over a near twenty-five-year career and—

He leaned on the sink and pressed his forehead against the mirror.

Stop.

Nothing to be done now, the annoying inner voice chirped. *Think of your blood pressure; remember what the doctor told you about getting angry.*

Sod off, he thought and paused. Arguing with the voice, that was new. He'd have to keep an eye on that. Here be dragons.

Still, there was no denying it *would* have been different if it hadn't been for the bloody fall; if Pauline, his next-door neighbour (nice woman, wouldn't hear a bad word against her, et cetera), hadn't been home that day; if she hadn't called for an ambulance. If *they* hadn't called for the fire brigade.

If he hadn't gone out there in the first place, half cut with a rusty saw and an untrustworthy ladder, none of it would have happened. Why on earth had he decided to drink? He'd hardly touched the stuff in years. Because he was upset? Was that his excuse?

Stupid.

Bone-headed stupidity.

Galling.

One fall, one stupid accident, and his carefully constructed façade had crumbled as though riddled with mica.

'Dad?'

He stared at his face in the mirror and tried to ignore the hunted look in his eyes.

'Dad?'

'I'll be out in a minute.'

He didn't move a muscle until he heard her footsteps on the stairs, heard the kitchen door open, heard music, because God forbid anyone should start the day with some quiet reflection ...

Stop it.

Don't blame Shona, she's doing her best.

He finished shaving and cleaned the rest of the foam off his chin with a facecloth (bending over the sink was still light years away). On his way back to his bedroom he refused to use the walls for balance and kept his torso as steady as a masthead. He might be down, but by God he was not out.

10

Dressing was a complicated affair, though he'd learned some tricks since his release from the hospital. His suit was laid out on the bed, his shirt and tie next to it, socks pre-rolled for ease of slippage. He had replaced his usual brogues with loafers, and while he didn't necessarily think that loafers were a good fit with his job, beggars and the injured could not be choosers.

There was, he had to admit, something to be said for the girdle the hospital had furnished. It was a lightweight piece of equipment with two Velcro straps, and it gave him a pleasing shape when worn under his vest and shirt. Not that he was vain – at his age there wasn't much point – but there was nothing wrong with a bit of self-improvement.

Elliot lay back on the bed and slid his feet into the legs of his pants and used a metal coat hanger to slide them up to his thighs. From there he could roll – carefully – onto his stomach and push himself upright with one arm while holding the blasted pants with the other. This had taken a certain level of trial and error to master, but he had the hang of it now.

Up, shirt tucked, buttons fastened. Now for the socks. They were a struggle, and an ungainly one at that, but he managed.

Christ, why was he sweating so much?

Probably your heart, the voice suggested. *Didn't your old man die of heart disease?*

Shut up.

Elliot glanced at the plastic pack of tablets on the bedside dresser. The prescription said he was to take no more than six tablets per twenty-four hours: he had already taken two. How the hell was he supposed to space them out over an entire working day?

Loafers on, tie on, jacket ... better leave that until he cooled down.

A quick brush of the hair, dab of aftershave and he was no longer 'Local man rescued in bizarre accident' but had become Detective Inspector Elliot Ryan.

Finally, he took a small red diary with gold lettering from the drawer of his bureau and slipped it into the interior pocket of his jacket. He felt the weight of it against his chest, a solid reminder that he had made a promise and he intended to keep it.

'Dad, come on! Your breakfast is getting cold.'

Instantly deflated, he hooked his jacket over his arm and made his way – carefully – down the stairs. Shona was bustling around his kitchen, already dressed, primed and armed for the day.

'Honestly, Dad, when was the last time you had a clear-out?'

'A clear-out of what?' He eased himself down onto a chair and looked with some dismay at his 'breakfast'. Fruit? Yoghurt? And a slice of what looked like plasterboard masquerading as bread.

'These presses, Dad, they're full of crap.'

He opened his mouth to complain but Shona was standing by the window trying to read a label on a jar. She was twenty-eight years old, dark-haired like him, short and sturdy like her late mother. A no-nonsense woman, efficient and capable.

Terrifying.

'I knew it,' she said, '2011.'

'What is this?' He poked the bread with his finger; it was stiff as a board.

'It's pumpkin-seed bread.'

'There should be a sliced pan in the freezer.'

'There isn't – I gave it to the birds.'

Elliot was outraged. 'Why?'

'Because it's white processed crap ... and what's this? This one is from 2008? Why would you keep a jar of capers from 2008? What are you keeping them for? Zombie attack? Armageddon? You're going to survive on out-of-date capers?'

'I don't – now hold on a second. What's this?'

'Butter.'

'This doesn't look like butter.'

'That's because it's plant based.'

'Shona, I may not be the sharpest knife in the drawer right now, but even I know butter starts out with a cow.'

'Why do you have so many tins of Spaghetti Hoops? Do you even eat Spaghetti Hoops?'

'Yes.'

'I've never seen you eat Spaghetti Hoops in my life.'

Elliot ignored her and smeared whatever the plant-based goop was over his single slice of rock-hard toast. He took a bite, chewed and put it down. This was not good; this was so far from good, good wasn't even invited to the plate.

'What time will you be home?' Shona glanced at her watch. 'I've got to head into the clinic for a few hours, but I'll be back in time to make dinner.'

'Oh no, don't go to any trouble on my behalf. I can grab a takeaway.'

She fixed him with an all-too-familiar expression. 'Dad, we agreed on this.'

Elliot felt aggrieved. Agreed? Agreed? He'd been off his head on morphine, a sitting patsy, and she'd come at him like a cobra. Now he was caught, trapped in the coils of her predatory concern.

'Shona, I can manage on my own.'

'Yeah, I can see that. If you hadn't fallen off a ladder you could have poison-caper-ed yourself to death.'

'I had an accident.'

'I read the hospital report.' She glared at him, the challenge open, the gauntlet thrown down.

He felt his heart speed up. The damned report. Evidence of his weakness. There were no words powerful enough to stop her.

'Until you're back properly on your feet I'm staying here, and I'd like you to recognise that your inability to ask for or accept help should not be a source of pride.'

Elliot winced. Shona had recently taken up with a therapist called Johann who seemed a nice enough fellow, a little quiet, a bit wishy-washy. Elliot wasn't exactly sure what his daughter saw in him, but he was beginning to suspect she was mining him for ammunition to use against the rest of the world, including him.

'Half-eight, I'll be back at half-eight at the latest.'

She smiled. 'Excellent. Now eat your fruit. I've packed you a salad for lunch – don't forget to bring the Tupperware home.'

He ate his fruit. Some battles were worth fighting and some were not.

4

Nola Kane opened her eyes.

It took a moment before the reality of her situation dawned hard and fast.

Oh no.

The man next to her muttered something in his sleep and turned over onto his side. Nola slid out of the unfamiliar bed and searched around the unfamiliar floor for her clothes, desperate not to make a sound. There were many bad things in the world, but morning small talk after a one-night stand was right up there with the worst.

Eventually she gathered her clothes up and retreated to the bathroom, where she locked the door and dressed. A quick glance in the mirror over the sink confirmed she looked as bad as she felt.

Crap.

She left the unfamiliar apartment, went downstairs and out of the building. It was still dark, the street empty, no cabs or buses to be seen. She walked nearly a mile before she managed to flag a taxi, so by the time she got home her mother was already up.

'Where were you until this hour?'

'Out.'

'Out where?'

'Just out, Ma.'

'Look at cut of you and you back in work today. What are you doing with your life?'

'No time.' Nola chugged a coffee and ran upstairs to the bedroom she shared with her sister. She stripped, showered and dressed as quickly as she could, brushed her teeth and ran back downstairs again as the doorbell rang.

She reached the door before her mother and yanked it open. Gracie Conway stood on the front step looking disgustingly fresh as a daisy.

'Morning,' she said. 'Ready to go?'

'Yeah, give me a—'

'Good morning, Gracie!'

'Good morning, Mrs Kane.'

Nola's mother elbowed her aside. 'Do you have time for a cup of tea? I've the kettle on.'

'Oh, no thank you, Mrs K. We'd better get shaking.'

Nola grabbed her rucksack from the end of the stairs. 'See ya, Ma.'

'Do you have your phone charger? What time will you be home? Will I put on—?'

Nola kissed her mother firmly on the cheek. 'Bye.'

She pulled the door shut and scowled. 'Don't.'

'Don't what?' Gracie grinned and spread her hands, all innocence personified.

'You know what.'

They crossed the street to Gracie's ancient Golf. Nola opened the passenger door and grimaced at the state of the interior. Because Gracie lived in a three-bedroomed house with six other

16

professionals, she spent a lot of time in this car, eating and making out with her weird culchie boyfriend, Tadgh. Biohazard didn't adequately cover it.

Gracie got in and started the engine. 'What time did you get home?'

'About an hour ago.'

'Should I ask?'

'I'd rather you didn't.'

They left the cul-de-sac and motored up the hill towards the bridge.

'Why didn't you tell me *he* was going to be there?' Nola said accusingly. No need for either of them to mention *him* by name. They both knew who she was talking about. Paul Deacon, a colleague and – until very recently – her boyfriend.

'I *didn't* know.'

'Yeah, right.'

'I swear, I had no idea he was going to be there.'

'You must have mentioned something.'

'I swear, Nola, okay?'

Gracie pulled away from the path. Nola leaned against the head rest and shut her eyes. She liked Gracie – they'd met in garda college and clicked straight away – but that didn't mean she trusted every word out of her friend's mouth. Nola Kane didn't trust *anyone* completely.

Not any more.

Her stomach roiled and the palms of her hands grew sweaty. 'I need to get something to eat.'

'You can grab something from the garage – we've got time.' Gracie slowed for a set of lights. 'Tell you what, Deacon couldn't keep his eyes off you all night.'

'He can stick his eyes up his hole.'

Gracie sighed. 'I think he's sorry, you know?'

Nola's head snapped around. 'Sorry?'

'You know, for how things turned out.'

The ember of internal rage fanned to life. 'Nothing *turned out*, Gracie,' Nola snapped. 'That cheating bastard nearly cost me my job.'

'You decking Samantha Copeland nearly cost you your job. You're lucky she didn't—'

'Whose side are you on?'

'Yours, of course.'

'You don't act like it.'

'I'm just saying—'

'Well, don't.'

'Right,' Gracie said quickly. 'Let's drop it.'

'Out of line.'

'Right.'

'I don't want to talk about it.'

The lights changed; they drove on.

'Well, at least you won't have to see him, now that you're moving to—'

'I don't want to talk about *that* either.'

'Right.' Gracie fell silent.

Nola glared out the window, fuming. It was her first day back after suspension and she was supposed to be excited? Excited about leaving (or being forced out of?) Homicide to work in the dregs with the rest of stiffs. Excited she'd put her career in jeopardy over a cheating rat-bastard? Sure, she was excited, so excited she could puke.

5

Elliot parked the Passat in the yard of the old station and entered the vast new station, overlooking a busy inner-city junction. He had, unlike many of his colleagues, liked the old station house and felt the new one, while admittedly modern and high-tech, lacked even a semblance of a soul, though of course he kept this rather fanciful notion to himself.

Several officers glanced his way when they saw him, one or two even nodded politely, but Elliot kept his gaze forward, his bearing upright. He knew he was considered an oddity among many of the rank and file. His nickname was, rather unkindly, the Fossil, and he had once overheard himself described in the men's bathroom as a 'queer fish'. The description offended him until he mentally redrafted it as 'one who swims against the tide'. After that he wore it like a badge of honour.

A first day back after medical leave meant he had to re-register with the main desk and get his clearance reinstated. Although he knew he had to comply with regulations, it irked him. Twenty-five years as part of an institution did that to a man. In the old days he'd have strode in no questions asked, but now everything was layers of red tape and hierarchy, every man for himself within the walls.

He put a lot of the blame for this on Assistant Commissioner Andrew Stall, a rail-thin hatchet-faced blade of ambition who'd sell his soul to the highest bidder if it meant he clawed another rung higher on the corporate ladder. No one trusted Stall; no one felt safe around him, and with good reason. The man's loyalty was to Ivan Dell, the minister for justice. Stall had no time for old donkeys like him and Elliot knew it.

Well, so what? In a few months he'd collect his pension and retire, take up a hobby or something.

Or something – the inner voice was leaden sarcasm.

Manning the main desk that morning was Sergeant Bill Givens, a behemoth and older than rock. He looked surprised to see Elliot and eyed his approach with impolite scrutiny. 'You're walking funny.'

'Am I?'

'Yeah, are you sure you're supposed to be back so soon? I heard you only got out Friday.'

Elliot had been prepared for this. He took the medical cert from his pocket and slapped it down. 'Read it and weep, Bill.'

'I heard you were banged up pretty bad.'

Elliot spread his hands. 'Do I look pretty bad to you?'

'Can't say you do but what do I know?' Bill picked up the cert and read it carefully. Elliot watched as his eyes moved from side to side. Even this was galling. Time was a man's word was good enough.

Time was if you were a decent—

Oh, shut up!

Bill handed the note back and tapped the auto-scanner on the desk; Elliot scanned his lanyard, heard a bleep and mentally punched the air.

He was back in the game.

'I suppose you heard Clancy's calling time?'

Elliot put the lanyard away. Paddy Clancy, his one-time partner, now one of the head honchos in Homicide. The prick had come to see him in the hospital, an audacious move all things considered. Elliot, high as a kite on morphine, wasn't sure he hadn't imagined it, but the flowers and the card confirmed the unholy visitation. 'That so?'

'Yeah, he's taking the thirty.'

'Right.'

'Deacon is throwing him a big party at the Duck and Piglet next Friday. He's hired a covers band.'

'Good for him.'

Bill gave him a speculative look. 'You know, you'd think after an accident like what you had you might learn some perspective.'

Elliot didn't rise to it – he never did. 'Take it easy, Bill.'

He took the lift to his department on the second floor, pushed open the heavy glass door and walked through a sea of occupied cubicles to his small office at the end of the first row, where he got his second shock of the day.

His office was pretty much as he'd left it, apart from the second desk shoved under the only window. It was clean, and the computer looked reasonably newish. No personal artefacts, drawers – he pulled both out – empty but for an official garda mousepad.

Elliot set his bag down, shut the door, picked up the desk phone and pressed a button. 'Olivia? It's Elliot Ryan. Yes, yes, thank you, I'm fine, yes, yes, I got the basket, yes, it was very thoughtful. Is he in? Yes, now, if you wouldn't mind. I'll wait.'

He waited. The on-hold music was painfully on brand, a pipe-band murdering a modern song. Elliot didn't recognise the butchered song, but he doubted what he was hearing did it much justice.

'Elliot?'

'Yes.'

'He says he can give you ten minutes.'

'I'll be right up.'

Elliot hung up. The pills he had taken that morning were starting to wear off and there were at least another two hours to go before he could – conceivably – take the next batch. The first ribbon of pain was unfurling, travelling along nerve pathways. It would soon be joined by another. Perhaps if he took one ...

Olivia, Superintendent Connors's secretary, glanced up as Elliot entered the outer office. 'Inspector Ryan, you look marvellous.'

'Thank you, is he—?'

'Oh yes, please, go on in. Can I get you a coffee or some water?'

'No, I'm fine, thank you.'

He breezed past, affecting a loose-limbed amble until he entered the main office.

Superintendent Connors was on the phone. He motioned to Elliot to take one of the two chairs facing his desk. Elliot – very carefully – lowered himself into the nearest one and sat with his hands on his knees, chest out, concentrating on keeping his expression as blandly neutral as possible. He liked Connors, whom he considered hard but fair, but the man missed nothing, and if he thought there was something amiss, he'd send him home, simple as that.

'Oh, for God's sake, Herring, what's the point of having a liaison officer if he doesn't know how to leak information?' Connors said, gripping the phone so hard in his tanned hand his knuckles were several shades paler. Elliot studied the hand. The boss was a top-notch gardener, and the office walls were adorned with photos of various flowers and shrubs. Elliot knew Connors often took part in flower shows and had won an award for creating some type of hybrid climbing rose several years before. For the life of him, Elliot could never understand what compelled a man to muck about with nature.

'What? What? Rule one-oh-one, Herring, you give the official line to the official source and slip the rest of the information to the bottom feeders. I don't give a shaved arse if it was off the record – it's 2022, nothing is off the record these days ... What? Don't give me that. Rein that clown in, put him on traffic for a couple of months ... I don't know, send him to Donegal, maybe that will soften his cough ... What? I don't care, see to it.' He slammed the phone down and eyed Elliot. 'You're back then, are you?'

'Yes, sir.'

'I wasn't expecting you back on duty so soon.' Connors looked past Elliot to the clock over the door. He'd had installed it the moment he became the super, limiting all meetings to ten minutes on the button. 'How are you?'

'I'm well, sir.'

'Tricky things, backs. Yoga might help. Nothing wrong with a bit of flexibility, especially as we age – strengthens the core.'

Elliot refused to dignify that with an answer. Yoga. Dear Lord. Whatever next?

Connors ran his right hand over his head. It was shaved tight and tanned like his hand. Golf tan, another of life's mysteries. He glanced at the clock again.

Elliot took the hint. 'I appreciate you taking the time to see me, sir. I think there's been a mistake.'

'What? What mistake?'

'Someone has put a second desk into my office.'

'Ah!' Connors held up a finger. He reached into his top drawer, rummaged around for a moment, came back with a file and opened it. 'No mistake, Elliot. Like I say, we weren't expecting you back so soon. Besides, you might benefit from an under sergeant.'

'Benefit?'

'You're recovering from a very serious accident, Elliot.'

'Yes, I know but—'

'And Sergeant Kane is available.'

The sweat from Elliot's spine reached the waistband of his underpants. He mentally shunted the pain to one side so he could concentrate on what Connors was saying. 'Sergeant Kane, sir?'

The second ribbon of pain joined the first. Soon a network would cross his body. He regretted his decision not to take the painkiller.

'She's young and, if we're laying our cards on the table, a bit of a hothead, but she's smart. I think with the right hand on the rudder she can readjust her ... er, focus. Just back from a short-term suspension, but don't let that trouble you – she's been cleared. It was a misunderstanding. No charges pending.'

Elliot ran through his personal computing system. He found Kane in seconds. Small, blonde, involved with Paul Deacon, which was a black mark against her in Elliot's book. Deacon was Paddy Clancy's current partner. A second black mark appeared by Nola's name. A Clancy stooge housed with him? Now, of all times?

Coincidence?

Elliot wished he could remember what they'd spoken about at the hospital. Had he mentioned anything to Clancy about receiving the diary?

Probably not. But anything was possible.

Now who's being paranoid? the inner voice queried.

'Isn't Kane Homicide, sir?'

'Was Homicide,' Connors said. 'Like I say, she needs some new direction and focus.'

'She chose my unit?'

'The position was offered and accepted.'

Elliot frowned. 'What's the catch?'

Connors gave his best crafty grin. 'No catch, Elliot. To my mind, there is no better man to help her achieve her goals.'

Oh God, Elliot thought. *Flattery*. That proved it: Kane was a spy. But who was she spying for, Clancy or Connors?

'Sir, I have a lot on my plate at this time and—'

'Exactly my thoughts, Elliot.' Connors glanced at the clock again. 'Kane understands the order of things. I imagine she will be a boon to you over the coming weeks, and' – he did crafty again – 'she in turn will benefit from your endless wisdoms.'

'Oh, so I have a choice in this, do I?'

'No, you do not.' Connors regarded him knowingly. 'Look, I know things have been ... difficult of late, so if you want my advice—'

'No, really.'

'—keep a low profile for the next few weeks, choose an easy case, wrap it up and finish your career on a high note.'

Elliot stared. 'My career, sir?'

'Going for the twenty-five, aren't you?'

'I haven't decided,' Elliot said stiffly.

'Hadn't you? Ah. I was sure ... I'm sure someone mentioned you were taking the twenty-five, and what with the accident and everything—'

'Will that be all, sir?'

'For now. Welcome back, Inspector.'

What a load of bollocks, Elliot thought as he left the office. Endless wisdoms? This was no 'boon'. He was being hobbled, pure and simple.

'Did you get everything you need, Inspector Ryan?' Olivia asked.

'No, Olivia, I did not, but it's a day with Y in it.'

'Lovely,' she said and carried on typing.

6

Nola Kane had arrived. Elliot found her standing at the door of his office with a canvas rucksack slung over her shoulder. He gave her a quick once over as he approached. She looked more like a teenager than a grown woman with sergeant's stripes. Smaller than he remembered, very blonde, with a slightly upturned nose.

'Good morning,' he said, aiming for cheerful.

'Howya.'

He tried not to scowl, but it bothered him when people responded to a polite greeting with such lazy vernacular.

'Are you Elliot Ryan?'

'Inspector Elliot Ryan, yes. You must be Nola Kane.'

'*Sergeant* Nola Kane.'

Spikey. He offered his hand. She took it, gave it a very firm rapid pump and released him.

'So, Sergeant Kane.' He took a beat before he moved behind his desk. 'I fear we might seem somewhat pedestrian after the high-wire tension of Homicide.'

She did not smile or even acknowledge his amusing comment. Elliot rubbed his hands together. 'Superintendent Connors mentioned you are returning from suspension.'

'Did he tell you I was cleared?'

'He did.'

'Maybe you should have led with that.'

Elliot was taken aback by her abrupt tone. 'I didn't mean to—'

'Don't worry about it. This my desk?' Without waiting for an answer, she pulled the chair out, removed her jacket and sat down.

Gingerly, Elliot lowered himself onto his own chair. From the corner of his eye, he watched Nola unpack her things. Several notebooks, a mobile phone. No photos or knick-knacks, nothing personal. He approved of *that* at least.

When she was finished unpacking, she switched her computer on without saying a word and soon was furiously tapping.

'Bikes?' She snorted. 'You lot are looking into stolen bikes?'

'Bicycle theft is rampant across the city, Sergeant, close to five thousand a year. And the assistant commissioner has made it something of a personal mission.'

'Stall? He's never been on a bike in his life.'

'Nonetheless, bike theft is an ongoing scourge and who are we to question his directive.'

'Yeah, right,' she said. 'Bikes, give me a break, this whole thing smacks of a PR stunt.'

'Crime is crime, Sergeant.'

'And water is wet,' she mumbled.

Elliot switched on his own computer and groaned inwardly when he saw the wall of emails waiting for him. There were hundreds, possibly thousands. If he was to take the twenty-five he'd probably see out what was left of his career replying to them.

He was in the middle of reading a long-winded email on budget cuts when the phone on his desk blipped. Grateful for the distraction, he snatched it up. It was Sergeant Robbie Keller, a brawny lug of a lad with a lukewarm IQ. A real hit with the ladies, though Elliot had never understood his supposed charm.

He listened. 'When was this, Sergeant?'

He listened some more. 'Give me the address.'

He reached into his drawer and took out his notebook. He pressed it open and wrote quickly in his clear, neat handwriting and hung up.

'Sergeant, I must go out. There has been a suspected B&E in Kilmainham and, sadly, a woman has been assaulted.'

'Thank God.' Nola reached for her jacket.

'I don't need a chaperone, Sergeant.'

Nola's expression was anything but friendly. 'Me neither, but here we are, Inspector.'

'Fine, we'll take my car.'

They went downstairs. Sergeant Kane got in the passenger side and slammed the door of the Passat loud enough to make Elliot's teeth hurt. His hand shook slightly as he got behind the wheel, but the worst was yet to come when Sergeant Kane reached out and changed the radio channel from Lyric FM to ... something else.

Elliot turned towards her. 'Sergeant?'

'What?'

'I don't wish to appear authoritarian ... but I do have a little rule.'

'Yeah? What's that?'

'He who driveth picketh the tune.'

'Seriously?'

'Verily.'

He put the station back to Lyric FM and was rewarded with a jaunty rendition of Bach's Brandenburg Concerto No. 5 in D Major.

Elliot beamed, put the car in reverse, and they were on their way.

7

Traffic was light as they crossed the city, though the atmosphere in the car was not. Any attempts at conversation Elliot made were rebuffed or met with monosyllabic replies and, on one occasion, an eye-roll worthy of a teenager. Momentarily defeated, he lapsed into silence and turned his mind to Clancy.

His old partner was not a stupid man and anyone who would think so vastly underestimated him, as Elliot once had done. Of course, that was then; now he had the upper hand, hadn't he? Clancy had no idea he was in possession of Natalie Dormond's diary.

Damn, why couldn't he remember what they'd spoken about at the hospital?

Automatically, he raised his right hand to his chest, his fingertips feeling for the gentle outline of the diary under his jacket. He knew it was the key to the questions that had dogged him for years; still, he needed time to figure out how to use it. It would be difficult, he knew that, for he had long compartmentalised his time working with Clancy for myriad reasons. But Clancy's reign was almost over, and it was up to Elliot to do something before the bastard galloped off into the retirement sunset.

They reached the crime scene and parked opposite a row of two-storey Victorian red-bricks. The front gate to the second last of the row was cordoned off and a uniformed officer stood outside it, watching the street. He looked bored and cold. Elliot and Nola pulled on gloves and blue booties over their footwear before they approached.

'Good morning,' Elliot said. 'Who's here?'

'Forensics, sir. The victim has been removed by ambulance to James's. Sergeant Keller is still on site.' He lifted the tape and let them through.

Sergeant Robbie Keller was standing inside the front door, taking notes. 'Inspector. All right, Sergeant Kane.' Robbie winked at Nola who stared back, stony-faced. 'I heard you were joining us. Welcome aboard.'

'What do we have?' Elliot asked.

'Victim's name is Jody Kavanagh, twenty-eight. Works as an interior designer for a company called Jolie Laide. Been here two years. No kids.'

Elliot nodded and felt a pang of sorrow. Twenty-eight, the same age as Shona. It shouldn't matter, but it always did. 'Can you tell me what happened?'

'Hard to say, sir.'

'Try, Sergeant Keller.'

'Well, it's weird, right? The victim's the owner-occupier. She was found unconscious and unresponsive in the kitchen by her husband' – he glanced at his notes – 'Simon Albright.'

'In the kitchen, right.'

'At 8.05 this morning.'

'Right, so ... did Mrs Kavanagh disturb someone?'

'Well, that's what I thought initially, but I don't think there's anything missing.'

Elliot tried not to sigh. He had forgotten what it was like to work with Robbie. The man's mind was like a sieve: everything had to be shaken loose. 'You mentioned she was found by her husband?'

'Yeah, see, the husband doesn't actually live here. He said he called over and found his missus unconscious.'

'So he's an ex-husband,' Nola said.

'Not according to him,' Robbie said. 'He said they were sorting through some issues. Said they were close to making amends.'

'Well, he would say that, wouldn't he? But he's the one living somewhere else, right? Not her.'

'Yeah, but—'

'So she ditched him, I'm guessing.'

'Yeah, but—'

'Sergeant Kane is correct. Details matter,' Elliot said. 'Is he here now, the husband?'

'Gone to the hospital, sir.'

'You let him leave?' Nola said. 'He's a suspect.'

'It was him who called the ambulance.'

'Oh, for God's sake, are you—?'

'Excuse me, Sergeant,' Elliot said. 'Sergeant Keller, did you take a statement from Mr Albright before he left for the hospital?'

'Not really – I mean, the poor guy was pretty broken up.'

Elliot frowned. 'He was injured?'

'No, like upset.'

'I see. You need to be more careful with your terminology, Sergeant.'

'Sorry, sir.'

'Do I hear a dog?'

'Yes, sir, big brute of a thing. It's out back. A member of the Dog Unit is on the way to remove it.'

'Okay, who is leading forensics?'

'Detective Macey, sir.'

Elliot nodded, pleased. Macey Butler was as thorough a forensics officer as you could find. He turned to Nola. 'All right, Sergeant, I'll leave the protocol to you.'

'Sir?'

'You do know the protocol, don't you, Sergeant? Forensics, eyewitnesses, statements, interviews.'

'Of course I do.'

'Good. Neighbours first.'

'Look, someone needs to go nab Albright before he has time to make up a—'

Elliot held up his index finger. 'I do not like to repeat myself, Sergeant. Time is of essence – gather statements, if you please.'

Nola flushed. She yanked off the gloves and booties and stuffed them in her pocket.

The uniform on the gate grinned as she passed under the cordon. 'How did you get stuck with the Fossil?'

'Luck of the draw.'

'Rather you than me – you know he's as mad as a box of badgers?'

'That's one way of putting it,' Nola replied and walked away before she put it another.

8

Nobody was home in the house to the left, so Nola trudged past the smirking uniform to the last house of the row. She couldn't find a bell, but when she knocked a bare-chested young male wearing black tracksuit bottoms and nothing else opened it and stood there chewing an apple. Nola kept her gaze high. If the pants had been any lower his Adonis Belt would have been a garter.

He was young, early twenties. Coal-black hair, one pierced eyebrow, one pierced nostril, both arms tattooed from shoulder to wrist and so good-looking he wouldn't need a personality for decades.

Nola showed him her identification. He barely glanced at it.

'I'm sorry to disturb you,' she began, then paused. 'Do you want to put something on? I can wait if you—'

'Nah, I'm good.'

'Is this your house?'

'I live here.' He thought about it for a moment while scratching his chest with his free hand. 'With my mom.'

'Is she here?' Nola asked hopefully.

'Nah, she's at work.'

'I was hoping to ask you few questions about your neighbour.'

'Yeah?' He took a bite of the fruit and chewed it. 'Are you really a cop? You don't look like one.'

'I showed my identification.'

'Could be fake.'

'Why would it be?'

He shrugged.

'What's your name?'

'Bane Russell.'

Nola narrowed her eyes. '*Bane?*'

'Yeah.'

'Is that your real name?'

'It's my chosen name – that makes it real, yeah?'

Nola wrote it down. 'What do you do, Bane?'

'I'm a life coach, content generator and personal trainer.'

'Content generator? What's that, like an influencer?'

'Ugh.' He rolled his eyes. 'Please don't use that term. It's so démodé.'

'Dey-mod-ey?'

'You know, last year.'

Nola asked him to spell the word, guessing, correctly as it turned out, that presenting as intelligent was by no means the same as being intelligent. Nola took a stab at it.

'Have you been here all morning, Bane?'

'Yeah.'

'Did you notice anything out of the ordinary?'

'I noticed you.' He grinned. A true wit.

'Yeah, apart from that.'

'No, not really.'

'No noise or—?'

'Nah.'

'What about last night?'

'What about it?'

'Were you here, at home?

'I was in and out.'

'Can you narrow that down for me?'

'Not really.'

'Excuse me?'

He held up both wrists to show they were empty. 'Time is a prison.'

Nola stared at him for so long he lost some of his composure.

'No cap.' He tapped the side of his head. 'Once you free yourself, you'll see the truth. See, that's how society controls you. Through time. If you accept time, you'll accept anything.'

'Did you hear anything or notice anything usual while you were dodging time? Did you see anyone coming to the house? Hear anything unusual – a row or an argument?'

'No.'

'What about your mum – was she here?'

'At some stage.'

Nola glared at him. He was getting on her last nerve. 'What's your mum's name.'

'Beverly.'

'Do you have a number for her?'

He recited one and tossed the apple core into the flowerbed.

'And do *you* have a number?'

He gave it, albeit reluctantly. Maybe phone numbers were as démodé as time.

'How well do you know your neighbour?'

He leaned on the door with such carefully affected

nonchalance it caught Nola's attention. When people worked *that* hard at being casual something else was usually at play.

'I know Jody to see,' he said. 'You know, casual, like.'

'What's she like?' Nola asked, making a note that he and his neighbour were on a first-name basis.

He shrugged. 'She's okay. Her husband's a prick.'

'Oh?'

'Stuck-up, thinks he's better then everyone. Jody was well rid.'

'They'd split up, I believe?'

'Yeah, a while back.'

'Do you know when they broke up?'

'Nah, Mom would know. Anyway, Jody's been seeing this other guy.' He frowned. 'Some Billy Big Bollocks in skinnies.'

Nola wrote 'Billy Big Bollocks' in inverted commas. Then added 'skinnies'.

'What can you tell me about him? Do you have a name?'

'I don't know his name, but he drives *a Tesla*.'

'Have you seen this guy around a lot?'

'Yeah, a bit.'

'Can you describe him?'

'I don't know, tallish.'

'Age?'

'Definitely.'

'I mean what age is he?'

'I don't know, older.'

Bloody hell, Nola thought, it was like pulling teeth. 'Can you describe him for me, hair colour, any distinguishing features? Would you be able to recognise him if you saw him again?'

'Yeah, I'd *know* him if I saw him.'

Nola nodded and thought for a moment. 'It's interesting,' she said.

'What is?'

'You haven't asked me why I'm here or what happened to Jody.'

'Not my business.'

'Even though you're friends?'

'Never said we were friends, said I know her, you know?'

'Have you ever been in the house?'

The question, innocently put, rattled him. 'Why?'

'Well, you are neighbours, so you might have been in for a coffee or something.'

'I mean, I helped her ... you know, set up her sound system.'

'Oh yeah?'

'Yeah.'

'When was this?'

'I don't know.'

'Oh, right, time's not your strong point. Were you upstairs or downstairs?'

'Uh ...'

'Is geography hard too?'

'No, look, I helped her out, you know – that's what I'm saying. Being a good Samaritan.'

'Right, well, thanks for the chat, Bane. I'll be sure to be in touch.'

'Yeah.'

He closed the door.

Nola made a few notes, put a question mark after Bane's name and wrote 'possible suspect', and after that she wrote 'idiot'.

9

Elliot moved through Jody Kavanagh's house with his hands loose by his sides, his posture upright, how he imagined a man of bearing and position might move if he wasn't fighting an almost phenomenal wave of pain.

The interior was elegant, modernised with a double-height extension to the rear that flooded the lower level in natural light. It was here he found Macey Butler studying a large brindle-coloured dog with a dark face through double doors leading to a garden.

'Hello, Inspector,' Macey said. 'It's been a while.'

'Indeed, it has.'

'I was sorry to hear about your accident.'

Elliot nodded curtly and surveyed the space to hide his discomfort. One side contained an L-shaped sofa, coffee table and rug, the other a smart, functional kitchen, likely bespoke, certainly showroom quality, built around a marble-topped central island. He saw markers on the floors and followed them to a large pool of blood. One of Macey's team was taking photos of a large black statuette lying on the floor.

Twenty-eight, what a tragedy.

'Her husband said he found her there.' Macey joined him. 'She was, we believe, struck several times by that.' She pointed.

'What is it?'

'Carl?'

The photographer paused and squinted. 'It looks like some kind of Egyptian god.'

'A god?'

'Yeah, you know, like, um ... a sphinx?'

'Bag it and tag it, Carl – we can delve into the history later.' Macy pointed. 'That's the dining room, leads into the living room at the front of the house. Nice place, actually. I wish I had this kind of space.'

'May I?'

'Go ahead, we've been through it.'

Elliot skirted the blood and entered the dining room. It was long and modern, painted in soft dusky hues of pink and grey. It held a long pale-wood table under three rose-coloured pendant lights and a funky fifties sideboard that reminded him of something his parents had back in the day. Several framed photos sat on it, many of them featuring a pretty blonde woman who he guessed was Jody Kavanagh. He picked up the nearest one: Jody accepting an award from an older gentleman. She was smiling at the camera, beaming, really. She had dimples. Pretty.

'What can you tell me, Macey?' he called out.

'Apart from the blood, there's no other sign of a disturbance that I can see.'

'Was anything taken?'

'In as far as I can tell, there's nothing missing. Money, computer, TV, laptop, wallet, all *anseo*. There's a jewellery box upstairs in the main bedroom – it was untouched. Some pretty good pieces in it too.'

'What about a phone?'

'*That* we haven't found, but I can't say it was stolen. She might have left it somewhere – at work, maybe.'

Elliot walked back into the kitchen and stood with his hands on his hips.

'There is one thing,' Macey said. 'Look up there.'

Elliot followed her finger and saw a small black camera on the ceiling beam.

'There's another one on landing and another in the front hall.'

'Cameras?'

'Wireless, which might explain the missing phone.'

'You think whoever harmed Jody took it?'

She spread her hands. That was his area, not hers.

'Do you mind if I look around upstairs?'

'Knock yourself out – we're pretty much through here apart from the garden.'

Elliot went upstairs, saw the camera in the hall, facing the top of the stairs. Jody Kavanagh was not taking any chances.

Three bedrooms – two doubles, one single – and a bathroom on the return. The main bedroom occupied the front of the house. It was a large room with a bay window, overlooking the street. He walked to the window and peered out, saw Nola entering below and stepped back before she saw him.

God, but she was a nuisance. He glanced at his watch, made a few calculations and went downstairs. Nola was staring at the dog with her arms folded across her chest.

'No one was in on the left, but I met a kid named Bane on the right,' she said without looking at him. 'He says he didn't see or hear anything out of the ordinary. He's been in this house, though, but he claims it was to help the occupant set up a sound system.'

'Bane?' Elliot furrowed his brow. 'Is that a name?'

'According to him, Jody Kavanagh and the husband split months ago. He reckons she was seeing someone else. A Tesla driver.'

'Ah, there's a new paramour on the scene.'

'Probably explains what happened here. Maybe the old *paramour* didn't like it.' Nola glanced over her shoulder as Robbie appeared. 'What's the deal with the mutt?'

'He was outside when I got here,' Robbie said. 'Nasty looking, isn't he? You wouldn't think a woman would have something like that as a pet.'

'Why not?' Nola asked, annoyed.

'Women normally go for cats.'

'In your wide experience, yeah?'

The doorbell rang. Gladly, Elliot went and found a woman in tactical uniform standing on the step.

'Sergeant Abby Fencer,' she said, offering her hand. 'I'm here about a dog.'

'Ah, please, this way.'

He led her though the house and introduced her.

'Have you a shield?' Robbie grinned. 'A suit of armour?'

Nola rolled her eyes.

'No,' Sergeant Fencer said. 'I have this.' She held up a thin length of rope and a plastic bag containing what looked like chunks of cheddar cheese. 'Do we know his name?'

They shook their heads.

'Not to worry.'

Everyone took a step backwards as she unlocked the door and went outside.

'She's some woman,' Robbie muttered, clearly impressed.

'Probably thinks she's dealing with a cat,' Nola said, but he ignored her.

Out on the patio, Sergeant Fencer angled her body slightly to one side, talking quietly, her movements small and easy. The dog initially backed up, then approached, hackles raised, tense but interested. Slowly he leaned in and sniffed at her leg. Sergeant Fencer opened the plastic bag and offered him a piece of cheese, which he ignored.

Then, as if the dog was nothing more than an afterthought, Sergeant Fencer made a loop with the length of line and dropped it over his head. She tightened the loop and made a gesture with her hand. The dog sat instantly.

She turned and gave her amazed audience a thumbs up.

'How on earth did you do that?' Elliot asked when Sergeant Fencer came inside with the dog walking quietly alongside her.

'Someone has trained this dog and trained it well. I'm going to bring him back to the kennels and scan him for a chip. You should keep an eye out for a contract or a licence for him. I suspect he's a personal protection dog – we're seeing a lot more of them lately.'

She and the dog left. Robbie followed her out to 'give her a hand'.

'Nice,' Macey said when she finally got access to the garden. 'I like it, low maintenance.' She walked down the path and tried a gate, which opened to a private lane running behind the houses.

It was padlocked from the inside. A brown wooden shed was also locked.

'I'll need the keys for these,' Macey said as she walked back towards them and around to the narrow side passage where the bins were kept. 'Inspector?'

'What is it?' Elliot asked.

'Come see for yourself, but, remember, don't touch anything.'

They went. Macey had the lid of the brown bin open. On top of a mound of mouldering leaves and hedge clippings lay a large bunch of yellow roses, their stems still wrapped in sisal.

'Beautiful display,' Elliot said. 'She obviously didn't want them.'

'She obviously didn't want *something*.' Nola took her phone from her pocket and started taking photos from various angles. 'Or someone.'

'Check to see if there's a card with them.'

Macey looked. 'No card, but there's a wooden holder for one.' She lowered the lid to preserve the scene. 'We'll go through the bins back at the lab.'

'Right.' Elliot glanced at his watch. The painkillers were waning and he needed to be away. 'Call me if you find a card or locate her mobile phone. Sergeant Kane?'

'Sir?'

'I need you to contact Miss Kavanagh's place of employment, Jolie Laide, and when you do that, I need ...' He put his finger to his lip, thinking.

They waited.

Time passed.

Nola cleared her throat. 'Sir?'

'Hmm?'

'What do you need, sir?'

'I need you to see about the missing phone. I'm going to go to the hospital to speak to Simon Albright.'

'How am I supposed to get back to the station?'

'Sergeant Keller's free, aren't you?' he asked Robbie, who had appeared from somewhere like a proverbial rancid penny.

'As a bird,' Robbie said. He winked at Nola for the second time in a day. Two times too many in Nola's book.

Nola glared at her boss. This was incredible. Was he really going to dump her with a gurning chimp like Keller? Dumped on her first day back? On her first case?

She opened her mouth to protest and closed it again, aware that anything she might say right at that second would likely come out wrong. All right, if that's how he wanted to play the game, let him play it. Promises had been made: if she played her part she'd be back on the fast track, and she had no intention of screwing *that* up.

10

At the hospital, Elliot spoke to an attending and was directed along the corridor towards the 'family room', where he found Simon Albright.

It was a small, slightly cramped room containing a sofa, two armchairs and a coffee table. Mint-green walls, one narrow window overlooking a car park. Efficient, but not exactly cosy.

Simon Albright was standing by the window, clutching a vape in his right hand. He turned as Elliot entered, a slightly built man, short with white-blond hair and a thin blond moustache, handsome in a slightly old-fashioned way. Elliot guessed him to be in his mid-forties. He wore gold-rimmed glasses, blue jeans, a pale-blue shirt, a blue and grey sports jacket and a wedding ring. There were bloodstains on his pants and on his shirt. He was also sporting some minor facial injuries and his left hand was heavily bandaged.

Elliot introduced himself.

'I gave a statement,' Simon spoke with an English accent, 'to the other officer at the house.'

'How is your wife?'

'She's in surgery – they're trying to stabilise her.' He closed his eyes briefly. 'They had to restart her heart in the ambulance.'

'I'm sorry, this must be very difficult.'

'You have no idea.'

I do, Elliot thought, studying the man, reading his body language. Simon Albright looked shattered, broken. A man teetering on the edge; but the edge of what? That was the question. 'Do you mind if we have a chat, I'll keep it brief.'

Simon moved away from the window and sat down on the chair. Elliot took the sofa. It squeaked under his weight.

'That's not a local accent,' Elliot said, taking his notebook from his inside pocket.

'No, London, by way of Surrey.'

'Lived here long, have you?'

'Three years.'

'What do you do, Simon?'

'I'm an architect.'

'And Jody's an interior designer, am I correct?'

'That's right.'

'How's life in Ireland working out for you?'

Simon Albright gave him a hard, bright smile. 'Oh, tickety-boo.'

'I only ask because I understand you and Jody have separated.'

Simon put the vape to his lips, thought about it and lowered it again. There was bruising to his knuckles and blood under his fingernails. Elliot made a note of it.

'Amicable split was it?'

'I didn't hurt Jody, if that's what you're asking. I would never physically hurt her.'

Elliot made a note of the word 'physically'.

'How long have you been separated?'

'Since January.'

Not even a full year, hardly time for anger to settle.

'Whose idea was it?'

Simon leaned his head back and stared at the ceiling for a moment. 'Does that matter?'

'It might.'

'I told you I didn't hurt her.'

'But you were there this morning, so you can see why I might have questions.'

'I was there because she asked me to come over.'

'May I ask why?'

'She said she wanted to talk.'

'At eight in the morning?'

'That's right.'

Elliot wrote in his notebook. 'Is there any way you can corroborate this?'

Sighing heavily, Simon took his mobile phone from his pocket, flicked it on, scrolled for a moment and passed it over. Elliot took it and read what was written on the screen.

Simon, I need to see you, it's important. Please come over.

It had been sent at 7.45 a.m.

'And this came from Jody's phone, did it?'

'Yes, that's her number.'

'Do you mind if I make a note if it.'

Simon watched him write it down.

'Run me through what happened. You got a message and ...'

'I tried to call her back, but there was no answer. I got dressed and went straight to our house.'

'Where are you living now?'

'Primrose Court, Ranelagh.'

'Okay, so ... you called over, then what happened?'

'I found Jody unconscious.' His voice trembled slightly. 'I thought she was dead.'

'How did you get into the house?'

'I used my key.'

'You have keys, even though you're separated?'

Simon shot him a baleful look. 'It's the accent, isn't it?'

'Excuse me?'

'You hear an English accent and suddenly I'm Oliver Cromwell.'

Elliot smiled. 'If you think I'm accusing you of being a genocidal maniac, I apologise. I'm just interested in why you still have keys to your ex-wife's—'

'Wife, not ex. She's *still* my wife.'

Ah, Elliot thought, there it was: the anger, the possessive nature of a man wronged. 'All right,' he said calmly. 'You found Jody unresponsive, what then?'

'I called an ambulance.'

'What time was this?'

'I don't know ... I called as soon as I found her.'

'What way was she lying?'

'What?'

'Her position, did you move her?'

'Oh.' Simon frowned and looked at his hands. 'I turned her over to check if she was breathing.'

'Where was the dog at this time?'

'Outside, in the back garden.'

'He's an interesting animal – had him long?'

'He's not mine. He belongs to Jody.'

'Ah,' Elliot said. 'What happened to your hand?'

'I had an accident at work.'

'Painful, is it?'

'Look I don't want to—'

The door slammed open and a huge man entered at speed, followed by a woman.

'What have you done?' the man said, balling a hand into a fist and shoving it in Simon Albright's face. The woman clung to the man's other arm, but he shook her off with ease. 'Well? What have you done?'

'Excuse me,' Elliot said, standing. 'My name is Detective Elliot Ryan, and you are?'

The woman glanced towards him, her eyes huge. 'Malcolm,' she said softly. The big man turned.

'Inspector Elliot Ryan,' Elliot repeated, hoping to take some of the steam out of the situation. 'Are you friends of Jody's?'

'I'm her brother-in-law,' the man said, glaring from under thick black eyebrows. 'This is my wife, Jody's sister.'

Again with the possessive tone, Elliot thought.

'I'm Fiona Hynes, and this is my husband Malcolm. We came as soon as we heard. What happened – what happened to my sister?'

Elliot took in the newcomers. Fiona Hynes was a good-looking woman and, from the photos he had seen at the house, very like her sister. But she was rail thin with sunken eyes. She wore her hair to her waist in a loose plait, and her clothes – Elliot was no fashion maven, but even to his inexperienced eye – looked terribly old-fashioned. In many ways she looked like she had stepped from the pages of a history book.

Malcolm was big, heavy-set, bearded. He might have been handsome under all the hair – Elliot suspected he was – but his expression was so guarded, so sour, it was hard to see past it. Unlike his wife, his dress was more modern: denims, with a red and black flannel shirt open to reveal a tuft of black chest hair. His boots were covered in dried mud, steel toed. Hard, like him.

Simon Albright looked like a bird of paradise in comparison.

'Someone attacked her at her home,' Elliot said.

Fiona's eyes widened. 'Oh my God.'

'Not *someone*,' Malcolm thundered. 'Not *someone*, it was him.' He jabbed his finger at Simon, who sat pale as a ghost but eerily composed.

'Look,' Elliot said. 'This is upsetting and I'm sure you've had a terrible shock, but, please, if we could—'

'Tell him,' Malcolm snapped. 'Tell him what you know.'

Fiona Hynes flinched. 'Malcolm, please—'

'All right.' He glared at Simon, who stared back. 'Jody kicked him out – did you know that?'

'Yes,' Elliot said, 'I was aware there had been a separation.'

'Did he tell you why?'

Elliot glanced at Simon, who looked like he had turned to stone; only the slight tremor in his legs gave him away.

'No,' Elliot said, 'he did not.'

'Malcolm, please,' Fiona said, her voice cracking. 'Please don't—'

'Lies, he sits on a throne of lies. One after another,' Malcolm said, sneering. 'Oh, the big shot, big lad coming over here with your notions and your big talk, full of pride. The Lord detests all the proud of heart. Be sure of this: they will not go unpunished.'

Simon got abruptly to his feet. Even at full height his head barely came to Malcolm's chin, but that didn't stop him going toe-to-toe with the bigger man. 'You have the audacity to speak to *me* of lies? You who—'

Malcolm Hynes picked him up and flung him over the chair so hard he hit the wall and crumpled to the floor.

'Malcolm, stop!'

Elliot tried to spring forward, felt his back spasm and ended up throwing himself between the two men, arms akimbo. '*Stop it, stop.*'

Thankfully, Malcolm stopped, but he stood over Simon, his chest heaving like a raging bull's. Simon groaned. His glasses had flown off in the fall.

'You speak to me or mine again, I'll fold you into pieces and send you back to the shithole you came from.'

'Mr Albright,' Elliot said, 'are you all right?'

Simon felt around for his glasses, found them and put them on before he got to his feet. He looked badly shaken but determined. 'I'm going to go outside now, Inspector. If you need to talk to me again, my solicitor's name is Harry Treadstone. You'll find him online. Excuse me.'

He limped from the room and closed the door quietly.

'He could have you for assault,' Elliot snapped. His back was throbbing, and he felt decidedly queasy and a little faint. He glared at Malcolm Hynes, who didn't seem to care much. 'Look, I understand how upset you are, but you can't take the law into your own hands.'

'I should leave it to you, is that it?'

'Yes, actually.'

Malcolm looked disgusted. 'Come on,' he said to Fiona. 'Let's go.'

'Wait, hold on a second,' Elliot said. He looked directly at Fiona. 'Your sister has been very badly hurt. If you know anything, anything at all, you need to talk to me. What was going on in her life?'

'I don't know.'

'Was she happy, unhappy? Worried about anything?'

'I ... I don't know.'

'What about – was she seeing a new man or—?'

'Are you deaf?' Malcolm said. 'She told you once.'

Elliot shifted his weight slightly. 'Mr Hynes, it's my job to ask questions.'

'For what?' Malcolm said. 'You had the man who did it and you let him walk out of here.'

Elliot knew it was pointless. He reached into his pocket and offered Fiona his card. 'Please, call me when you have a moment.'

Malcolm snatched it out of his hand. 'We've said all we need to say.'

'Nevertheless, I'll be in touch,' Elliot said and left the family room, grateful to be away from Fiona Hynes's desperate eyes.

11

The drive back to the station was excruciatingly awkward – for Nola, at any rate. Robbie either didn't notice how cross she was or, as she suspected, he did notice but didn't give a toss. There was only one plus side to the journey as far as she was concerned: at least Robbie didn't play Lyric FM.

Every cloud had a silver lining.

'So,' Robbie said after a while. 'How are you getting on?'

'Fine.'

'Must be weird, moving over like that.'

'It's fine.'

'How long were you in Homicide?'

'Two years.'

'Yeah?'

Nola looked out the window, willing him to stop talking.

'Ryan used to work with your old boss, back in the day. Him and Clancy were partners.'

'I know.'

'Apparently, they were as thick as thieves until they fell out. Probably over a woman or something.'

Nola tried to picture Elliot Ryan working up enough energy to fight over a sandwich, let alone a woman. Clancy, she could picture it. Her old boss was cut from the cloth of a bygone era. Not that she had minded much, not from the inside looking out. But now? Now she had a slightly different view on her old 'crew'.

How long had they known Paul was sticking it to someone else? How long had they laughed about it, made stupid jokes about it, about her?

Had Gracie known?

Had she?

Nola's face burned.

'So, what's the story with you?'

'None of your business.'

Robbie grinned. 'I heard you punched Samantha Copeland spark out. One Punch Kane they're calling you. The OPK!'

Nola took her notes out and reread them. She did not want to talk about her ex-colleagues (friends?) and she definitely didn't want to talk about Samantha Copeland.

'Speaking of Clancy, are you going his retirement party on Friday?' Robbie asked as he stopped for traffic lights at Suir Road bridge. 'They've booked the Duck and Piglet.'

'I'm busy on Friday.'

'Oh, come on, he's got a band, caterers, the whole shebang. You'd be mad not to come.'

Nola closed the notebook and looked out the window. God but Dublin was a truly depressing dump in winter. She couldn't believe people chose to live here if they didn't need to. What did anyone find enjoyable about it, the damp footpaths and relentless grey skies. If it wasn't for her mam she'd move abroad, somewhere sunny, Australia or somewhere like that. Some place where she knew no one and no one knew her, somewhere to start again, a blank slate.

'Got to be a weird one for Deacon.'

Nola's head swivelled. 'What did you say?'

'I said it's got to be weird for Deacon taking over. The squad, like.'

She couldn't believe her ears. 'Deacon's going for inspector?'

'Yeah.'

'He's too young – he'll never get it.'

'He might. I was told Connors called him in for a quiet chat the other week. And Clancy's got some serious pull with brass – you ask me, the badge will be his for sure.'

Nola looked out the window again.

She tried to imagine Paul Deacon as an inspector. And though the thought of it turned her stomach, she supposed it made a kind of sense. Her ex was a company man through and through, blue blood running through his veins and all that guff. Still, the idea of Paul Deacon with more power at his disposal did not sit easy with her.

So much for karma.

'What's the story with your pal, Gracie?'

'What do you mean – what story?'

'Is she straight or, you know, a bit AC/DC?'

Nola stared at the side of Robbie's handsome head. A jogger dressed in very short shorts and a thin vest, despite the cold, ran down the canal. Robbie watched her progress with obvious carnal interest.

'Are you serious?'

'What?'

'It's 2022, you absolute muppet. Are you seriously asking me if Gracie is gay?'

'Well, is she?'

'What business is that of yours?'

He shrugged as they pulled away from the lights. 'I was going to ask her to come to the party with me, that's all.'

'Forget it, you're not her type.'

''Cause I have a mickey?'

''Cause she has a brain.'

He grinned, impervious to insult. 'So, what you're saying is I'm in with a chance?'

'How do you get that from what I'm saying? How are you like this?'

'Like what?'

'Thick!'

He put his right hand over his heart. 'God loves a trier.'

She looked at him with genuine wonder. *They walk among us*, she thought, *they really do.*

At the station, they parted company. She went to the office and was about to call Jolie Laide when her phone bleeped.

It was Olivia, Connors's secretary. She informed Nola, in her stilted, unfriendly way, that Connors wanted to see her.

Nola tidied her hair with her fingers and hurried upstairs. 'How do I lo—?'

Olivia waved her in.

'Ah,' Connors said when he saw her. 'Sergeant Kane.'

'You wanted to see me, sir.'

'Sit, Kane, I like eyes at a level.'

Nola sat, folded her arms, unfolded them again, couldn't decide where to put them and ended up with them hanging by her sides like two limp noodles.

'How are you getting on?'

'Fine, sir.'

'I'm told you and Inspector Elliot have a case?'

'That's correct.'

Connors's eyes bored into hers. 'I wonder, Sergeant, if you recall what I said to you when I assigned you to Inspector Ryan's division?'

'You said I was to assist him during his recovery and be of assistance until he reached his retirement next March.'

'Bikes, Sergeant, the current operation was the recovery of stolen bikes.'

'Yes, sir, but Inspector Ryan left this morning and I felt it was my duty, as we discussed, sir, to accompany him.'

'I see.' Connors stared at her. Nola stared back, or rather she stared at a point over his right shoulder. 'What can you tell me about this morning's case?'

'Break-in and entry, Kilmainham. The owner, a twenty-eight-year-old woman, was assaulted. Unclear what was taken.'

'I see.'

'I suspect it was the victim's husband.'

'Oh?'

'They were separated, and he was the one who called it in.'

'A simple case, you imagine?'

'I imagine it's cut and dried, sir.' She paused. 'But it will likely occupy a good deal of Inspector Ryan's time, with interviews and what not.'

Connors pressed his tanned fingers together. 'And you will pay close attention to its progression.'

'As we agreed, sir, I will stick to Inspector Ryan like a limpet.'

Connors smiled. 'See to it that this case *stays* simple, Sergeant. And when it's wrapped up, remember, the bikes the bikes are calling.'

Nola forced herself to smile at his terrible pun. 'Yes sir.'

She stood to leave and had almost made it to the door when he called her.

'Sergeant Kane?'

'Sir?'

'How does Inspector Ryan *seem* to you?'

Nola considered a variety of responses. 'Thorough, sir,' she said eventually.

Connors glanced the clock over her head. 'That will be all, Sergeant.'

12

Elliot left the hospital. He knew he should head back to the station, but instead he drove west to a small private housing estate consisting of twelve townhouses built in the shape of a horseshoe. He parked by a well-cared-for green opposite the estate, where he could keep an eye on both the houses and the bus stop on the main road. While he waited, he took another painkiller and tried to get comfortable, and when that didn't happen, he popped another.

His thoughts drifted as a pleasant warmth enveloped him, keeping him happy company until shortly after midday, when a bus pulled up and a woman wearing a quilted coat over a nurse's uniform got off and crossed the street. She was carrying a plastic shopping bag in her right hand. Elliot watched her enter one of the townhouses before he got out and followed, walking slowly up the tiny rise, conscious of where his feet went. One step, then another.

Oh boy, he was a bit fuzzy around the edges when what he needed was clarity, focus. If any mistakes were made, if he messed things up, he'd never forgive himself. Time was not on his side.

She deserved his best.

They deserved his best.

The door opened. Rebecca Black was older than when he'd last spoken to her, naturally. Her dark-red hair was shorter than he remembered, no longer wavy but straight, worn in a shoulder-length bob with a side parting. But her eyes, her remarkable eyes, had not changed one iota. They still reminded him of a hawk.

'You,' she said.

'Yes,' he said, unsure if that was the correct reply. Too late to come up with a better one.

'What are you doing here?' She looked past him towards the street. 'How do you know where I live?'

'You're not that difficult to find.'

'You have some neck showing up at my door, do you know that?'

'Rebecca, I'd like you to listen to me.'

'Fuck off.' She started to close the door. He put his hand against it to stop her. 'Get your hand off my door.'

'Rebecca, if you could just hear me out—'

'You don't get to do this, Ryan. You don't get to come back into my life and do this.' She slapped his hand away with such force that he wobbled and had to grab the wall to stop himself from falling. 'Hey, are you all right?'

He realised with a start that he was not and closed his eyes for a moment to gather himself. He had not expected her to be friendly – indeed, why should she be? Her anger was justified. It was just that he didn't have the capacity to fight with her. Thinking was hard enough. Standing was hard enough.

He opened his eyes. She narrowed hers. 'What are you taking?'

'What?'

'Oh, please, I'm a nurse so don't give me that. I'm not blind. You're as high as a kite.'

'I had an accident a few weeks ago, a fall. I hurt my back. I was in hospital for a while.'

She nodded but didn't ask for any more details, or probably didn't care.

A small black dog came down the hall behind her and stood sniffing the air. Elliot smiled at it. 'Oh, that's nice, you have a dog. What's its name?'

'What do you want?'

'Natalie Dormond's mother came to see me several weeks ago.'

The name caught Rebecca's attention, but not her trust. 'So?'

'She gave me a diary, Nat's diary.' Elliot tried to smile. 'It turns out she was a meticulous recorder of detail.'

'Stupid bitch,' Rebecca said, but not unkindly. 'She was always scribbling in that thing. I'd wondered what happened to it. I thought maybe her mam destroyed it.'

'She didn't find it until recently.'

'And, what, she brought it to you?'

'She did.'

'Waste of time.' Rebecca sniffed. 'Too late now.'

'I know.'

'So now what?'

'I thought maybe you could look through it and corroborate—'

'No, no fucking way. Whatever it is, whatever *this* is, I can't be involved. For God's sake, Ryan, I have a family, a life. I needed you to listen back then, after Nat was killed. You weren't interested. Too busy covering for your pal.'

'I never covered for anyone a day in my life.'

'Easy to say.'

'It's not I ... I didn't understand what I was dealing with back then.'

She gave a short, bitter half-laugh. 'No, that won't wash, Ryan, not with me. You didn't want to know; you didn't want to dip into the shit at the Black Top in case any of it stuck to you. You think I don't remember? You think I don't remember you and that pig coming to the house to talk to Dave? You knew what was happening in the care home. You knew what David Ash was doing. Acting like he cared about us, acting like he was on our side. Making us trust him until he could use that trust against us. Oh yeah, you knew. You knew he brought us there, plied us with drink, smoke, passed us around between his so-called friends. The man was a groomer, and you knew.'

'I swear to you I had no idea.'

'How many complaints did you get?'

'Rebecca—'

'There was a social worker, Carol. She knew – fat lot of good it did.'

Carol. Elliot tried to remember. Carol ... he thought he knew the name, but when he tried to grasp it slipped through his fingers like smoke. Rebecca was watching him. 'I don't remember.'

'What happened the night Nat died? She was in the Black Top earlier that evening – people saw her ... Next thing she's dead under a railway bridge? Come on.'

'I didn't know.'

She shook her head. 'See? Still lying, still full of shit, still covering for *him*.'

'I'm not covering – I'm trying to piece everything together.'

'Why bother, why now?'

'Clancy's retiring on Friday.'

'Good for him. I hope hell welcomes him with open arms.'

'He'll walk away with a pension and the good will of the force.'

'And?'

'He won't if I can help it.'

'What difference does it make now?' she said. 'What's done is done – you can't raise the dead.'

'I know that. I'm not trying to raise them.'

'Then what do you want?'

He was flustered. How could he explain how important this was? 'I think your brother was innocent.'

'No shit, Sherlock.'

'This might clear his name.'

'He spent fifteen years in prison, you stupid fuck. It's too late.'

'I wrote to the parole board. I spoke for him.'

She laughed. 'Oh my God, my God, you don't get it, you don't get a thing. Listen to me, Ryan, it doesn't matter, it's too late. All you're doing now is playing catch-up.' She held her hand up, palm flat. 'Don't come here to my house with bullshit. If you can't be honest with yourself, how the fuck do you expect to be honest with me?'

He hung his head. Her eyes, those eyes that burned him fifteen years before, lit him up now in shame.

'You knew Clancy was involved,' she said softly, not accusingly, but as a flat certainty. 'You knew.'

'I didn't have any real evidence.'

'You didn't look for any – you didn't want to know what your pal was into.'

Elliot started to tremble. 'I'm sorry.'

'For what?'

'For being a coward.'

She sighed heavily. 'We're all cowards, if the truth be known.'

'What do you mean?'

'I saw him when he was dying.'

'Who?'

'Who do you think? David Ash, he was on the ward.' She pulled her cardigan tight. 'Saw him lying in the bed, all bones and skin, not much else. Yellow he was. Half-dead. His liver was shot.'

Elliot stared.

'I could have finished him, made him suffer – I know how. But I didn't, did I?' She gave a strange little half-laugh. 'Do you know, the bastard didn't even know it was me.'

'I'm sorry.'

'I'm not. Not now. I'm not talking about some higher-ground shit either. He wasn't worth it; he wasn't worth a second of any of it. Let him meet his maker, I say, like I'll meet mine knowing I could have done wrong and didn't.' She glared. 'Can you say the same?'

Elliot lowered his head. He could not bring himself to look at her.

'What are you going to do?' she asked.

'Expose him.'

'Why? Nat's dead and Ronan's got parole.'

'I know.' He raised his head.

'Why did you write to the board, why did you do that?'

'I thought if I helped Ronan, he could help me.'

Rebecca didn't say anything for a moment. He could see her thinking. First, she looked thoughtful.

Then frightened.

'What?' he said.

'Have you ... does Clancy know you're rattling this cage?'

'I don't know, it's possible. He came to see me at the hospital when I was ... I was sedated.'

'Fucking hell, Ryan, you're the same gullible gobshite, aren't you?'

'I don't know what you mean.'

'If Ronan's out ... if Clancy thinks he's a threat, if he thinks I'm a threat to him, what do you think he'll do? A man about to retire, on a hefty pension no less. And you're going to threaten all that? Use us to put to right what you did wrong?' She shook her head. 'We didn't have this conversation; we haven't seen each other. My name doesn't appear anywhere, okay? You got it?'

'But—'

'But nothing,' she snapped. 'I don't know what fucking game you're playing at, and I don't care. But you are messing with a dangerous man, and you have no right, *no* right to involve me or Ronan in it. I don't care how much guilt you carry, Ryan, that's yours. Leave us the hell alone.'

'I'm not doing this for me,' he said. 'Rebecca, I'm doing this for Natalie.'

'*Natalie is dead.*' She flung the words at him, spittle flying. Somewhere back in the house, the little dog whined.

Elliot sagged. 'I'm sorry I bothered you.' He turned to go, gingerly stepping off her step. Rebecca called out to him. He turned back.

'You say you have Nat's diary. You've read her own fucking words, so use what she said – at least she has *nothing* left to lose.' She gave him a long, hard look. 'Don't call here again.'

This time he made no attempt to stop her from slamming the door.

13

Nola met Gracie in the canteen for coffee.

'How are you holding up?' Gracie asked, watching Nola empty four sachets of sugar into her coffee and stir it with a pen.

'Shit, I hate it.'

'What are you working on?'

'Some DV case, it's stupid. I mean, it's obvious who the suspect is, but Ryan is ... he operates a certain way.'

'How do you mean?'

'Old school, you know? We have to follow procedure to the dot.'

'Ah.'

'I should be happy; you should have seen what they were working on before this case.'

'What?'

'Bikes.'

'Bikes?'

'Stolen bikes, like ... actual bikes.' Nola stirred the coffee furiously. 'Apparently it's a VBD.'

'A what?'

'A Very Big Deal.'

'Oh.'

'What are you doing?'

Gracie shrugged. 'Oh, you know.'

'No, I don't know, tell me.'

'We're working on the Clyde House shooting.'

'No way.'

Gracie spread her hands.

'I thought that was special branch?'

'We're support.'

Nola's scowl deepened. The Clyde House shooting had been *all* over the media during her suspension, with multiple sources connecting the killing of a young MMA fighter to a high-profile gangland crime family. The sort of case Nola would give a left arm to be involved with. The sort of case that *made* careers.

She drank some of her coffee; it was disgusting, even with the sugar. She put it down and pushed it away. 'I don't know if I can do this.'

'You can do it; you know you can.'

'I'll go out of my mind working with the Fossil.'

'It's a couple of months and then you're back with the squad.'

'You don't know that.'

'Paul won't let you fall through the cracks.'

Paul. Nola couldn't remember Gracie ever calling Deacon by his first name before. She must have done ... but Nola didn't think so. Something else to chew on.

'I'm guessing you've heard the news – he's running for inspector.'

Nola laid her head in her hands. The hangover she'd been trying to ignore all morning was back and pounding on the inside of her skull. She had never felt more miserable in her entire life. Ever since she had been a little kid, she had wanted to be a cop, dreamed about it, convinced she could make a difference. Now here she was, twenty-six, demoted and stymied, shunted aside.

A fuck-up.

Just like her old man.

She groaned.

'Nola.'

'What?'

'Is Inspector Ryan working on something other than the case?'

'What?' She lifted her head, confused. 'What do you mean?'

Gracie shrugged. 'I've heard rumours, you know?'

'What rumours?'

'About him going over old cases.'

'What old cases?'

'Dunno, cold cases, I guess.'

'No idea. I can ask Robbie if you like. Oh, speaking of Robbie, he wants to know if you want to go to Clancy's party on Friday night. Don't worry, I told him he wasn't your type.'

'Why did you tell him that?'

'He's not ... is he?'

Gracie shrugged.

'You have a boyfriend,' Nola said, trying and failing to keep the disapproving tone from her voice.

'We're not exclusive.'

'Since when?'

'Nola, come on.'

'What?' Nola was genuinely baffled, annoyed. 'You and Tadgh have been going out for yonks.'

Gracie sipped her tea. 'Are you coming on Friday?'

'No.'

'Seriously?'

'Seriously.'

'Why not? You could—'

'Yo, One Punch!'

Gracie and Nola looked around. Two sergeants had strolled into the canteen and spotted them. One of them did a quick shuffle before throwing a punch into the air. When Gracie gave them the finger, they laughed and carried on walking. Nola watched them go, her cheeks aflame.

'Ignore them, they're idiots.'

Nola picked up her disgusting coffee and stood. 'I've got to get back.'

'Nola—'

'I'll see you, Gracie, mind yourself.'

She left, head held high, mortified.

14

Elliot arrived back at the station and found Nola sitting at her desk with her foot curled underneath her, eating something that looked disgusting and smelled worse. His stomach immediately revolted. The earlier high had eased to tolerable, though he felt drained, unwell and demoralised.

'Sergeant, please tell me what that is.'

'Chilli dog.'

'Do you have to eat it here?'

'I'm waiting on someone to get back to me from Jolie Laide. Hey, while I have you, I ran Simon Albright's name too – he's got form. Took a tyre iron to a Renault Trafic two weeks ago and got a hiding over it. Got booked, but no charges pressed. He went to hospital.'

'When was this?'

'Friday the eleventh.' She reached for a sheet of paper and passed it behind her with one hand. 'Case 11278J, Sergeant Lucy Powell.'

'Good work, Sergeant.'

Elliot took it, sat down at and stared at it unseeing. After a moment he shook his head. It was after two and he'd eaten nothing since his pathetic breakfast. No wonder he was feeling a little ropey. He reached down, opened the lower drawer and took out the Tupperware bowl and the bottle of water Shona had given him. He did not generally approve of eating at his desk, but in this brave new world it was clearly every man for himself.

'How'd you get on at the hospital? How's the vic?'

'Stable.'

'Did you talk to Albright?'

'Yes, and to Jody Kavanagh's sister, Fiona Hynes, and her husband, Malcolm Hynes.'

'Oh yeah? What's their deal?'

'They were very upset, as you can imagine, very shocked.' He opened the lid and peered in hopefully. There was not a whole lot to it – some leaves, some shredded carrot, a single boiled egg and some slices of chicken he could have skimmed over flat water.

Pitiful.

'There seems to be a level of animosity between the Hyneses and Albright.'

'Did you ask him what he was doing at her house?'

'Of course. He said Jody asked him over.'

'On a Monday morning, before work?'

'He showed me the message she sent.'

Nola looked sceptical. 'Could have come from anyone, or maybe he sent it himself. It's not like we have her phone and can check.'

Elliot inclined his head. She had a point.

'Did he say what she wanted to talk about?'

'No.'

'Did you ask him?'

'No.'

'Why not?'

'Things got a little heated.' He picked up the salad bowl. 'Any word on the Tesla owner?'

'No, like I said, I'm waiting on Diandra Cliff to get back to me – she's Jody's boss or whatever in Jolie Laide. She might know who this Billy Big Bollocks is.'

'Don't swear, Sergeant.'

'We should bring Albright in and put the squeeze on him.' She sucked sauce from her thumb. 'In Homicide we'd have the creep crying over his signed statement by now.'

The temperature in the office cooled significantly.

'In this unit,' Elliot said stiffly, 'under my watch, we do things by the book. It's dull, no doubt, but it's valid and it doesn't leave irregularities.'

'He's our man, I bet you twenty yoyos.'

'And if he is we will build a case against him, piece by piece. Who else did you speak to?'

'I left a message for Beverly Russell, Bane's mam. She says she's busy today so I'll get her tomorrow. I spoke to a few of Jody's friends – same story each time: she's great, she's sweet, talented, everyone loves her but nobody, and I mean nobody, is too sweet on Simon Albright. I'm going to see her best friend, Gabriel Frost, in a while – he should be good for info. I'm telling you, no one likes the ex, period.'

'Being unpopular is not the same as being guilty.' Elliot stabbed at a chicken piece and watched the tines of his plastic fork buckle without breaking the skin. What had Shona cooked it in, Teflon? 'Have we located the mobile phone?'

'No, it's turned off. I ran a "trace my phone" app on her

number, but it's either deactivated or she never had it on in the first place.'

'Why would it be missing? Why would someone take a phone but not money or jewellery or her laptop?'

'Probably because the phone has information on it. I bet you anything Albright has it.'

God, Elliot thought, *she's like a dog with a bone.*

Nola finished her food, balled the tinfoil and tossed it expertly into the metal bin. 'Did you hear? Paddy Clancy is having a leaving do on Friday.'

'And?'

She raised her eyebrows. 'Whoa, no need for snark. Just passing conversation – I didn't mean anything by it.'

'I ... you're right, I apologise, Sergeant. Will you be attending with your paramour?'

'What paramour?'

'I thought you were involved with Paul Deacon?'

Now it was Nola's turn to bristle. 'I am not *involved* with that ape in any way, shape or form.'

Elliot realised he'd insulted her and wasn't entirely sure how to backtrack. Before he could figure something out, she wiped her hands with her napkin and grabbed her jacket.

'I'm going to go talk to Gabriel Frost, I'll have my phone if you need me.'

When she was gone, Elliot took his fifth painkiller of the day, abandoned the salad and went downstairs to Records.

Sergeant Curran raised her eyebrows as he approached the desk. 'Behold, as I live and breathe, you're alive.'

'In the flesh.'

'How are you keeping?'

'Out of trouble, you?'

'Oh good Lord, no!' She laughed. 'Where would be the fun in that?'

'How's Mike?'

'Grand, chafing at the bit a little now he's retired. He's been talking about buying a holiday home in West Cork. Can you believe that? Mike? I think he's lost his mind.'

'Retirement does things to a person, or so I'm told.'

She grew serious for a moment. 'I was sorry to hear about your accident.'

'I think it was in all the papers,' he said, aiming for jokey but aware he hadn't quite pulled it off. 'I was careless, that's all.'

'I suppose you've heard Clancy is pulling the pin?'

'Yes, I heard.'

She tilted her chair backwards slightly. 'I can tell you, I won't be sorry to see that one go.'

Elliot was surprised. Most people, including the brass, loved coppers like Clancy since he was a big numbers guys, the sort that always cleared cases, which made everyone, especially the brass, feel good about themselves. Let them sleep a little better at night. Paddy Clancy, poster boy for the boys in blue, dogged, hard-working, photogenic, verbose, a fuzzy peach of a man with one eye firmly on the prize at all times.

'Elliot?'

'Hmm?'

Sergeant Curran was peering at him. 'Are you okay? You look a little ... glassy.'

'Yes, I'm fine.'

Was he?

'You left the room there for a moment, Elliot.'

'I'm sorry. It's been a hectic morning. First day back, you know how it is.'

'Ah, of course. Sorry. Did you need something?'

'I'd like to see the Dormond file, if you could rustle it up for me. Here's the case number.' He passed her a yellow Post-it.

She took it, turned to her computer and tapped the keys. After a moment she leaned closer to the screen. 'That was one of yours, wasn't it?'

'Yes.' He waited for her to ask why he wanted it, a lie already prepared, but she did not. Bless her lack of curiosity.

'Okay, hang tight and I'll be right back.'

He waited, counting time, feeling the weight of the diary against his chest. He thought about Rebecca Black, the fear in her voice. Without her, the evidence was light, one less string in a weak bow. Still, he owed her the privacy she deserved. He owed all of them so much.

For what that *is worth*, the inner voice sneered.

A door opened behind him. He turned his head and found himself looking into the alarmingly blue eyes of Paul Deacon. Elliot didn't like Deacon: didn't like his style, his attitude or the smug look on his stupid face. He kept his own face entirely impassive, decided that was worse and let it slide back to dislike. A guilty conscience was easier to hide behind dislike. Less theatrics.

'You're back then?' Deacon said, smirking because that's what he did, smirk.

'Very observant, Sergeant. I can see why you get all the big cases.'

'How's the noggin?'

'Fortified.'

'Is it true they had to winch you out?' Deacon glanced at the Post-it on the desk.

Elliot reached out, grabbed it and put it in his pocket. 'Did you want something, Deacon?'

'How are you and One Punch getting on?'

'Who?'

Deacon laughed. 'Sergeant Kane.'

'Oh, yes, she's … fine.'

'You'll like her, she's a tough cookie. Tell her I was asking for her.'

'I'll be sure to let her know you were enquiring.' Elliot turned back towards the desk, stony-faced. They waited in silence until Julie returned and handed Elliot the file.

'There you are now, Inspector. Oh, hello, Sergeant, what can I do for you?'

'Excuse me.' Elliot stepped past Deacon with the file pressed firmly to his chest and went into the annexed room left of Julie's desk where he could read in peace. As he closed the door, he felt Deacon's eyes boring into him and knew with absolute certainty the younger man's presence in Records was not an accident.

Someone was keeping an eye on him, and someone wanted him to know he was being watched.

15

Nola pushed open the door of a bar on Molesworth Street and stepped inside. It was a long and low-ceilinged, and what little light the teeny-tiny tasselled lamps dotted about the place gave off did little to dispel the slightly gloomy atmosphere.

Nola gave her eyes a second to adjust before she walked up to the bar where a man with a black quiff, wearing a sequined waistcoat, glanced up from the menu he was writing. Most of a Bloody Mary sat on the counter next to his elbow.

'We're not open yet, hun, call back at four.'

'I'm looking for Gabriel Frost.'

'That's me,' he said, peering at her. 'Are you Sergeant Kane?'

'Yes.' She took her ID out.

'My God, you're a child!'

Nola put her ID away. She had run across this reaction before and tried not to let it get to her. 'Mr Frost—'

'Call me Gabe, hun, everyone does.'

'I appreciate you taking the time to see me so promptly.'

'Well, of course, my God, it's all so tragic. I called the hospital earlier and they hardly told me anything.'

'I understand, this must be—'

'It was him, wasn't it? I bet it was – I bet it was Simon.'

Nola's scalp tingled slightly on hearing the name. God, was Ryan blind? Stupid? Everyone and their dog knew Simon Albright was guilty, so why the hell was she wasting time like this? 'Why would you think that?'

'Well, who else?'

Nola pulled out a stool and sat down. 'You said on the phone you and Jody have been friends since you were children. What can you tell me about her?'

'Jody?' He grinned. 'She's an amazing woman – kind, sweet and so talented. My God, give her a cardboard box and she could transform it into the Taj Mahal. I mean, did you *see* the house she did for Tamara Ford? Out of this world!'

Nola frowned. 'Tamara Ford the actress?'

'Icon, love her.'

'What do you mean Jody did a house for her?'

'You didn't see it? It was a television show, *All Buildings Great and Small*.' He rolled his eyes. 'Right? I know, not exactly a wildly original title, but it was a *huge* hit, especially Jody. People loved her. And that huge pile belonging to Tamara Ford and her geriatric husband was the icing on the cake. Jody was inundated with work after that.' He leaned on the counter and lowered his voice. 'Between you and me, Jody was considering leaving Jolie Laide and setting up on her own.'

'Really?'

'Oh sure, it was always a dream of Jody's to have her own company, and after *All Buildings Great and Small*, believe me, she could afford to pick and choose clients.'

Nola took out her notebook and wrote in it. She wondered how happy Diandra Cliff was about Jody leaving the company. 'When did this show air?'

'December, actually not long before the big brouhaha.'

'Brouhaha?'

'When Jody and Simon split.'

'Why did you automatically assume Simon Albright harmed Jody?'

'Stands to reason. For leaving him, for being more successful than him. You know, I never understood what she saw in that man in the first place. I mean, he's not ugly, I suppose, but God is he dreary.'

'Mr—'

'Gabe.'

'Gabe … did Jody ever say anything to you about being afraid of Simon?'

'Oh, please, she didn't have to.' He took his phone from his pocket, and after a few swipes and one muffled 'Oh, not that one', shoved the phone across the bar. 'Look at this.'

Nola leaned in.

In the photo Jody was standing by a Christmas tree wearing a Christmas jumper with a reindeer on it. Gabe stood next to her, resplendent in a Christmas onesie that was unzipped to his navel, and on Jody's other side stood an unsmiling man, dressed head to toe in black. He was blond, dressed in jeans and a pale-blue shirt and looked like he'd rather be anywhere else in the whole world.

'Look at his face, look at it!'

'He looks older than her.'

'Eighteen years.'

'When was this taken?'

'December, before they went to Sligo,' Gabe said. 'Old sourpuss, that's what Jody called him behind his back. Never cracked a smile in all the time I've known him. I do not know what on earth Jody ever saw in him, but there you go. The heart wants what the heart wants, am I right? He even tried to get her into jazz – can you believe that? Jazz? I mean talk about affected and—'

Nola tried to get him back on track. 'Did Jody complain about his behaviour a lot?'

'Well,' he paused, a little annoyed at the interruption, 'I wouldn't say she complained – that isn't Jody's style, you know? But anyone with eyes could see she was getting fed up of him. Especially after Diandra gave him the boot.'

'Diandra Cliff? Jody's boss?'

'Right, you know she fired him?'

'I didn't know Simon worked with Jody.'

'Not day to day, but Diandra had him in on some design projects – probably to keep Jody onside, you know?'

'And she fired him?'

'Fired, let him go, whatever. But she definitely cut him off at the knees, especially after they split. If you ask me, Diandra was probably glad to see the back of him. I know I would be.'

Nola wrote it down.

'Mind you, Diandra is a bit of a weapon herself.' Gabe sniffed. 'Not exactly Miss Sunshine.'

'Tell me about the ... brouhaha – what happened?'

'Oh gosh now. Don't ask me for deets, but Jody and Simon had some major blow out down in Jody's mother's place. Course, the Ice Queen probably had something to do with it, but if she did, I won't hold *that* against her.'

'The Ice Queen?'

'Morag Kavanagh, Jody's womb with a view.'

'Her—?'

'Her mother, richer than the pope but with all the maternal instinct of an iceberg. She and Jody didn't speak for years and years, but they made up when Jody's dad passed away. I guess sometimes grief is the bridge, right?'

'When did Jody's dad die?'

'Two thousand and seventeen, but he'd been sick for years, dementia. Jody was in London when it happened. It was me who had to break the news. Jody and Simon came back for the funeral, and that's when she and her mother started talking again.'

'What about Jody's sister? Are she and Jody close?'

'Her?' Gabe managed to look and sound hugely judgemental. 'Hardly. She didn't even bother to attend the funeral.'

'Oh? Is there drama there, between the family?'

His suspiciously black eyebrows shot up into his suspiciously black hairline. 'I couldn't say.'

'But what do you think?'

'Well, Fiona's a funny duck and no mistake. She married into this ultra-strict religious sect, if you can believe that. Jody's mother acts like she's dead. Jody's seen a little more of Fiona since she came back to Ireland, but I can tell she's exasperated by her. Fiona keeps popping out all these children like gremlins. Anti-vax, anti-modernity, anti-social, home-schooling fruit-bats insane.'

'When did Jody come home for good?'

'Summer 2019, she and Simon moved over from London. Big mistake if you ask me. Imagine leaving London for Dublin? It's no wonder they broke up.'

Nola wrote the date down and tapped the pen against the page. So far, nothing Gabe had told her really gave her any insight into

83

Jody Kavanagh. She was talented, kind, gorgeous. So why would anyone want to do her harm, apart from Simon Albright?

'So, Jody left Simon in December or January, and now it's November. Why would he hurt her now, after all this time?'

Gabriel Frost leaned across the bar, his eyes twinkling with gleeful gossip. Nola grinned despite herself. She wished all witnesses were this ready to spill the tea.

'Well, I don't like to tell tales out of school—'

'Of course not.'

'But between you and me, Jody landed herself a very rich fish recently.' He made a reeling motion. 'Snatched that baby right out of the pool.'

'Billy Big Bollocks?'

'Excuse me?'

'Never mind, please go on. Do we have a name for this fish?'

'Jools Byrne.'

Nola wrote that down and underlined it. Gabe said it like it should mean something to her.

'It's like my mama always told me, like attracts like. Jody met Jools at one of Tamara's parties – big hitter, I think he could be richer than her mother. There was only one problem and it's a doozy.'

'What's that?'

'Jools used to be married to Amber Feenan.'

'And she is ...?'

'She *was* one of Jody's friends back in the day. You better believe there's a big fat *was* there. Amber lost her shit when she found out that Jody and Jools were seeing each other.'

Finally, Nola thought. Maybe Jody wasn't all sweetness and light after all. 'Are you friends with Amber?'

'We know each other a little.' He made a face. 'But she's closer to Monica, Monica Fell?'

'Ah, yes, I spoke to her. I'm seeing her tomorrow morning.'

'Sweetheart, you'll love her. She'll have the goss on Amber too but you'll have to drag it out of her. Mon's a type, doesn't like to talk out of school.'

Not like you, Nola thought. 'Would Amber have harmed Jody, do you think?'

'Amber's crazy – like, certifiable.' He leaned across the bar. 'I once saw her reef a girl down a flight of stairs at some awards show for flirting with Jools. I'm not speaking out of school either, but if you ask me that woman is capable of anything.'

'One last thing, does Jools Byrne drive a Tesla?'

Gabe Frost laughed and took a swig of his Bloody Mary. 'Oh God, what else, hun, what else?'

16

Elliot read the file. After a while, he closed it and sat staring at nothing. He was glad he had taken the extra painkiller. It allowed him time to float free, gave him space to let his mind drift.

Natalie Dormond had been thirteen years old – already known to the guards for truancy and various juvenile-court appearances – when she was sent to David and Melinda Ash's juvenile care home, where she met Rebecca Black. The two outcasts hit it off right away, and within months, the bond between them deepened until they were inseparable, according to everyone who knew them.

Natalie had been a few weeks shy of fifteen when he and Clancy discovered her body in a disused yard under a railway bridge in East Wall. She had been stabbed to death. Her autopsy and tox screens revealed a gruesome story. The child – and that was the only way Elliot would ever think of her – had various injuries, injuries that raised many questions, questions that should have been asked and had not been because, well, she was a street kid who did drugs and fell through the cracks. Sad, sure, but that was life.

He took the red diary from his inner pocket and flicked about one-third of the way through it, landing on 19 September.

F-day. Black Top. WD40.

It had been written three days before Natalie died, and here Elliot ran aground.

The Black Top had been a pub over on the East Wall, owned, it was said, by a local crime lord, but run by a man named Fats AKA Francis Clancy, older and heavier cousin to one Paddy Clancy. It had an upstairs 'lounge' where it held private parties on a regular basis, parties attended by people from all walks of life, all backgrounds, but with 'commonalities'. It was also, according to a single witness, the last place anyone ever saw Natalie Dormond, who was there with another girl. The witness said the girls were part of a larger party. The witness would not give a name, and after a brief investigation (hah) the phone call was discounted. Especially when Natalie's relationship with Ronan Black, Rebecca's older brother, was uncovered. Black had a long history of drug use and mental illness. When arrested, he was carrying a blade covered in Natalie Dormond's blood.

Neat and tidy.

Elliot drummed his fingers on the desk as he tried to conjure Natalie's face. He'd remembered her as a slight girl, pretty, younger than she looked, with pale skin and a shy smile.

He remembered the house: a plain semi-D with an overgrown front garden and a dirty Opel Corsa in the drive, net curtains. Saw the door open, the suspicious, hostile face of David Ash, his twitchy and frankly unpleasant chain-smoking wife, Melinda, behind him. He remembered breaking the news of Natalie's death, noted their obvious and frankly offensive disinterest. But enough about them, to hell with them. It was Rebecca who followed him down the street to where he'd parked the car. Thin, spotty, wearing a green duffel coat several sizes too big for her.

She caught his arm. She had, he remembered now, a gap between her front teeth. She had been crying.

'What happened?' Straight out, no beating around the bush.

'Natalie was found dead last night.'

'Where?'

'East Wall, in an old railway yard.' He looked past her towards the house, saw the curtain in the front window twitch. 'Rebecca ... we've arrested Ronan.'

The look on her face – no girl that age should have been able to look so disgusted, so cynical.

'You stupid bastard.'

She turned and began to walk away. She had taken several steps when she whipped back around. Elliot remembered her blazing eyes. 'She was killed at the Black Top, but you don't care, none of you do because you're all the fucken same.'

'Rebecca—'

'Fuck off.'

Elliot felt a stab of shame. Rebecca had looked to the uniform for help, seen through the bullshit and nailed his colours to the mast.

We didn't care.

The case was tidy, wrapped, neat. Ronan Black killed his underage girlfriend. Case closed. Go home and kiss your wife, sing a lullaby to your child, eat some food, put your feet up, have a beer, maybe two.

You deserve it.

Ring the bell, all is well.

Shit.

Then the visit from Natalie's mother happened.

She was a woman to whom time had not been kind, nor grief

gentle. When she asked to see him the week before his accident, she had looked too old for her years, worn.

'You remember me then,' she had said when he came downstairs.

'I do, of course.' They shook hands. 'How are you?'

The corners of her lips dipped. 'Is that a question?'

Elliot sat down beside her. He had never forgotten her voice, the accent, her quirky mode of speech. He scanned his memory. She hailed from some island off the coast of Croatia, a hardscrabble place with a tiny population. Married to an Irishman who'd worked abroad for years before moving back to Dublin with his wife and three children to set up a laundromat on Dorset Street. Hard workers both, and did well until Alec Dromond was stabbed during a robbery while locking up one night. Survived ten long, miserable days until sepsis took hold. Leaving Kaya to bring up three children on her own in a country that was not hers.

He remembered her opening the door of her neat terraced house, remembered the faint smile that fell when she saw their uniforms, remembered the cry of distress and anguish when he broke the news that her oldest child, her runaway daughter, had been found dead, murdered like her husband. All these things he recalled in a single instant.

'You wanted to see me. What can I do for you?'

She opened her handbag and took from it a small red diary. It had gold lettering on the cover and the year. It was the same year Natalie had died.

'The day before she was … died, Natalie came to the house. She was, I think, very troubled. I asked her to stay, but she would not stay.' She looked down for a moment, swallowed and regained her composure. 'I thought she wanted money, things to sell for drugs. But now I think she knew – she knew she was going to die and she came to say goodbye. I did not know and I did not understand.'

'How could you?'

'I am leaving Dublin, selling my home, Inspector Ryan. The agent suggested I give the place a subtle *glow-up*, as he put it.' Her eyes bored into his. 'As part of this *glow-up*, we had to do something about Natalie's old room. I found this under the carpet, hidden with ... other things. Last night I read it and—' She blinked, blinked again.

Elliot waited.

'I have known for a long time my daughter lived a complicated life, but she did not become what she became alone.' She passed the diary to him, pressed it into his hands. 'There are names, numbers, dates in here, some that you may find useful, or perhaps not. It is not for me to tell you how to do your job. But she was my child, and I loved her. And this I will do for her.'

Elliot closed his fingers around the diary, felt the weight of it in his hand. He looked into Emily Dormond's eyes and read the pain there, as raw as the day he'd called to her neat little red-brick home to break the worst news a parent could ever hear. 'I'll do what I can,' he said.

She nodded and stood up. He stood up too; this time he did not offer his hand.

'Thank you.'

'Do you want me to call—?'

'I do not want to hear from you. I will return to my homeland and forget this place. I want nothing more than this.'

'Okay.'

'Goodbye.'

He watched her until she left the building, then put the diary in his inside pocket so he could read it in private later.

And he had read it.

And he had understood his role in her grief.

And it all but destroyed him.

17

When Nola got back to the station Elliot was once again nowhere to be found. She wondered briefly where he kept disappearing to, then sat at her desk and googled Jools Byrne.

Several newspaper articles popped up about Jools and his family, photos of his property-tycoon father with his German mother at various black-tie events, looking impossibly glamorous and chic. A death notice for his father. Photos of Jools coming and going from various nightclubs over the years, handsome, always with a thin blonde woman clinging to his hand. Notices for his wedding to 'society darling Amber Feenan'.

Huh, Nola thought, scrolling. Jools Byrne was a walking cliché right up until his mother died, then he seemed to vanish from society until an interview two years later in a weekend supplement. It was a high-profile, but sober, piece talking about his ambitious rewilding plan for the Leitrim estate he had inherited from his mother and three throwaway lines about how sad he was that his marriage didn't work out.

Her phone vibrated in the pocket of her jacket. She took it out and read the messages. One was from Gracie, wanting to know if Nola wanted to go for a drink after work, and one was from Macey Butler asking her to call the lab.

Nola replied to Gracie first. She typed 'Sure', then deleted it and typed 'Maybe'. Then she deleted that and didn't type anything at all for a moment.

Gracie, gorgeous, sweet, funny up-for-anything Gracie, mad as a box of badgers, top-notch mate, always ready for a bit of craic. Why was she dragging her heels?

She sent a thumbs-up emoji.

Next, she called forensics and doodled while she waited for her quarry. On her notepad she wrote 'Amber Feenan' and underlined it. If someone had done the dirty here it was Jools, but – as she could herself attest – sometimes the hurt lashed out at the wrong person. By all accounts, Simon Albright was still her top suspect, but this changed things, widened the field.

'Sergeant Kane?'

'Yes?'

'I'm sorry, I did try to get Inspector Ryan, but I can't reach him.'

'That's okay – what have you got?'

'We located a card in the main kitchen bin – we believe it came with the flowers. It reads ... hold on now ... ah, my Latin is a little rusty so you must forgive me – it reads "*nescit amor habere modum*".'

Nola laughed. 'I'll see your rusty Latin and raise you a "what?"'

'Basically, it means love does not know how to keep within bounds.'

'Great, and what's that in English?'

'Your guess, Sergeant, is as good as mine. An out-of-bounds love? Something or someone forbidden?'

'Was it signed?'

'Unfortunately, no.'

'Do you have any idea where the flowers came from?'

'That I can help you with. They came from a very expensive little boutique in Donnybrook called Ava's Blooms.'

'Brilliant, thanks a million.'

Nola hung up and sat for a moment, bouncing her thumbs off each other. Decision made, she snapped out of her chair, grabbed her jacket and went looking for Robbie. He was in his cubicle, reading a sports paper.

'What?'

'Keys.' She waggled her fingers.

'For what?'

'I got a line on the flowers and I want to nab them before they close.'

'I'll drive.'

'Yeah, right, give me the keys.'

Robbie put the paper down. 'No. I'm responsible for that car – if something happens it's on me. I'll drive you wherever you need to go.'

'You're being ridiculous.'

'Take it or leave it.'

'Arsehole.'

As soon as she said it, she realised she was being rude for no reason. Robbie Keller was not Paul Deacon, even if they did share the same sex.

'Fine ... if you're not too busy.' She nodded to the paper.

'I can always make time for a pretty lady.' He wiggled his eyebrows at her.

Nola instantly regretted her decision.

As they walked down the hall towards the lift, she told Robbie about Simon working with Jody.

'Wow,' he said. 'That puts a different spin on it, doesn't it?'

'Maybe.' Nola was thinking of Connors's reaction when he learned of this little complication. 'I wish I knew where the damn phone was.'

'Yeah,' Robbie said. 'The more I think about it, the less I think this is about a break-in.'

'You think?' Nola was sarcastic, but Robbie didn't appear to notice.

'Why was the dog outside?' He furrowed his brow.

'What?'

'The dog's bed was in the kitchen, so she must have put it outside. I wonder why.'

'Maybe it needed a wee.'

'Maybe, I don't know ... I'll sing on it.'

'You'll what?'

'I usually sing in my head if I'm working something out.'

'You sing?'

'Yeah, I read somewhere that your brain is two separate hemispheres, but they work differently. So, if I need to concentrate on something I sing. That usually sorts it out.'

Nola was amazed. She tried to picture *any* of her old colleagues admitting to such a thing and came up blank. 'What do you sing?'

'Beatles songs mostly. My da was a big fan – he used to play them all the time.' He lost a little of his cheery nature. 'He died last year.'

Nola gave his shoulder a squeeze. 'I think that sounds like a really good idea.'

'Yeah,' he said, not looking at her. 'It helps me – it might help you.'

'No doubt,' she said.

'I wonder why she put the flowers in the bin.'

'I'm wondering a lot of things.' Nola pressed the button for zero. 'A lot of things don't sit right with this stupid case.'

18

Elliot was walking towards his car when he became aware of footsteps behind him. He took his right hand from his pocket, tightened the fingers of his left on his briefcase and slowed, giving no indication he had heard a sound.

At the driver's door, he angled his body to use the wing mirror, hit unlock on the fob and then and only then did he turn. 'What do you want?'

Clancy stood to the rear of his car. Looking at him now, Elliot thought his former partner looked more carnal than ever before. How had he ever mistaken the nature of this man? How could he have been so wilfully blind to what he truly was?

'Me?' Clancy gave an easy grin. 'Came to see how an old pal was doing. I heard you were back, and I wanted to pay my respects.'

'Don't trouble yourself on my account.'

'Got to say I'm surprised. I thought you were a goner when I saw you in the hospital.'

'Well, you know the saying: rumours of my demise are greatly exaggerated.'

'Thank God for that.'

If there was any justice, Elliot thought, a bolt of lightning would now strike Clancy dead, solving a whole host of problems, for the word God coming from this man's mouth had to be the highest form of blasphemy. But apparently God was busy elsewhere because Clancy clapped his hands together, untoasted.

'Have you heard? I'm retiring.'

'I heard. You must have put a bulletin out.'

'The boys are throwing me a little party on Friday at the Dog and Piglet – why don't you stop by?'

'No.'

'Come on, stop by and have a drink for old times' sake.'

'No.'

Clancy leaned back on his heels and lowered his hands to his sides. He was dressed in a well-made navy suit, clean lines, white shirt. Neat, despite the pallor and the beginning of a belly against the buttons. Whatever else you could say about the bastard, and Elliot could say plenty, he knew how to dress.

'Look, Elliot, I think we should talk.'

'Anything we had to say to each other was said a long time ago.'

'I don't want things to end on this note between us. You and me were pals once – what happened?' Clancy looked pained. It was an act, a good one, but Elliot had seen it too often to fall for it.

'Ask yourself that question and see what you come up with.'

'Arra, get off the cross, Ryan, someone might need the wood.'

'I'll see you, Paddy.' Elliot reached for the door handle.

'We're not so different. For all your fucking piety and your chest beating, you're no better than me.'

Elliot opened the car door.

'I got a call from the board; he's getting out tomorrow.'

Elliot paused. 'He', no need for names. Not between them. Not even now.

'Did you know?'

Was that fear in Clancy's voice? Was that even possible? Elliot turned towards the man he had once revered, a man he'd have taken a bullet for. 'Did you think they'd keep him in forever?'

A door slammed in the distance. Clancy flinched and glanced over his shoulder. *Remarkable*, Elliot thought, *he* is *scared*.

'A little bird told me you've taken an interest in history.'

Deacon. He could lie, he supposed, but why should he bother? *Cui bono*? 'And?'

'And now Black's getting out early. Funny that.'

'Are we done?'

Clancy took a few steps closer. 'Let sleeping dogs lie, Elliot. Black was a bad 'un. He'd no business messing about with a kid. Her DNA was all over his shithole squat.'

Elliot smiled. It wasn't a kind smile, or even a genuine smile. It was the smile of a man who knew this day would come and the arrival far exceeded the stress of waiting. 'How much were you making, Paddy, funnelling kids to the Black Top? Fifty per cent? More? Enough to clear your debts, though, right?'

'You stupid prick,' Clancy said, no longer pretending. He was now almost nose to nose with Elliot, their breaths mingling. 'You're a stupid prick, Ryan, going around acting all holier than thou – a joke, that's what you are. Crying over a fucking degenerate, turning your back on your own people. You never learn, Ryan, never.'

'Oh, I learn, Paddy. It might take a while, but I learn.'

He opened the door – forcing Clancy to take a step backwards – and got in too quickly, igniting a vicious pain flare. He put his briefcase on the passenger seat and started the car.

'Elliot, you're making a mistake.'

'No,' Elliot said. 'I made a mistake when I looked the other way.' He looked up into the eyes of his former partner and felt an overwhelming sense of revulsion. He put his seat belt on and reached for the door handle. 'My eyes are open now, Paddy, wide open.'

He slammed the door, reversed out of the space and drove away, leaving Clancy standing in the shadows.

19

'What's keeping her so long?' Robbie asked, lurking around the buckets of cut hydrangeas and spiky irises, sounding more and more like a bored, whiny child by the moment.

Nola turned her back to the counter and glared at him. 'Will you stop? The kid's doing us a favour.'

Robbie put his hands in his pockets and looked sulkily about. 'I don't like flowers; they creep me out.'

'Flowers creep you out?'

'Cut ones, I don't mind them in gardens and shit ... obviously.'

Nola knew what she was about to ask was probably stupid, but she was intrigued. 'What about houseplants?'

'Nah, gross.' He shuddered.

Nola looked at him in wonder. 'You mean to tell me you've never had a bunch of flowers or a plant in your life?'

'I live in a one-bed in Rialto – what do you think?'

Nola didn't need much of an imagination to imagine exactly what kind of home Robbie kept. She could picture it now. One black leather-look sofa, one television, one Xbox. One mattress on the floor of the bedroom, scratchy sheets, one lamp brought from his ma's house, musty towels. Oh yes, she could picture it perfectly. No plants.

But just as she felt a smirk coming on, a second thought usurped the smug. At least Robbie *had* a place of his own.

Yeah, that.

A door clicked behind them and the dark-haired shop assistant was back with the phone clamped to her ear and a pained expression on her face.

'Right, one moment.' She held the phone to Nola. 'She wants to talk to you.' She handed the phone over and mouthed 'I'm sorry' as she did.

Nola took the phone and smiled at the girl. 'Thanks – Mella, isn't it?'

'Yes.'

'Don't worry, you've been a great help.' She lifted the phone to her ear. 'Hello?'

Nola listened, letting her eyes roam as her ears absorbed outrage, D4 style. The shop was large, well-stocked, well-maintained, well-lit, with expensive floors. More like a fancy clothes boutique than a flower shop. A local shop for local people ... with money. The owner, currently sniping down the phone line, was very unhappy to have cops snooping around her business.

That might be useful.

'Right, right,' Nola said, when there was a suitable break in the hot air. 'No, I understand. No, I do, it's – well, actually, we wanted to keep this *out* of the media, you know?' She listened again. 'That's right ... Who? ... Oh no, I don't know the commissioner personally, although I believe he's very good friends with *my* boss, Superintendent Daragh Connors ... Oh, you do? Yes, ma'am, I report directly to him.' She glanced at Robbie and grinned. 'No, ma'am, I doubt it. It wouldn't make any difference. If I need to get a warrant it automatically becomes public record ... Oh no, this will likely go to court.'

Robbie's grin widened.

'That's not for me to say – I don't control what *they* write, but you're correct it would be of public interest ... For a warrant, yes, ma'am, it might appear that way ... No, ma'am, I'd make sure of it ... Oh, really?' She listened some more. 'Well, that would be the preferred method ... No, I agree. Not *all* publicity is good publicity.' She smiled. 'Sure, one moment.' She passed the phone back to Mella. 'She wants to talk to you.'

Nola left the counter and drifted over to Robbie, who was trying hard not to laugh.

'Wow, you pulled out the big guns, huh? Media mafioso.'

Nola shrugged. 'Rich people, they're all the same. As soon as they think you're gonna drag their business into the light they start cooperating.'

'But we don't even have a warrant.'

'So?'

'Inspector Ryan won't like it.'

'Won't like what? I didn't tell her I had a warrant, did I?'

Robbie thought about it. 'I suppose not.'

'Besides, if Ryan wants me to dance to his tune, he needs to be around to play the music.' Nola looked him dead in the eye. 'Look, Robbie, I don't appreciate being second guessed either.'

'Fair enough.' Robbie held up his hands. 'You made your point.'

'Sergeant?'

They walked back to the counter. Mella reached underneath it and hauled up a huge ledger.

'You don't keep orders on computer?' Robbie asked.

'The roses were paid for privately,' Mella said. She flicked back a few pages, found what she was looking for and turned the ledger around so Nola could read the quote for the card and the name of the person who paid for the flowers.

'Tamara Ford,' Robbie said and began to whistle until Nola stood on his foot.

'Thank you, Mella, you've been very helpful.'

She wrote the name and the date the flowers were ordered into her notebook, and they left.

'Nice work,' Robbie said, as they walked back to the car. Nola allowed herself a smile. 'You know, people are wrong about you.'

Nola's smile faded. 'Oh yeah?'

'Yeah, you're more than just a hothead.'

She thought about a reply and decided against it. Why ruin a perfectly good bloody evening?

20

Ambush

It was the single word that came to mind when Elliot pulled up outside his house and saw there was nowhere for him to park. He sat with the engine idling and his hands on the steering wheel. There was usually space for two cars in his drive, but now it was fully occupied. Next to Shona's Nissan Leaf was an older, much less socially acceptable gas guzzler. His sister's Range Rover.

He had heard it said that pets, over time, began to resemble their owners, or perhaps it was the other way round. He had never really given it much credence, not being a pet owner himself. He did, however, put a lot of stock in being able to gauge a person on the jalopy they drove. Shona was a young woman who cared about the environment and didn't like to waste resources, ergo the Leaf. As the driver of a Volkswagen Passat, he considered himself solid, reliable, a little dull but with enough welly under the hood to get the job done.

And then there was his sister.

Margaret had married young, hitching her wagon to a bright introvert who made an absolute fortune from designing a type of packing tape that was light, incredibly strong, yet, and this was the kicker, resealable. Overnight, or so it seemed to Elliot, Margaret and Chester became alarmingly rich, and though it didn't seem to affect Chester much, bar allowing him to quit his day job and spend more time inventing and tinkering with adhesives, obscene wealth became Margaret.

As a child, his sister had always been a rather plain girl who grew into an even plainer woman. But with more money than God, suddenly Margaret discovered that being plain was purely a state of mind.

First, she had her teeth fixed, then the wiry Ryan hair was relaxed, treated and carefully dyed. After that she had the bend in her nose straightened, her brow smoothed and added a new jaw-line that fitted perfectly with her determined soul.

She would not be beautiful, not even close, but by golly she made the absolute most of a shoddy blueprint.

In many respects, Elliot had always admired his sister. Margaret had gumption and absolutely refused to accept the state of play, so to speak. Also, she had been nothing but kind to him when Laurie was sick, devoting her time freely to watching Shona, always the listening soul when fears were spoken about.

This is to say, he loved his sister dearly.

But like Shona, Margaret was a force to be reckoned with. One female Ryan, he might hold ground against; two as a united front was ... well, it was daunting.

He glanced at the house. Through the bay window he could see the lamps were on and the fire lit in the sitting room (why did Shona never close the curtains?). What a dilemma. Here he faced a warm, safe, clean house, with people who loved him waiting inside.

Why then did he hesitate? Why did he want to drive to the nearest hotel and order room service and mix minibar alcohol with his pain medication until he sank into fresh oblivion?

Because you're a coward, the inner voice reminded him. *A coward.*

It was hard not to agree with the sentiment.

The street was empty, dark. He had options.

What?

Run?

Like before?

Stop. This is not the time.

With a heavy sigh, he pulled the handbrake up and switched off the engine. There were times when it was not possible to run. His sister was a good person, his daughter too. They were on his side.

He locked the car and trudged up the drive, let himself in and closed the door quietly. From the kitchen he heard ABBA playing, Margaret's influence no doubt. Irritated, he hung his coat in the downstairs cloakroom, put his bag on the walnut side-table and paused to take in his reflection in the hall mirror.

Fine, he looked fine. Okay, tired maybe, but that was allowed, wasn't it, after an honest day's toil? Dammit!

Elliot walked towards the kitchen door like a man condemned, raised his hand to the handle and paused again.

Beyond the door he heard Margaret's husky voice, asking Shona about some Greek island she had visited after the pandemic rules were lifted. Heard Shona's sigh, the prelude no doubt to some long-winded monologue about how things 'abroad' were so much better than here.

Stop it.

He forced himself to grip the handle and press down. The click was uncommonly loud, so loud he gritted his teeth.

Too late now.

Enter the lair.

It was bright, much brighter than he preferred. Overhead lights, not the lights under the presses. Dazzling, unpleasant.

'There you are,' Shona said. She looked hot and sweaty in her mother's old plastic apron (where had she dug that out?). 'You said half-eight, it's nearly nine.'

He blinked to give his eyes time to adjust. Took too long.

'Dad? Are you okay?'

'Hello ... yes, I'm fine.' He smiled to prove it and turned towards Margaret, who was sitting with her back to the wall, a glass of red before her. She looked, as she often did these days, a little puffy. If Elliot had to guess, she'd found a new strategy to ward off ageing but would never dare ask.

'Hello, brother mine,' she said, tapping her talons against the stem of the glass. 'How are the geese flying?'

Despite himself, Elliot felt a genuine bloom of affection. This was an old line, and one they'd learned from their mother's lips. 'South, my angel, towards warmer climes.'

Margaret smiled. Her teeth were worth every penny. 'I'm glad to hear it. How was the first day back in the fray?'

Elliot loosened his tie. The room was ridiculously warm; he wanted to open a window but worried this might cause concern. So many things did these days. 'Fine.' He sat down. 'What smells so good?'

'I'm making that couscous dish you like,' Shona said, filling the kettle from the sink. She pressed the lid down and turned it on.

'What dish is this?'

'You know, I made it for you and Johann before your accident – you told me you really liked it.'

Ah, pre-accident. Who knew what the dish had been or how he'd enjoyed it? Who knew anything about those halcyon days?

'Shona tells me you have a new partner?'

Elliot felt an unpleasant jolt. 'What did you say?'

'You have a new partner?' Margaret frowned and looked past him to Shona, who was breaking up a chicken stock cube with the back of a fork. 'At work?'

'Really?' Elliot turned his head to look at Shona, who refused to acknowledge his gaze. 'I don't believe I mentioned it. Shona?'

'What?'

'Have you been checking up on me?'

'Of course not.'

'Then how do you know I have a new partner?'

'Someone must have mentioned it.'

'Someone who?'

'Elliot.' Margaret put her hand on his. 'It doesn't matter. I shouldn't have—'

'It matters to me,' Elliot snapped. 'Shona?'

Shona poured boiling water onto the smashed cube. 'Superintendent Connors told me.'

Elliot stared.

She put the kettle back and wiped her hands on a tea-towel. 'Look, Dad—'

'You spoke to Superintendent Connors? You spoke to *my* boss behind my back?'

'Hardly behind your back.'

'What did you talk about?'

'Nothing, nothing much.'

'What did you talk about?'

'Elliot, please.'

'Stay out of this, Margaret.'

His sister withdrew her hand. Shona looked aggrieved.

'I wanted to make sure they didn't ... you know, push you too hard.'

'Push me too hard,' Elliot repeated. 'You called to make sure my boss didn't push me too hard.'

'Yes.'

Elliot got to his feet.

'Where are you going?'

'Upstairs.'

'But your food is nearly ready.'

'I'm not hungry.'

'Dad—'

'Good to see you, Margaret. Give Chester my best.'

He closed the kitchen door firmly and went upstairs.

He was in bed with a book on his chest when he heard Shona walk Margaret to the front door. He strained to hear what they were saying, but they were talking too quietly. When he heard Shona's footsteps on the stairs, he put the book down, switched the light off and lay as still as a mouse, fully expecting her to tap on his door and apologise. But she went straight to her own room and shut her door with a determined thump.

In the darkness, Elliot sensed her anger and was suddenly ashamed of himself.

None of this was her fault.

It was his.

It had always been his.

21

'I don't think I can do it,' Nola said, spearing a chip with another chip. She was a little bit drunk, a little bit tired and more than a little bit hungry. 'He's unbearable. I mean, who knows what he wants? Half the time I can't even find the bloody man.'

Gracie peered into the brown bag on her lap and frowned. 'How many tenders do we normally get with this order?'

'He's so slow and super cringe, always going on about procedure – like, hello, I'm a sergeant, I *know* about procedure, buddy, and I don't need you to hold my goddamned hand like I'm a rookie. Oh and you should hear the way he speaks, like, so cringe.'

'There's normally six, yeah? I'm sure there's normally six.'

'Then there's the music, holy shit. And if I *try* to change the station, he's all "Whoa, he who drive-eth picketh the fucking tunes". Have you ever, like, in all your life, heard that kind of shit?'

'They skimped me.' Gracie wrapped the bag up and opened the car door.

'Hey, where are you going?'

'Those fuckers skimped me.'

'Gracie!'

She watched Gracie stomp across the road and enter the fast-food restaurant, waving the bag about like it was the ten commandments. The kid behind the counter, who could not have been more than seventeen, all acne and twitchy hands, started to protest, pointing to the chalkboard behind his head.

'What is she doing?' Nola muttered, watching Gracie throw the bag on the counter.

Her phone vibrated. She reached into her pocket and took it out. It was a WhatsApp message from her mother.

R U coming home soon?

Nola scowled and considered not answering, but she did.

No, having food with Gracie.

She saw from the blue ticks her mother had read the message and waited.

K, pasta in m-wave, C U tmw X

Nola read it and ate a chip.

Why, where're you going?

She waited for a reply. Nothing happened. She looked up and saw Gracie holding her badge in front of the kid's face. The kid looked scared.

What was this shit now?

Her phone vibrated. Another message.

Seeing a friend, talk tmw X

Nola typed:

What friend?

But this time her mother didn't reply, though Nola could see she'd read it. She put the phone back in her pocket and watched the kid in the restaurant hand Gracie another brown bag across the counter.

Gracie walked across the road and got in. 'Shit, it's cold out there.'

'What's the story? What happened?'

'Oh, he made a mistake.'

'Yeah?' Nola glanced back at the restaurant. 'Why did you badge him?'

'I think he thought I was pulling a fast one, so, you know.' She dipped a chicken tender into smoky barbecue sauce and bit it in half. 'Mm, perfect. Go on, you were talking about the Fossil.'

'Oh yeah, he's … insufferable.'

'Clancy reckons he's not right in the head.' Gracie shrugged. 'Said after Ryan's wife died, he went off the rails.'

'Oh. How did his wife die?'

'Cancer. Clancy said it got pretty bad towards the end.'

'Really?' Nola had lost an aunt to cancer. She felt a pang of sympathy for Ryan.

'Clancy reckons the Fossil lost the will to live after she passed. He reckons that's probably why he had the accident in the first place.'

Nola didn't reply. She had heard about Elliot Ryan's accident – everyone in the station had once word got out about how it took two branches of the fire brigade to free him from the narrow shaft between a boundary wall and a garden shed. Clancy and Deacon had fallen about the place laughing when they heard, particularly Deacon who, like all bullies, enjoyed the pain and misery of others.

Especially if he was the one inflicting it.

Had she laughed?

Possibly, she wasn't sure. If she had, she was sorry about it now, even slightly ashamed. That was the difference between her and Paul Deacon: she had the capacity for shame.

And anger.

That too.

So what if Ryan was a bit of an oddball? So what if he was an antique? That didn't make him a bad soak, just a dull one. People liked casting aspersions; she was proof of that, wasn't she?

'What does he do when—?'

'I think Mam's seeing someone,' Nola said, desperate to change the subject.

'No way!'

Nola popped another chip in her mouth and chewed it. 'She's being all cagey and shit, but last week I heard her talking on the phone, and when I came into the sitting room she hung up. And tonight she's out, but she won't say where or with who.'

'She's entitled to a private life.'

'She's my mam.'

'Right, your mam, not your kid.'

'Besides, she's married.'

Gracie paused with a tender halfway to her mouth. 'I thought your old man was well off the scene?'

'He is.'

'Well then?'

'Well ... she's ... you know.'

'I don't.'

'She's my mam.'

'What age is she?'

'Old enough to know better.'

Gracie laughed. 'Look, Nola, I know things are weird right now, but it will settle back to normal if you let it. You're working a case, right?'

'Yeah, supposed to be. That's the other thing – Ryan keeps disappearing, never says where he's going or what he's doing.'

'How do you mean? Disappearing where? Is he working on something else?'

Nola opened her burger box and lifted her dirty burger out. Bacon double with cheese, smothered with jalapeños. She'd regret it as soon as she'd eaten it, she knew from experience, but it was *so* worth it.

'Spill it, Kane, what are you not telling me?'

'Wednesday night's lottery numbers,' she said, before taking a huge bite.

'Smart arse,' Gracie said.

Nola nodded, chewed. 'Mmft ... okay. So c'mere, were you serious earlier about Robbie Keller? Do you really want to hook up with *him*?' She took another bite, bit straight though a jalapeño so hot her eyes watered.

'You know the goss, yeah?'

There was too much food in Nola's mouth to respond so she shook her head.

Gracie laughed. 'Wow, okay, so the story is Kelly Doyle went out with him last year – you remember her, right?'

Nola nodded: she could feel the top of her scalp tingling.

'Yeah, well, Kelly said the reason they broke up is cause his willy was too big, like horse big, she said—' Gracie glared. 'Right,' she said, after a moment. 'So, first, that's fucking gross, and second, I know this car is not exactly, you know, high end, but spraying half a dirty burger over my dash is super mank!'

22

Tuesday

'Sign here and here.'

Ronan Black took the biro he was offered and carefully put his signature to the places marked. He waited as his scant belongings were passed through the grille, wrapped in see-through plastic, his name and inmate number stuck to the front.

'You got your pay?'

He nodded. Two-hundred and eighty-five euro for ten years' work. He would have laughed if it had been funny.

'Here.' The sergeant passed him the paper with the address of the halfway house. 'You got someone picking you up?'

Ronan shook his head.

'You know where that is?'

A nod.

The sergeant sighed. 'Well, on you go, and I hope we don't see you again.'

Ronan collected his things, followed a different guard to a small cloakroom and got into the clothes his sister had sent through for him. The clothes he had been arrested in had been taken away for forensics years before and never returned, along with several wraps, some benzos and a silver bracelet Natalie had given him days before she was killed. He had not wanted to part with it, but the arresting officer was a brute who brooked no argument. Back then, Ronan had been in no condition to fight for his rights, even if he'd known he had any.

Once changed, he left his jail clothes in a neat bundle on the bench and waited for the officer to come back and walk him out. The warden had already been by that morning to congratulate him on his freedom and wish him well. The warden was a decent man: he truly believed he made a difference. And maybe he did, for *some* men – who could really say?

Three separate electronic gates later he was free.

He looked up. The sky was grey, the air cold. For some reason he thought he'd feel something, something profound.

After a moment, he turned right and walked down the hill heading towards town. There was some time to kill before he had to sign on in the cop-shop, time he owned and time he needed to put his next step into motion.

Ronan Black was a free man in body only. A man with only one thing on his mind can never be free. Not in this life. Ronan had accepted this the first time he'd taken a hiding in the jail, the first time he'd woken up in the hospital, eyes swollen, concussed and broken. He'd accepted his fate and vowed that if he survived those who had decided this fate would pay for the privilege. This fed him, gave him succour, kept him sane on the bleakest days.

And now he was free, and now it was time to set things right.

23

Monica Fell opened the door of her house with a single gushing statement. 'I have five minutes.'

Nola, a little taken aback by the abruptness, recovered fast and offered her identification. Monica waved it away. She was a tall woman, with dark shoulder-length hair, dressed in a casual preppy way that cost real money.

'Don't be silly. I know why you're here, and I'm telling you right now you're wasting your time. I don't know a single person who could do something like that to – my God, Jasper! Jasper! Tick-tock, darling, tick-tock!'

'I'm sorry,' Nola said. 'Have I called at a bad time, only—?'

Two King Charles spaniels hurtled down the hall, yapping their heads off. Monica reached out, yanked Nola inside and slammed the door before they reached it. 'Sorry,' she said. 'If they get out they're a nightmare to catch. Come on, come this way.'

Nola followed her down the huge hall and into a kitchen larger in scale than anything she had ever seen in real life. 'You have a beautiful home.'

'Thank you, do you want tea or something?'

'No, I'm fine, thanks.'

Nola stood with her hands in her pockets as Monica paced from one side of the vast space to the other, picking things up, tripping over dogs, who, denied freedom, seemed intent on killing their owner instead. She was, Nola realised with a jolt, not much older that she was, which made the house, the kid and the Range Rover parked on the manicured gravel outside a little harder to swallow.

'My God,' Monica said suddenly and threw up her hands. She turned to Nola, looking overwhelmed, defeated. 'I called the hospital – they said Jody is in a coma but stable. Whatever that means.'

'Yes, I spoke with them myself this morning.'

'This city, you know? Nobody's safe any more. I don't understand why this keeps happening. Can't *your* people do something about this?'

Your people. Nola suppressed a snarky reply. Joe Public never ceased to annoy the shit out of her. People resented paying tax with every fibre of their being, stations were being drained left and right of good people and resources, but as soon as there was a single crime, a personal crime, *her* people were supposed to swing into action like crime-gibbons.

'It's awful,' Nola said instead.

'I can't believe it – you know, I saw Jody last week and she was in such good form.'

'When was this?'

'Tuesday. She called and asked me to lunch to give me her good news and she was just ... so happy, you know?'

Nola, reaching for her notebook, paused. 'Her good news? Can we back up a moment?'

'One sec!' Monica and the dogs hurtled down the hall out of view. 'Jasper! Shake a leg, darling. Think of the traffic!'

She was back, dogs too.

'Did you say Jody Kavanagh had good news?'

'She told me she was pregnant.'

'By Jools Byrne?'

Monica laughed, faintly baffled, and echoed Gabe Frost. 'Well, who else?'

'I don't know.' Nola wrote that snippet down. She'd need to call the hospital and have them confirm it. 'Wasn't she still married?'

'Oh, well ... for now, obviously, but she and Simon were going to divorce.'

'He doesn't think so.'

'Oh ... well, that's unfortunate.'

'You've known Jody most of her life, am I right?'

'We went to Hedley High together.'

Hedley High, a prestigious private school. Nola knew of it by reputation alone. A student from Hedley had been caught importing high-grade Fentanyl into the country several years before – caught red-handed yet somehow, mysteriously, managed to avoid full prosecution, contending with 'community service' in lieu. Nola, who came from an area where kids were routinely banged up for carrying small bags of weed, had been sour about it for weeks.

'What about Amber Feenan?'

'Amber?' Monica's hand went to a chain around her neck; she pulled it free, revealing a diamond the size of a small grape. 'Why are you asking about Amber?'

'Didn't she go to Hedley?'

'Uh, yes.'

'Was she friends with Jody?'

Monica looked genuinely pained. 'They were friends, mostly. Jody played lacrosse, Amber too – actually Amber was the captain of the team in final year.'

Nola wrote 'lacrosse teammates', put a question mark after 'friends'.

'How did Amber feel about Jody dating Jools?'

Monica's smile faltered slightly; she fingered the diamond again. Nola noticed she did it whenever a question rattled her slightly. Clearly not much of a poker player.

'She ... it's complicated, really.'

'I'll bet.'

'They had drifted apart and of course Jody was away for years.'

'She came back to Ireland in 2019, right?'

'Yes.'

'Amber and Jools Byrne divorced in 2020?'

'Oh ... no, Jody had nothing to do with what happened between Amber and Jools if that's what you're suggesting.'

'I'm not suggesting anything. What happened, in your view, between Amber and Jools?'

Monica's face clouded over. 'I'm not one for gossip, Sergeant Kane. Amber's story is her own.'

'But she and Jools Byrne were married for four years?'

'Right.'

'How do you think she feels about her ex-hooking up with one of her best friends?'

'They were hardly best friends.'

'Friends then.'

'I'm sure she's devastated,' Monica said with a rush. 'But like I say, she and Jools had split up long before Jody and Jools got together.'

'Still,' Nola said. 'It's got to hurt.'

Monica glanced at her watch.

'Tell me about Simon,' Nola asked quickly. 'Gabe doesn't think much of him.'

'Oh, Gabe said that?' She reached for the necklace again. 'Well, he's older, of course, self-assured in that London way, you know?'

'Not really.'

'I think he had certain expectations of a life here. But then Jody went to Jolie Laide and the television show happened and, you know, her star ascended.'

'You think he resented her?'

'I think it was hard for him to find his place in Dublin. I suspect they might have had some financial issues.'

'Oh?'

'Well, Dublin is expensive and I think it was hard for Simon to get regular work.'

'Is that why they split up?'

'I don't why they split – I genuinely don't. Simon is a very private man. I think it's fair to say they seemed happy – the split came right out of the blue, and poor Jody was devastated.'

'I thought she left him?'

'She did.'

'So why was she devastated?'

'Nobody leaves a marriage unscathed, Sergeant. It doesn't happen.'

Nola glanced through some of the notes she had written before she left the house that morning. 'What about Fiona Hynes?'

'Who?'

'Fiona, Jody's sister?'

'Oh, right, sorry, yes, of course. Sorry. Gosh, Fiona, yes, so she was in a different class to us.'

Nola felt there was a lot of weight to *that* statement, but let it slide. 'Were you friends with her too?'

'Uh ... no, not really. Fiona was, um, quiet, you know? Like ... quiet.'

'You're saying she wasn't sporty or head-girl material?'

'No, she didn't ... I mean, I don't remember her being really involved in things, you know? She was ...'

'Quiet?'

'Right!'

'That's strange, isn't it? I mean, you'd imagine sisters would be pretty close.'

'I suppose so.' Monica looked as though even the concept of Fiona had to be dredged from the deep. 'Gosh, it feels like a lifetime ago. Some days I miss it so much, you know?'

'What, school?'

Monica stared into the middle distance, transported out of her million-euro-plus house to a vast fee-paying cloistered modern-day playground for the haves and the have-mores.

Nola, who had hated school with a passion, tapped her pen against her notebook, dragging Monica back to reality.

'Oh, don't get me wrong,' Monica said quickly. 'I love, you know, being Mom, of course – that goes without saying.'

'Right.'

'It's, well, one misses the freedom sometimes. Right!' Her hands fluttered out to each side of her body. 'I really need to get moving.'

'One last thing, I promise,' Nola said. 'Did Jody mention anything to you about being scared lately? Or worried about anything?'

'Lately? No, but you know ... she had Cooper.'

'Cooper?'

'Her dog.'

'Ah, yes. The dog.'

'After that incident, she thought it would be wise to have some protection, you know?'

'Incident?'

'Someone broke into her house.'

'What?'

'Someone broke into her house. Oh ... I'm sorry, I thought you knew. I'm sure she reported it.' Monica reached for her necklace again. 'They didn't take much, as far as I know, but ... well, you know. A woman alone.'

'When was this?'

'Um ... back in September, I think, I'm almost sure of it. That's when she got Cooper.' She stared down at her own little dogs, who were snoring at her feet. 'Poor Jody, he couldn't save her after all.'

24

Across town the atmosphere in a different and much smaller kitchen was decidedly frosty. Shona was banging pots and pans around with abandon until Elliot, who had been awake since 3 a.m. with only his anxieties for company and was feeling more than a little fragile, reached the end of his tether.

'Shona, will you please stop that.'

'Stop what?'

'That.' He waved his arm. 'If you're annoyed, say so. Speak your mind.'

'All right.' She whirled on him. 'Do you think this is easy, Dad? I've uprooted my life to help you and you act like I'm an imposition.'

'Nobody *asked* you to do a thing, Shona. In fact, *if* we're going to lay our cards on the table, I believe I was very clear that I did not want anyone fussing over me in the first place.'

'Oh, of course you don't.' He noticed she was ladling on the sarcasm. 'That way you can carry on pretending there's nothing wrong.'

'There *is* nothing wrong.'

'You really think people are stupid, don't you? You think I am stupid.'

'What? What are you talking about now?'

'You think I don't notice things; you think I haven't noticed what's been happening over the last few years.'

It was on the tip of his tongue to ask what she was talking about when he realised he was certain he didn't want to hear what she had to say.

'Shona,' he said, softening his voice. 'I know you're trying your best—'

'Dad, you almost died.'

'Look—'

'No, okay. I won't *look*. I won't listen, I'm not going to go away and I'm not going to pretend, okay? Not any more.' She pulled out a chair and sat down, reached across the table and took his hands in hers. 'You punctured a lung and you almost died, Dad. If Pauline hadn't called for the ambulance you would have.'

'Don't be silly.'

He tried to withdraw his hands, but she held them firmly. Suddenly Elliot felt light-headed, even a little queasy. The wretched tablets on an empty stomach were lethal.

'Dad, I know things have been difficult since Mam died. I know you're doing your best. I'm here for you – tell me what's going on.'

'There's nothing going on.' He wished she'd stop talking. 'I'm fine.'

'Your blood alcohol the day of the accident was 1.2.'

He forcibly removed his hands from hers. 'I had a few drinks after work – can't a man spend his off-time as he pleases?'

'Speaking of work, why are you back on duty so soon?'

'Shona—'

'You're not short of money, are you? Because if you need anything—'

'Don't be ridiculous.'

'Then why?' She cocked her head. 'You put a lot of pressure on the hospital to discharge you and you practically forced your GP to sign your medical cert. He told me he had misgivings, but you were adamant.'

'Dr Dunn had no business discussing my medical information with you, and you certainly had no business asking.'

'I had no choice! You *leave* me no choice. You refuse to tell me anything so what am I supposed to do? I don't have a crystal ball, Dad.'

'You could try minding your own business!'

'Dad, when you were sedated, you kept talking about someone called Natalie, and you were upset. Who is—?'

'That's enough,' Elliot snapped. 'I don't want to talk about this.'

Shona flung up her hands. 'See? This is what I'm talking about. You're so quick to close everyone down.'

Elliot's heart was hammering so hard he was afraid he'd black out, but he had to try and make her understand. He had to win some breathing space.

'Shona, listen to me. My twenty-five is in March and, if you insist, I will take it on medical grounds. After that I promise to do nothing but read, potter around and acquiesce to your every bloody whim.'

'Dad—'

'But right now' – he tapped the tabletop with his index finger firmly – 'right now, at this moment in time, I have a job to do, and I intend to do it. You say you want to help me, fine. Then help me but stop *undermining me every step of the way.*'

His voice had risen without him realising it. Shona was staring at him, crestfallen.

'I'm not trying to undermine you, Dad. I'm sorry if you feel that way.'

'Shona—'

She stood up and left the room. Elliot put his head in his hands.

This was not how it was supposed to be.

He was exhausted. The previous night had been a bad one, and sleep, when it eventually came, brought dreams filled with one image.

Natalie Dromond. The night they found her, under the bridge, her small body lying on the wet ground, crumpled.

He tried to remember that night, tried to piece it together. He had been on duty with Clancy, mid-shift. Had he been in the car when Clancy took the call? He wasn't sure, couldn't remember. He'd been drinking earlier that evening, he knew that – not much, not enough to be drunk, but enough to take the edge off. Clancy knew, but Clancy never said shit to him about it.

Elliot closed his eyes. He couldn't remember if the call had come over the radio or not, but in the report he'd verified that it had. Someone had called it in, kids acting suspiciously near the old railway bridge, throwing bottles, that kind of shit. Stupid stuff, kids' stuff – you drove by, flashed the lights and they legged it. Job done. No need for paperwork.

Usually.

It had been raining, he remembered that. The ground was

slick, treacherous. Had he slipped? He thought so, remembered Clancy cursing, telling him to go down, search the sheds by the old chain-link fence. He'd gone willingly, glad to be alone. Glad to wind the clock down so he could go home and have a drink.

Maybe that's why he never questioned it. Maybe that's how he compartmentalised it in his mind. People fell through the cracks all the time.

Right?

Natalie Dormond had fallen through the cracks. She had run with a bad crowd, engaged in risky behaviour.

Died under a wet railway bridge, stabbed to death by a man she thought she loved and she thought loved her.

Or had she?

Yes.

That was the question.

25

The short drive through the Phoenix Park normally offered solace to Elliot, but that morning it did nothing except make him think of death. That was the trouble with bare trees and dead grass and low-lying fog; it did nothing to lift a broken spirit, nothing at all.

Shona's words rattled around in his brain like pennies in a metal tube, pinging loudly thither and yon. Somewhere along the way he had failed her, failed her as a father. He had overlooked – no, nice dodge, Elliot, he had ignored her pain, swept it under the rug with his own.

She had been fourteen when Laurie got sick, sixteen when she died. It would be accurate to say those two years between diagnosis and death were complicated, and at the time he was certain he was doing his best. But teenagers were complicated creatures, secretive, volatile half-humans with minds of their own in bodies they could barely control. Elliot, reeling from his own emotional implosion, had no idea how to handle his child, though it occurred to him now that he had – in fact – made a complete mess of things.

But what was he to do? Back then the problems were legion, insurmountable at times, and while he had tried to make all the right moves, say the right words, was she correct? Had he cut her out? Shut her down?

It was possible.

So many mistakes.

The day Laurie found the lump in her left breast was indelibly scratched into his cortex. But what about the day after? Or the day after that? He remembered the first visit to her doctor, the first visit to her oncologist, the first day of aggressive chemo. The firsts were never an issue; it was the days in between that fogged. The decision to keep the worst of it from Shona had not been his, he was certain of that. Laurie said she had no intention of dying, and even when it was clear that her intention would not save her, she refused to discuss death with Shona, proving to Elliot that even the smartest, bravest women he knew could be stupid, stubborn and a coward too.

What had she feared? That Shona would turn away from her? Love her less?

Madness.

Folly.

This too was on him. Those last days in the hospice he could have reneged on their agreement and over-ridden her wishes. Laurie hadn't been in any position to stop him, so why hadn't he?

Why indeed.

Because he'd promised or because he was a coward.

I think we know *the answer to that,* the inner voice said.

He passed the central roundabout and proceeded down Chesterfield Avenue, keeping the Passat well below the speed limit. His back was particularly painful that morning so he'd already taken four of the 'good' painkillers before he left the house and was now operating well, if a little spacey. It occurred to him he'd have to ease back on them over the coming weeks – a terrifying prospect – but right now he would do whatever, take whatever, it took to see his mission through.

He slowed to let a group of joggers cross the road, marvelling at their ensembles, put his foot on the accelerator and edged closer to the roundabout by the zoo where he waited to let a lorry come right and—

Something hit him and shunted him over the line. Elliot slammed on the brakes and glanced in the rear-view mirror, saw a white – was that an Audi? It struck again, another shunt. Horns blared. In a panic, Elliot accelerated. The lorry clipped the rear end of the Passat. Metal screamed as his car spun wildly until it ended up on the central verge, facing in the wrong direction. Shaken, Elliot opened the door and put one unsteady loafer-shod foot onto terra firma.

The lorry driver had already jumped out of his cab and was heading his way, furious. 'What the bloody hell are you at? I had right of way, you gobshite.'

'I'm sorry ... someone hit the car.'

'What are you talking about?'

'I was slowing and—' Elliot staggered and clung to the roof.

The lorry driver narrowed his eyes. 'Here, have you been drinking?'

'Drinking? No, I—'

'Go away out of that, your eyes are like two piss holes in the snow.'

The lorry driver stomped back to his vehicle and got his phone. The traffic around them was building, backing up in either direction to the gates of the park and along Chesterfield Avenue. Horns honked and blared; people, impatient to be moving, rolled down their windows and began to make their objections known.

'What's going on? Move this lorry out of way!' a woman shouted. 'I've got to get to work.'

'Hold your horses, missus,' the driver said. 'I'm calling the guards.'

'I am the guards,' Elliot said, his voice drowned out by the noise. 'Listen to me, I am the guards.'

'Hello? Yeah, I'm reporting an accident on Chesterfield Avenue. My lorry was hit by a drunk driver.'

'I'm not drunk,' Elliot said. But nobody was paying any attention to him, though several people were filming him on their phones.

Elliot tried to focus.

Someone had hit him from behind – he was sure of it. He limped to the rear of the Passat and, sure enough, the bumper was damaged. 'See?' he said, pointing. 'Someone rammed me.'

'I'll ram you if you don't shut up,' the driver said.

'You need to move this lorry,' the woman yelled. 'You can't hold us up like this.'

'You,' the driver said, pointing his finger at Elliot, 'don't go anywhere. The guards are on their way and, here, pal, you better have insurance.'

Elliot ignored him. Cars were scraping past the lorry on the footpath. There was no sign of the Audi or its driver.

His legs began to shake.

Had he imagined it? Had he made a mistake?

A clearer voice fought its way through the mental fog.

Do you see the dent on your bumper?

Yes.

Then hold on to that – hold on to that and don't let go.

So, what was this then, an accident? Hit and run?

There are no accidents, the inner voice raged, as Elliot slumped into the driver's seat, feeling scared and unwell.

This was deliberate.

26

'There's no shame in taking some personal time for recovery, Elliot.' Superintendent Connors leaned back in his chair. He was wearing his most compassionate, yet put-upon, expression. 'Under this uniform we are but flesh and blood, mortals.'

Elliot sat stiffly in the same chair he had been in the day before. He had never been a politically minded man, never played any kind of chess move to advance his career. But neither was he a fool. The morning had proved forces were at work against him because, while his body might not have been his own, his brain was operating on full capacity. Elliot understood human nature; he understood humanity. He had seen the best and the worst in mankind and had risen, if not above it, to the surface at least.

He would not now or ever again let shenanigans or foul play interrupt him.

'It was not an accident, sir, and I refuse to have it recorded as one.'

'Inspector Ryan, be reasonable. No one here doubts that you are a fine officer, but you've been under enormous mental and physical pressure of late.'

'I gave a breath sample at the scene, sir.'

Connors sat upright and steepled his tanned fingers. 'I'm told you insisted upon it.'

'That's right.'

'Even after you had identified yourself to the officers?'

'Yes, sir.'

'Do they sound like the actions of a sound mind?'

'They sound like the actions of an innocent man, a sober man.'

'Nobody suggested—'

'Do I need to call my union rep?'

'Dear Lord, Ryan, this is not the Inquisition and I am not out to hang you!'

No, Elliot thought, *you're out to protect the organisation and your arse*, but he wisely kept that thought under wraps.

'You told the driver of the lorry you had been pushed into the traffic, shunted, according to your report.'

'That is correct, sir.'

'Can you expound upon that?'

'Not really. It happened very suddenly.'

'Did you get a look at the car, make or model?'

'I thought it might have been an Audi, sir. White.'

'Might?'

'I wasn't paying attention; I was busy trying to avoid getting flattened by a truck.'

'Ah.' Connors looked down. 'Ah.'

'My rear bumper *was* damaged.'

'Yes, you mentioned that.'

Elliot resisted the urge to put his hand to his forehead. The headache from earlier had increased severalfold and he was finding it difficult to concentrate. Besides, what more was there to say? He had made his statement, filed an accident report, contacted his insurance company, who were, to say the least, as sceptical as Connors about the rear-end shunt. There was nothing more he could do or say, so what was the point in making more trouble for himself? His boss was either going to clear him for work or he was going to send him home. It was out of his hands.

Connors shook his head. 'What am I going to do with you at all?'

Elliot waited.

'Are you sure you're well?'

'Yes, sir.'

'And you are sticking to the story that you were not the cause of today's accident?'

Elliot bristled at 'story' but simply nodded.

Connors sighed. 'All right. Carry on, Elliot, but don't make me regret this.'

'I won't, sir.'

'The case you have now, remind me?'

'A young woman, Jody Kavanagh, sir, assault during a possible break-in.'

'Right, that. I want you to clear it, Elliot. Make a good job of it, no stone unturned, no wiggle room. I'm told the ex-husband is a suspect?'

Someone had been busy, Elliot thought sourly. Kane, no doubt – a dog barking for its master.

'Yes, sir.'

'What has he to say for himself?'

'We haven't interviewed him formally yet.'

'Well, there you go, that should be your next priority.'

'Yes, sir.'

'Keep things tidy, Inspector, no more ... incidents.'

'Sir.'

'All right, well. Don't let me keep you.'

Downstairs, Elliot found Nola and Robbie huddled together outside the office in deep conversation. So deep he had to clear his throat twice to announce himself. From the way they sprang apart, it didn't take a psychic to guess they had been discussing him.

'Are you all right, sir?' Nola asked. 'We heard you had been in an accident.'

'A minor fender bender, Sergeant, nothing to worry about.' He glanced at his watch, realised he couldn't read what it said and lowered his arm again. 'I got your note that Simon Albright also worked for Jolie Laide.'

'On and off. Diandra Cliff ditched him when he and Jody split, at least according to Gabe Frost.'

'Interesting, he never mentioned it when we spoke. Proceed.'

'I spoke to Monica Fell this morning—'

'Who?'

'She's one of Jody Kavanagh's friends – you remember I told you I had to meet her today?'

'Right,' he said. 'Of course, Monica. Was she able to shed any light on yesterday?'

'Two things. She said Jody's house was broken into in September and that's why Jody got the dog, but I checked and she didn't report any break-in.'

'I see.'

'She also told me Jody Kavanagh met with her last Tuesday to tell her she was preggers.'

'Please don't use slang, Sergeant.'

'Gestating a human. According to Monica the father was Jools Byrne.'

'A baby – that's an interesting development. Have you confirmed?'

'I called the hospital, they'll let me know.'

'Excellent.'

'What kind of sicko attacks a pregnant woman?' Robbie pondered.

Nola rolled her eyes. 'The kind that attacks any woman.'

'Warped.'

'I've got another one for you, Sir. The baby-daddy is only the ex-husband of one Jody's friends, Amber Feenan: Jools Byrne aka Mr Billy Big Bollocks himself. According to Gabe Frost, Amber Feenan is a bit of a nutter and he says she's capable of anything.'

Elliot winced at 'nutter' but let it slide because Nola was smirking like a cat with *all* the cream. 'Capable of assault?'

'Why not? Hell hath no fury and all that sh– stuff.'

Elliot thought about it for a moment. 'Right, we should talk to Amber Feenan, and where is this man, Byrne? Why has he not been in contact? I mean, his, er ... lady-friend has been attacked and badly injured so where is he?'

'I called his office,' Robbie said. 'Apparently he's in Dubai but he's back tomorrow.'

'Dubai? When did he go to Dubai?'

'Yesterday, at 1 p.m.'

'So, he was *in* the country when Jody was attacked.'

'Yes, sir.'

Elliot nodded. 'Well done, Sergeant, fine sleuthing.' He turned his attention to Nola. 'I take it Jools Byrne is our Tesla driver.'

'Confirmed.' Nola glanced at Robbie. 'Tell him the other news.'

'We got a definite ID on who sent the flowers.'

'Ah, let me guess, Simon Albright.'

'No, sir, they were sent from Tamara Ford.' Robbie grinned. 'The actress, sir.'

'Tamara Ford. What on earth is her involvement with this?'

'Jody Kavanagh renovated a house for her on that television show, remember?'

'Ah, yes. Of course.'

'Doesn't explain the note, though,' Robbie said. 'All that lovely-dovey stuff.'

'She's an actress.' Nola rolled her eyes. 'She probably talks like that all the time. Oh, sir, I spoke to Diandra Cliff, Jody's boss at Jolie Laide. She said she could give us a few minutes today.'

'How gracious of her.'

'What do you want me to do?' Robbie asked.

'I want you to call to number thirty-three, the neighbouring house that was empty yesterday, and take a statement. I want you to pay particular attention to any arguments or disturbances they may have noticed this last weekend.'

'I thought I might see about the dog—'

'Sergeant Keller, I have given you an order.'

Robbie glanced at Nola, who widened her eyes slightly. 'Yes, sir.' Robbie slunk away, his usual bounce somewhat deflated.

'So?' Nola closed her notebook. 'Jolie Laide?'

'They can wait, Sergeant. First I'd like to have another chat with Simon Albright.'

Nola sprang out of her chair. 'Are we taking your car, sir?'

'No, Sergeant, it is out of commission for the moment – choose one from the lot.'

'Yes, sir.'

'I'll meet you downstairs.'

'Roger!'

When she was gone, he took two painkillers together and swallowed them with a gulp of spring water from the bottle Shona had provided.

What are you doing? the voice asked. *Two?*

I'm functioning.

He took the lift to the garage and found Nola standing by the passenger door of a newish Hyundai.

'Keys are in it, sir,' she said respectfully.

Elliot knew when the game was up. 'Would you mind driving, Sergeant? I've had quite enough adventure for one morning.' He hesitated. 'You can drive, can't you?'

'Can I?' Nola grinned. 'I thought you'd never ask.'

She ran around the driver's side and leaped in with such abandon that Elliot, despite his woes, smiled. It was refreshing to see such enthusiasm.

Of course, he'd never been in a car with Nola driving before that day.

The smile did not last long.

27

It took several minutes for Simon Albright to answer his door, and when he did it was clear they'd woken him and blatantly obvious he was suffering from a kill-me-now hangover.

Blearily, he invited them in.

The apartment was, Nola thought, the saddest shithole she had ever set foot in, and she had been to Paris.

'I think I can guess why you're here,' Simon said, leading them down a tiny hall into a grim kitchen-cum-living-room, the tiny conjoined space so beloved by landlords the world over.

'We have a few questions,' Elliot said. 'I thought you might prefer here to the station.'

They watched him clear away the remains of a half-eaten takeaway and a near-empty bottle of gin.

'You mind if I make some coffee?'

'Go ahead.'

'You want some?'

'No, thank you.'

'No.'

Nola and Elliot sat beside each other on a small leatherette couch, their knees touching no matter which position they tried. The kitchen area was about the size of a postage stamp, and the single window faced the wall of the building next to it. Even at this hour it was so dark Simon had the lights on. Everything about the place screamed 'down at heel'. It was hard not to compare it with the tasteful splendour of his ex-wife's home.

Simon made a cup of instant coffee, took milk from the fridge, sniffed it and put it back without using it.

'If you don't mind my saying, Mr Albright,' Elliot said mildly, 'you look like you've been through the wars.'

Simon sipped the coffee before he answered. 'I've had better years.' He put the coffee down and rubbed his eyes.

Nola stared at the bandages on his right hand.

'Let's hear it.'

'Sergeant Kane?'

Nola cleared her throat. 'I spoke to Monica Fell this morning. She told me that Jody had recently gotten engaged to a man by the name of Jools Byrne. Were you aware of this?'

Simon smiled wryly. 'I was aware, Sergeant.'

'You didn't mention it yesterday,' Elliot said. 'In fact, you made a point of calling Jody your wife.'

'She is.'

'Technically,' Nola said. 'But she was going to divorce you.'

'Is that so?'

'You were in a bit of a kerfuffle a few weeks ago, Mr Albright. You were charged with criminal damage. What can you tell me about that?'

'Nothing, it was a misunderstanding.'

'You took a tyre iron to a commercial vehicle. I'd hardly call that a misunderstanding.'

Simon lowered his gaze and stared at the grimy carpet for

a moment. 'A van was parked in my space and they refused to move when I asked them to. I ... I lost control.'

'Do you often lose control, Mr Albright? Did you lose control when Jody told you she was engaged? Is that it?'

'I told you, I didn't hurt Jody.'

'Why were you there, Mr Albright? At her home so early in the morning?'

'I told you.' He looked at Elliot. 'Jody asked me to come.'

'In a message.'

'Yes.'

Nola frowned. 'Why?'

'Excuse me?'

'Why did she need to see you that morning? What was so important that she had to see you there and then?'

'I don't know.'

'But you went straight there, according to you.'

'Yes.'

'Again, why?'

Simon Albright leaned back and closed his eyes for a moment before he answered. 'I met Jody at a weird time in my life, you know? I was searching, questioning. I'd come out of a long relationship and ...' He sighed. 'Jody is the answer to a question I hadn't even realised I'd asked. I love her, I would never hurt her.'

'Why did she boot you out?' Nola asked, unmoved by his admission. In her experience, men who claimed to 'love' women often put them in an early grave.

'I can't—' He gave a tight smile. 'It's complicated.'

'You seem to have a lot of complications in your life,' Elliot said mildly.

To their surprise, Simon Albright laughed. 'Oh my goodness, if ever there was a definition of understatement needed that would be it.'

Elliot leaned forward. The sofa was incredibly uncomfortable and he was sorry he'd sat in it. 'You neglected to mention you used to work with Jolie Laide.'

'I didn't know it mattered.'

'It matters. Did you work with your wife?'

'I did some consultancy work for the company, yes.'

'Were you involved in the television show?'

'I worked on the Ford property.'

'The one that made Jody so famous?'

'Yes.'

'I watched that show yesterday,' Nola said. 'I didn't see your name mentioned in the credits.'

Simon shrugged. 'It happens in television; you're not always credited in the final production.'

'Was that the last job you did for Jolie Laide?'

'Yes.'

'Did that bother you?'

'Why would it bother me? Jolie Laide was Jody's thing, not mine. Besides, I had wanted to strike out on my own for some time.'

Nola made a point of looking around the horrible apartment. 'How's that working out for you?'

'Fine,' he said firmly, giving her a look.

'It must have been difficult,' Elliot said, rather kindly. 'You probably sacrificed a lot to come to Ireland. Then you lose your job, lose your wife, your home ... I can imagine how you feel.'

'No, no you can't.' Simon turned his head and looked out the window at nothing. 'You have no idea how I feel. Jody is my North Star.'

Nola's phone vibrated. She took it out and read the message from Robbie before she tapped her knee against Elliot's. He glanced at the screen and raised his eyebrows.

Hospital confirmation – pregnant.

'Would it surprise you then, Mr Albright, to learn that Jody is pregnant?'

Simon Albright trembled so violently the cup fell from his hand. It didn't break and he had drunk most of the coffee so Nola didn't buy it. It struck her as dramatic, like something from a Hallmark film.

'Are you all right, sir?' she asked drily.

Simon managed to pull himself together, though he was pale and shaky. 'I'd like you to leave now.'

'Did you know?'

'You have my solicitor's name,' Simon said to Elliot, ignoring Nola completely.

'I do.' Elliot took his card from his pocket and wrote on the back of it. 'I think you should come down to the station with him – when you're recovered, of course. We'll see ourselves out.'

Outside, Nola was fuming. 'We should have hauled his arse in, sir. He's lying left, right and centre.'

'All in good time, Sergeant.'

'And that bullshit about going to her house, I don't believe a word of it.'

They got in the car and left the estate.

'Are we in a hurry?' Elliot asked.

'No ... why?'

'I wonder if we could drop down from warp speed, Sergeant?'

'Sorry, sir.' Nola eased off the accelerator a fraction.

'Do you know, I don't think he's our man.'

'Are you serious?'

'He looked very shook to me.'

Nola was scornful. 'He was hung-over to shit.'

Elliot winced. 'Even so, I don't get a feeling from him here in my gut – I don't feel it.'

'With respect, sir, what have your guts got to do with it?'

Elliot closed his eyes. 'Just so, Sergeant, just so.'

Nola drove on. 'What now, sir?'

'Drop me off at the station. I want you to go speak to ... the woman, what was her name? With the magical son.'

Nola glanced at him, concerned. Magical son? What was he talking about? 'Do you mean Bane?'

'Yes, I thought you said you were going to speak with her.'

'I thought we were going to Jolie—'

'No.'

He opened his eyes and sat up a little straighter. He looked waxen and as pale as Simon Albright had been. 'Can you pull over, Sergeant?'

She pulled in.

He undid his belt and put his hand on the door handle. 'I believe I will walk from here, get some thinking steps under my belt, maybe some fresh air.'

'We're not far from the station.'

'Exactly so.'

He got out, closed the door, gave her a jaunty wave and set off. Nola watched him through the window for a moment until a 15 bus tooted its horn behind her and she had no option but to pull into traffic and leave him behind.

28

The Athena beauty studio operated over a butcher's shop on South Circular Road. Nola pushed open a glass door on the street level and climbed a narrow flight of stairs. On the upper landing were two doorbells, one for a chiropractor named Meadows and the other for Athena. She gave the pink bell a short press and was buzzed in immediately.

The studio door was opened by a very tan man in a yellow vest and extremely short shorts. He beamed at Nola as though she was the most wonderful being to have ever existed, and this apparent happiness to see another human made Nola instantly suspicious.

'Threading?'

'I'm sorry?'

You're here for threading?' He pointed to her eyebrows.

Nola raised them automatically. 'No, I'm here to speak to Beverly Russell.'

'Oh,' the man said. 'Is Bev expecting you?'

'Yes.'

'Only she's with a client right now—'

'I'm on official business.' She offered him her ID, which he gave a cursory glance. What was it with people not looking at ID? she wondered.

'This way.'

He left her in the lobby and disappeared. Nola looked around. The walls were covered in posters with sparkly handwritten happy-clappy slogans that only the truly vapid would find inspiring. Two incense sticks burned on a ledge behind the desk, working overtime to mask the smell of sweat and mildew. The entire place gave Nola the heebie-jeebies.

Tan-man was back in under a minute, his walnut-coloured forehead crinkled with contrition. 'I am so sorry. Beverly begs your indulgence – she had an emergency.'

What the hell kind of emergency does a beautician get? Nola wondered.

'How long will she be?'

'Fifteen minutes?'

Nola scowled. 'I'll wait.'

The man smiled. His teeth were very white and very straight. Around Nola's way this kind of smile was known as a Croatian Special, an all-inclusive package deal involving cheap flights, a cheap hotel and a cheap dentist. Coupled with the tan, the teeth could be seen from space.

'Would you like chai?'

'No, thank you.'

'We have a mindful chair, if you'd like to try it while you wait?'

'A what?'

'A mindful chair. Come, come this way.'

With extreme reluctance, Nola followed him down a hall, through a curtain of multicoloured beads and into a square room overlooking the back of the launderette next door. Someone had tried to give it a tropical feel, adding several glossy plants, and framed pictures of white sandy beaches. In the middle of the room on a raised platform sat a beige chair that looked a bit like an old-fashioned dentist's chair, but with cables and pleather accents.

'Have you heard of Neuro Energetic Integration Technology?' Tan-man asked, moving around the room, adjusting lights and the window blind.

'No. What is it?'

'It's incredible. Stress is the number one thing our clients suffer from. The life–work balance is so completely out of whack that we're making ourselves sick. Toxicity is rising, both in our food and in our environment. Basically, we're drowning in modernity.'

'Right.'

'But we can repair our synapses when we rebuild our inner harmony.'

'With a chair?'

The weird smile stretched. He waggled a tan-finger at her. 'Not a chair, a sensory experience. Come, be seated.'

'I don't think I need—'

'This will change your life.'

It was such an outrageous claim she was intrigued. Besides, it was this or spend fifteen minutes scrolling through Twitter, and her blood pressure was probably high enough.

She removed her jacket and stood awkwardly as he began pressing buttons and dials. 'If you please, be seated.'

She sat, lowering herself slowly into the chair, feeling like an absolute wally. 'Now what?'

'Now relax, close your eyes and try to empty your mind.'

Fat chance of that, Nola thought as she closed her eyes. She heard Tan-man make some adjustments, soothing music began to play and the chair began to vibrate.

Nola heard him leave the room. She opened her eyes, stared at the ceiling and closed her eyes again, knowing full well this was a waste of time.

'Sergeant Kane?'

Nola jerked awake. She half-threw herself from the chair and stood, disorientated and alarmed. 'Was I asleep?'

'I think so.' The woman who stood before her was tall, with long dark-red hair and perfect skin. 'It happens a lot in the chair.'

Nola was mortified. 'I'm sorry.'

'Why apologise?'

'I'm on duty.'

'I should be the one to apologise – I kept you waiting. I'm Beverly Russell.'

Still flustered, Nola shook the offered hand. Beverly's skin was cool and dry to the touch. Her nails were long and pearly pink. Everything her screamed 'perfection' and Nola found she resented it slightly.

'How is Jody? I tried calling the hospital, but nobody will give out any information.'

'She's stable.'

'Thank God, I've been worried sick since I heard what happened.'

'Were you in on Sunday night?'

'I was out until late Sunday night. My mother is unwell, Sergeant. I like to spend as much time with her on the weekend as I can.'

'I'm sorry to hear that.' Nola opened her notebook. 'What time did you get home?'

'A little after ten. I had a glass of wine, watched some television and went to bed.'

'Did you notice anything unusual?'

'No, nothing at all. Poor Jody, she's had the worst year. First the break-up with Simon and then … It's horrible. It doesn't bear thinking about.'

'And then?'

Beverly hesitated.

'If there's something you know—'

'She told me she thought someone had been in her house, going through her things.' Beverly shivered and folded her tanned arms across her chest. 'So creepy.'

'When was this?'

'September. I told her she should report it, but I don't know if she ever did.'

'Did Jody have any idea who was behind the break-in?'

'She never said, but come on, it's obvious it was Simon. He was very unhappy about their separation. For months he would turn up at her house, banging on the door, acting like a total fool. I told Jody she should have gotten a restraining order against him. I would have.'

His North Star indeed, Nola thought, making notes. 'Did you ever hear Simon threaten Jody?'

Beverly pursed her lips. 'He's too clever for that. No, this was more like … coercion, you know? "Oh, I love you, I'm sorry, you need me, forgive me" – it was relentless. To be completely honest, at one point I was genuinely scared she might take him back.'

'Scared? Are you saying he scared you?'

'I won't lie, I don't like Simon, I never did. The first time I met him I knew he was looking down his nose at me. Jody is the sweetest, kindest, gentlest soul you could possibly meet and I love her, but she has a blind spot when it comes to men – she can't seem to see when she's being manipulated. Simon Albright, in my opinion, is a master manipulator.'

'Yet she left him.'

Beverly looked thoughtful. 'She did. Something must have happened to break the spell.'

'She never confided in you about what happened? What the catalyst was?'

'No, we were friends, but ... Jody could keep her cards close to her chest when she wanted to. I assumed she grew tired of carrying him.'

'What about Jools Byrne – have you met him?'

'Once.'

'What's he like?'

'Handsome, rather like a young George Clooney.' She smiled. 'I could see why Jody was completely smitten.'

'Did you know he was married to one of Jody's old friends.'

'Amber Feenan.' Beverly shrugged. 'As they say, all's fair in love and war, Sergeant.'

'I wonder did Simon feel the same way?'

'Of course he didn't. But Jody *deserved* to be happy.'

'Did you know she was pregnant?'

Beverly expression was priceless. 'No! I had ... I had no idea.'

'What about Jody's family – did she ever talk about them much?'

Beverly's shock vanished in an instant. 'You know, I feel really bad talking behind her back like this,' she said after a moment. 'It's not like any of us can choose our families.'

'Oh, tell me about it.' Nola feigned impatience. 'Seriously, don't get me started about my sister – she'd put years on you.'

'Fiona, that's Jody's sister, is a total whack job. She married into some weird religious cult when she was young, doesn't believe in vaccinations or public school or modern medicine like birth control. She's a year older than Jody, but she has, like, I don't know how many kids. It's bonkers. Jody said she can barely feed the ones she has.'

'Did Jody see much of her?'

'As much as she could tolerate. I don't think Fiona's husband likes Fiona being around Jody much. He's got a weird mindset about liberal women.'

'Oh, have you met him?'

'Again, only once, but I did not like him. Easy on the eye but boorish and unpleasant. He came to the house with Fiona for a housewarming party not long after Jody and Simon moved in. Strange man. Very hostile. They didn't stay long. I think he and Simon had a row.'

'About what?'

'I have no idea, but it was heated, I know that. My God, is she really pregnant?'

'Yes.' Nola tapped the pen off her lip. 'Can you think of anyone who'd want to harm Jody?'

'Absolutely not, not a single person. Everyone likes her.'

'Someone didn't,' Nola said.

Beverly shivered dramatically. 'There's only one person who was angry with Jody, Sergeant. And that's Simon Albright. Trust me, he's your man.'

Yep, Nola thought, *and everyone can see it. Everyone except Elliot Ryan.*

29

'Carol?'

The woman sitting at the table looked up and stared at him from behind large slightly old-fashioned glasses. Elliot smiled, though he was shocked by her appearance. He remembered Carol Joyce as a sturdy, rotund country woman with ruddy cheeks and an honest, slightly earnest demeanour. The woman before him was a shadow of her former self, grey, sickly, slightly sunken, like fruit about to turn.

'Inspector Ryan,' he said.

'I know who you are – you called me, remember?'

'I wasn't sure if you'd remember me.'

Her expression hardened. 'I remember you. I remember *you* very well.' Her tone was anything but friendly.

Elliot reached the chair opposite her, but hesitated. 'Do you mind if I sit down?'

'You called me, I'm here. Sit or don't sit – I don't have all day.'

He sat, cleared his throat. This was going to be more difficult than he had anticipated. 'You look well.'

Carol Joyce laughed, but it wasn't a genuine laugh. Elliot

mentally gritted his teeth but smiled to be polite when the laugh went on too long. He was glad when a waitress came to take an order for coffee, glad the only other customer in the coffee shop was an older man by the window, reading the *Racing Post*.

'Well,' Carol snorted when the laughter dried up, 'I'm not well, Inspector. I'm marking time.'

'Oh?'

'Stage four liver cancer.' She pushed the glasses up her nose. 'Nothing to be done.'

'I'm so sorry.'

'Why?'

He was stumped. What sort of question was that to ask? Why wouldn't anyone express sympathy to a dying woman? While he was scrambling around for a reason, Carol Joyce pushed her half-drunk tea away and folded her arms.

'What do you want, Inspector Ryan? I know you didn't call me up for the pleasure of my company.'

The waitress returned and set a black coffee before him. Elliot thanked her and added milk from a metal jug. He stirred his coffee and put the spoon down. 'Natalie Dormond's mother came to see me a few weeks ago.'

Carol didn't so much as blink.

'She gave me a diary Natalie had hidden in her bedroom.'

Again, nothing.

'There were a number of entries. Some of them mentioned you.' He looked across the table.

It was as though someone had removed her batteries; but for the faint rise and fall of her chest, she might be a corpse.

'I wondered if she spoke to you about her ... time at the Ash care home?'

'She didn't. The other one did, Rebecca.' She looked annoyed. 'But she wasn't my client, and then Natalie got involved with her eejit of a brother, so I didn't know what to believe.'

'Did you know she was being abused?'

'I had my suspicions.'

'Why didn't you do something? Why didn't you move her?'

'To where? She was a teenage delinquent with an adult boyfriend – nowhere was safe.'

Elliot felt a sliver of disgust. 'There must have been something you could have done.'

'Like you, you mean? What did you do?'

He glared at her.

'You were at the inquest,' she said after a prolonged silence.

'I was.'

'Heard the same things I heard, I imagine.'

'I did.'

'Well then, what do you want of me?'

'You left social services not long after Natalie's inquest.'

She unfolded her arms and laid them flat on the table. 'You've been checking up on me.'

'A little,' he admitted. 'I'd forgotten about you until I reread the file.'

'Huh, doesn't surprise me much. You were a dose back then, you and that other one.'

'Clancy.'

Her upper lip wrinkled. 'Never understood why either of you became guards. You'd no interest in anything, and the only thing he was interested in was himself.'

'I'm sorry,' Elliot said again, the inadequacy of the word shamefully apparent.

'Too late for sorry now,' she said, but with no malice. 'What's done is done.'

'What can you tell me about the Black Top?'

'The pub? Not a whole lot – some of the kids used to mention it. Not to me, mind, but to each other. Word eventually filters through, but you know what they're like. They guard their sources like dogs.'

'What sources?'

'Money, smoke, gear, whatever they think they need.'

'You think they were getting it from the Black Top?'

She looked at him askance. 'Why are you asking about this now? The place burned down, didn't it?'

'A few years back, that's right.'

'Well then.'

He reached into his pocket and put the diary on the table between them. She looked at it but didn't touch it. 'There's an entry in here: two days before Natalie was killed she wrote "Black Top, 8 p.m., WD40". Do you know what that means?'

She laughed again. Her teeth were a nightmare. 'Oh for God's sake, come off it, Ryan, how long are you on the job?'

'Long enough.'

'It's code.'

'For what?'

'Oil, for a hinge. It's a hand job. She was pulling dick, like a lot of them.'

'Jesus.' He let out a shaky breath. 'She was a kid.'

'Are you really this thick?' Carol shook her head in amazement. 'Ask yourself why David Ash was never properly investigated, why any complaint that may have been made about him was withdrawn.'

He looked past her to the counter. The waitress was on her phone, scrolling. 'He was protected.'

'Bingo.'

'By who?'

She snorted again. 'Who do you think?'

'Clancy.'

'Ding-ding-ding.'

'If you knew you could have—'

'Please, you think the agency is going to let themselves be dragged through the mud? Over teenagers?' She shook her head with disgust. 'No one gave a shit about them then; no one gives a shit about them now.'

'I do.'

'You do, yeah. You know, I remember seeing you at the stationhouse one time. You were sitting on a chair with your chin on your chest. I could smell the drink off you halfway down the hall. Oh, I'd heard about your troubles, about your wife. No doubt they covered for you, kept the lid on things. But you were a fucking disgrace, Inspector Ryan. You sit there now, all clean and contrite, bleating on about caring. Well, listen to me, you can't care for the dead. You can't do shit for them. It's over. They're gone.' She waggled the fingers of her right hand. 'Dust to dust.'

'I should have stopped him.'

'Clancy's a carrion fly. It's the whole rotten corpse I couldn't stand. It sickened me, mentally and physically.' She leaned forward. 'That job destroyed me. You sit there and you talk about care? You, Inspector Ryan, you turn my stomach more than the rest because deep down I think you know you could have done good; you know you could have made a difference, but you didn't. And now it's too late.'

'I was a different man back then.'

She reached behind for her coat. 'You weren't,' she said. 'You only think you were.' She left, leaving him to pay for both their unfinished drinks.

30

'Beverly Russell confirms it,' Nola said, around a mouthful of crisps. 'Albright is our man. We should bring him in, sir, do a proper interview.'

'Do we have the phone yet?'

'No.'

'And no report of this break-in in September?'

'Nada.'

'I shouldn't have to point this out, but Jody Kavanagh did not report Simon Albright to us at any stage. If she was frightened of him, why didn't she get a restraining order against him or make a nuisance report? I mean, goodness, Sergeant, she didn't even change the locks.'

'Maybe she thought he'd get over the break-up or something, but things escalated when she got involved with Jools Byrne.'

'Guesswork.'

Nola scowled. 'Why are you so convinced Simon Albright is not our man?'

'Why are you so sure he is?'

'Because he's her ex-husband and he was at her house on the morning she was attacked, covered in her blood – hello?'

Elliot rubbed the back of his neck. After the meeting with

Carol Joyce he had walked to the Church of Mary Immaculate, Refuge of Sinners and sat for almost an hour, mulling things over in his mind. He was not a religious man, not these days. He had thrown his lot in with God when Laurie was sick and come away an atheist. But there was a lot to be said about sitting in a spiritual space with time to contemplate life and all her trappings.

Robbie tapped on the open door, grinning ear to ear.

'What is it, Sergeant Keller?'

'I spoke to Justine Cullen, that's the neighbour on the other side, and, oh, she had so many things to say.'

'Such as?'

'She told me Jody Kavanagh was,' he looked at his notebook, 'a doxy.'

'A what?' Nola asked.

Elliot cleared his throat. 'A loose woman, Sergeant, someone free with her ... er, sexual favours. What age is this lady?'

'Eighty-one but sharp as a whip and get this. According to her there was an altercation on Friday evening. A row that was so bad she called us.'

Nola and Elliot sat forward in tandem. 'Friday night, this Friday night gone?'

'Yup.' Robbie's grin widened. 'Mrs Cullen said she spoke to Sergeant Sandra Flynn. She said in all her years she's never heard anything like the carry-on at that house.'

Elliot reached for his phone. 'Bill, it's Elliot Ryan ... Yes, no, I'm holding up. Thank you. Is Sergeant Flynn in the building do you know? ... Sandra, yes ... Got it, thank you.

'She's in dispatch.' He put another call through. 'Hello, who's this? ... Inspector Ryan ... Yes, it's fine, yes, thank you ... Indeed, good to know. I'll take it under advisement. Tell me, is Sergeant Flynn there? ... Oh, she is? Could you ask her if she might pop upstairs for a moment? ... That's very kind, thank you. I will ... Yes, yes.' He hung up. 'She's on her way.'

'According to Miss Cullen,' Robbie said, 'there was a right old ding-dong happening, screaming, shouting, the dog was barking. She thinks the husband – sorry, ex-husband, was involved.'

'What did I say?' Nola clicked her fingers. 'Simon Albright's bandaged hand. I'll bet you a slab of cans the dog took a chunk out of him.'

Moments later, Sergeant Flynn arrived. She was a small sharp-eyed woman in her thirties. 'You wanted to see me, sir?'

'I did, thank you. Did you take a report about an altercation at a house in Kilmainham last Friday evening? Possible domestic.'

'Yes, sir.'

'What can you tell me about it?'

She spread her hands slightly. 'Not a whole lot to it, sir. We were called regarding a DV complaint, but when we got there the suspect was gone, and only the woman and her ... friend remained, and they didn't want to press charges.'

'Of course not,' Nola said hotly. 'Jools Byrne is a wealthy man; he won't want a scene.'

Sergeant Flynn frowned. 'That is not a name I'm familiar with.'

'Oh.' Nola looked at Elliot. 'Then who did you talk to?'

'I spoke with' – Flynn took out her notebook and flipped back a few pages – 'Jody Kavanagh and her companion, Simon Albright.'

'Simon Albright was there on Friday night? With Jody?'

'Yes, he was comforting her. It looked to me like there had

been a row or a fight of some kind, but neither party wanted to pursue it so ...' She shrugged.

'What time was this, Sergeant?'

'Shortly before nine.'

'And Jody Kavanagh was unharmed?'

'She was upset, but I spoke to her in a different room away from him and I don't think he was any threat to her at all – if anything, he seemed as upset as she was.'

'Very good, thank you.'

Sergeant Flynn left.

Nola sat back. 'I don't get it.'

'It's certainly a conundrum.' Elliot glanced at his watch. 'Go have some lunch – it's impossible to think on an empty stomach. Not you, Sergeant Keller, I need you type up that report.'

'What, now?' Robbie scowled.

'No time like the present. If you'll excuse me.' He rose unsteadily and made his way to the bathroom where, once he had checked the stalls were empty, he vomited copiously until there was nothing left, washed his hands and went outside to make some calls in private.

31

Nola went down to the canteen and was looking at a video on her phone over a plate of steak, chips and a fried egg when a shadow fell over her.

She looked up and found herself staring into the cold blue eyes of Paul Deacon.

Looking at him now, she could scarcely believe she'd ever had feelings for him. Real feelings. Adult feelings. He hadn't been her first boyfriend, far from it, but she had felt ... well, she had thought he was different.

He was different. But not good different.

'What?'

'What yourself.' He grinned. 'Can't we even talk now?'

'We've nothing to talk about.' She glared as he sat down on the chair next to her. When she made to stand, his hand reached out as fast as a snake strike and caught her by the wrist, holding her in place.

She looked at it, looked at him. 'If you think I won't scream blue murder, you don't know me at all.'

'You won't.'

'Try me.'

'You know, for a smart girl, you're fierce thick when you want to be. Or is it an act?'

She tugged her hand free. He had gripped it tight enough to leave marks. It infuriated her. 'What do you want?'

'What's the old soak up to?'

'What?'

'Ryan, what's he at?'

'We're investigating an assault on a woman in Kilmainham.'

He leaned closer. She could smell his aftershave and recognised it as the one she had bought him for his birthday back in the summer, back when she thought she gave a shit what he smelled like.

Back when she thought she loved him. 'What a joke.'

'What?'

She blinked. 'What?'

'You said "what a joke" – what is?'

'You are,' she said, recovering quickly. 'What business is it of yours what we're working on?'

'Just interested. I like to keep tabs on my people.'

'*Your* people?'

'People I care about, sure.'

Nola laughed. 'Since when?'

He grinned. 'You know, with Clancy retiring there's going to be a reshuffle.'

'I heard you're throwing your hat in the ring for inspector.'

'I'll need a good team around me, if I get it. Homicide attracts the best.'

'That's your territory, pal, not mine.'

'It could be yours again. I could put in a good word with the brass, smooth things over.'

Nola narrowed her eyes. 'Why? Why would you do something like that? Why now?'

'You're cute when you're paranoid.' He smiled his insincere shark smile, the one she had once found charming. 'I'm looking out for you, kiddo, that's all; everyone knows Ryan is ...' He twirled his forefinger by his temple. 'It would be easy to get sucked into his madness.'

'What madness? What are you talking about?'

'The man's not a team player, Nola, you know that. I don't want to see you get hurt.'

'Don't bullshit me – you're fishing, Deacon. What are you fishing for?'

'Look,' he said. 'I care about you—'

'Go fuck yourself into the sea.'

He attempted to look contrite. 'Nola, I can't change what happened. I can't undo it. I wish with all my heart I could, but I can't. But that doesn't mean I don't care about you.'

'You screwed someone else.'

'It was an accident.'

'Did she fall onto your dick when you weren't looking?'

'I'm sorry, Kane, you know I never wanted to hurt you.'

She felt her heart try to climb its way out of her chest. Was she hearing things? Was he admitting he was in the wrong?

Why did this feel like a trap? She wracked her brains. *You know this man; you know what he is capable of. What does he want?* Another thought, faster and brighter than the others, pinged her cortex. *Yeah, you do know this man, you know exactly how he thinks, so bounce the ball back into his court.*

She softened her features and lowered her voice. 'You broke

my heart, Paul, you ruined my life and now you want to interfere with my job?'

'I'm trying to help you, Nola.'

'I don't need your help. I don't *want* your help.'

He leaned back slightly, eyes locked with hers, oozing concern. 'Okay, that's fine. I get it. But listen to me, take some advice. Don't get involved in Ryan's bullshit, okay? The man's not well.'

'I don't understand. I don't understand what you're warning me about.'

'Ryan has some kind of vendetta against Clancy, has done for years.'

'What kind of vendetta?' He was watching her closely, so she kicked it up a notch. 'I've never heard him say a bad word about Clancy.' She paused as if pondering. 'Or anyone else for that matter.'

'That's good.' He stroked his chin. 'Has he ever mentioned any other names to you?'

'Names?'

'Yeah ... Black or ... Dromond?'

She shook her head. 'You know, with all the medication he's on right now, I'd say even remembering my name might be a struggle.'

'Oh yeah? Is he taking a lot of pills?'

She shrugged, hating herself for what she was about to do. 'I think so. Makes him a bit spaced out at times. I can't always tell if he's in the room.'

'I didn't know that.'

'So why do you think he has a vendetta? About what?'

He moved directly to back-peddle. 'I don't know why or what

it's about – it was before my time, before yours, you know? The poor fuck was never right after his wife died. Well, you know, you work with him you must have noticed that he's a bit ... squirrelly.'

Nola pretended to think about it. 'I think he's depressed.'

Deacon clicked the fingers on his right hand and pointed at her, grinning, relaxed now that he was sure he had her 'onside'.

'Yeah, yeah, depressed.' The grin vanished. 'So you've got to take the shit he says with a pinch of salt.'

'He doesn't really talk to me anyway.'

'Yeah?'

'He doesn't really talk to anyone.' She shrugged. 'To be honest, I think he's trying to get to his twenty-five in one piece.'

Deacon glanced at his watch. It was new, she noticed, and looked very expensive. The man liked nice things. Nicer than her at any rate.

'Look, I've got to go, but Nola, I'm glad we had this chat.' He curled his index finger and lifted her chin with it. 'I've really missed you a lot.'

'Get out of here,' she said, shaking her head, a faint smile playing on her lips.

He grinned, gave her a rapid kiss on the cheek and was gone, walking his cocky walk across the canteen, Mr Bo-fucking-jangles, player of women.

Nola waited until he left the room, then dropped the smile and wiped her cheek with the back of her hand, disgusted. Her food had gone cold. She cursed him for that as she pushed the plate to one side and sat staring straight ahead.

If anyone had seen her, it would have looked as though

she was shut down, blank. But Nola Kane was anything but. Nola Kane was wondering why Paddy Clancy was hell-bent on painting Elliot Ryan as a nutcase and why he was so interested in what her boss might be doing. She was wondering why Paul Deacon and Gracie were singing from the same hymn sheet and why, when Clancy was only a few days from retirement, did it matter now?

32

It was raining when they pulled into the tiny car park of Jolie Laide, a single-storey building, squat and unlovely, painted matt black. The car park was surrounded on three sides by spiked black railings.

'Gloomy,' Elliot said, undoing his belt. 'Why is everything black or grey these days?'

'That's fashion for you.'

'There is nothing wrong with a bit of colour. Livens up a day, a life. We will all be dead soon enough.'

'Sir?'

'Never mind.'

They entered the building through a revolving door so tight they had to enter and exit into the tiny reception area individually. A blue-haired woman with various facial piercings, wearing a headset, watched the approach. She did not seem overly pleased to see them. 'Do you have an appointment?'

Elliot showed his badge. 'Detective Ryan, and this is Sergeant Kane. We're here to speak to Diandra Cliff.'

'Regarding?'

'Regarding one of your employees,' Nola snapped. 'Is she here or not?'

'Jeez, relax.' The girl pressed a button and adjusted her microphone. 'Di? Some *people* here to see you.' A pause. Then, 'Yeah, they *say* they're cops.'

Moments later, Diandra Cliff pushed through a smoked-glass door neither of them had noticed. She was slight, with jet-black hair tied in a ponytail with a fringe that almost met the top of her black-rimmed glasses. Her clothes were also black, understated in a way that made a wallet wince, and if Elliot had to guess her age he'd have struggled. She wore no jewellery except for a delicate gold watch on her right wrist.

'Ah, I was expecting you earlier,' Diandra said. 'Please, come this way. Would you like anything? Tea, coffee?'

'No, thank you, we're fine.'

'I'll have some water, please,' Nola said. 'Sparkling, if you have it?'

'Taika, some water, please, and hold my calls.'

They followed Diandra back through the invisible door and down a carpeted hall, the walls of which were covered in moody photos of interiors. She led them into a conference room and stood holding the door open with her hip until they had taken a seat.

'Miss Cliff,' Elliot began.

'Please, call me Diandra.' She sat opposite them and linked her fingers. 'My God, I am in complete shock. It's just so awful. Can you tell me what happened exactly – are you allowed to do that?'

'Miss Kavanagh was assaulted in her home between Sunday night and Monday morning, badly assaulted. She was found on Monday morning, unresponsive.'

'How brutal.'

'We were wondering, Diandra, if you could give us some background. How long has Jody worked for you?'

'Let me see, November 2019.' She smiled. 'A fresh returnee from London.'

'You hired her immediately?'

'I snapped her up the second I could. I should tell you, Detective, Jody and I are old friends.'

'Ah, I didn't realise.' Elliot scratched his chin. 'You also worked with her husband, Simon Albright, correct?'

'He did some minor consulting for the firm last year.'

'You sacked him, though, right?' Nola asked. 'Why was that?'

'I declined to use his services.' Diandra tilted her head. 'That was a business decision.'

'Probably for the best,' Nola said. 'I mean, if him and Jody were on the outs.'

'That had nothing to do with it.'

'Did Jools Byrne have anything to do with it?'

Diandra visibly stiffened. 'Excuse me?'

'Jools Byrne. Drives a Tesla, looks like George Clooney,' Nola said. 'You know him, don't you?'

'Yes, we've met.'

'Do you know Amber Feenan?'

'Yes, socially.'

'How did she feel about her old pal hooking up with her husband?'

'Ex-husband and I don't know.' She smiled thinly. 'Why would I concern myself with such matters?'

'I thought you lot all ran in the same circles – Tamara Ford, Jools Byrne, Amber Feenan.'

Diandra Cliff's face went completely blank. 'I don't think I can talk about this without breaking a confidentiality clause.'

Nola sat forward. 'There is no confidentiality in this case – there's only withholding information. Miss Cliff, your friend and colleague has been badly injured. If you know something, you need to tell us. Now.'

'I *don't* know that I can, Detective,' Diandra replied, with more than a little frost in her own voice. 'There may be legal ramifications.'

'There *will* be legal ramifications if you know something and don't tell us what it is.'

'When did you last talk to Jody?' Elliot asked, pressing Nola's foot under the table with his. *Dial it back*, his foot said.

'Friday. She was still here when I left. We didn't talk for long.'

'I'd like to see her office, if I may.'

'Of course.'

'How did she seem to you?'

'Tired, Detective, it's been a difficult few weeks.'

'How so?'

Taika entered the room carrying a tray of glasses and a bottle of sparkling water. She put them on the table and stalked out. Nobody touched them.

'You were saying?' Elliot probed. 'It's been a difficult few weeks?'

'Meaning exactly that.' She exhaled heavily. 'Look, I understand you have to ask your questions and I wish there was something I could do or say that would help Jody, but in truth there's nothing. Jody was a workaholic, a perfectionist, incredibly talented and we at Jolie Laide are lucky to have her.

The wheel would not turn smoothly without her, I can assure you.'

'She's the grease, is she?' Nola asked. She found she was taking a perverse pleasure in rattling Diandra Cliff's cage a little.

'I think it's fair to say Jody has incredible connections.'

'What kind of connections?'

'Jody's grandmother is Hilary Hamilton-Ray.'

Elliot and Nola looked blank.

'Dudley Ray's second wife?'

The blankness continued.

Diandra sighed. 'The Rays are involved in the pork-processing industry. In fact, the Rays *are* the pork-processing industry.'

'Ah.'

'So, as you can imagine, Jody knows all of the right people.'

'In pork?'

'In money.'

Elliot felt a flicker of admiration for the bluntness. 'I can see how that would be an advantage in your line of work. No wonder you welcomed her to the business with open arms.'

'I work within a small but highly competitive market. Naturally, I use whatever connections I can. Jolie Laide is for the discerning customer.'

'Why is it called Jolie Laide?'

'It's a bit of a joke, really. It means a sort of ugliness that signifies beauty.'

'I see,' Elliot said. 'Odd name for an interior design company I would have thought.'

'Not really. We find beauty in the ugly and use it to transform a dwelling, elevate it.'

Elliot, whose idea of 'transforming a dwelling' involved gallons of magnolia paint and white gloss, merely nodded. 'Is there anyone you can think of that might have a personal problem with Jody? Someone with a grudge or a vendetta?'

'No. I can't think of anyone who would harm Jody.'

Her phone buzzed. She took it from her pocket, glanced at it, grimaced and put it back in her pocket. 'I'm sorry, I really don't have time to—'

'Did you know she was pregnant?'

Diandra stared. 'I ... pregnant? Are you sure?'

'The hospital confirmed it.'

'My God, I had no idea. She never mentioned anything to me.' Her phone buzzed again. 'I'm sorry, I have to take this. If you'll excuse me.'

'We'll take a look at Jody's office.'

'Of course, it's down the hall, last door on the right.' She stood up and left the room, flustered.

'What?' Elliot said, putting his notebook away.

'She's hiding something.'

'Everybody's hiding something, Sergeant, it's human nature.'

'Well, Jody didn't trust her, that's for sure.'

They wandered down the hall and entered Jody's office. It was small, cluttered, dominated by a large table covered in swathes of fabrics and pictures. A small desk stood in a corner of the room, it too covered in magazines and colour charts.

'How does anyone work in this mess?' Nola asked, looking around.

'Creatives,' Elliot muttered, studying the photos on the walls. Mostly interior shots of expensive homes, lots of muted colours and awkward-looking furniture.

'I've got a planner here,' Nola said, lifting it. 'I'll take this back to the station, see if it can offer up something interesting.'

Elliot paused at a photo and took a closer look. It showed Jody and Simon sitting at a picnic table, sharing lunch. Jody was grinning at the camera; Simon was looking at her with such utter devotion it made Elliot feel a little strange. Had he totally got this wrong? Did Simon Albright attack the woman he swore he loved?

They left the building as the rain began again in earnest.

Nola got in and slammed the door.

Elliot got in beside her and put his belt on. 'I wonder ...' he began. 'I wonder if I'm wrong.'

'About?' Nola said, starting the engine. She threw her hand over the back of his seat and reversed out.

'Simon Albright. Right now I would like some forensics we can use. Something concrete. Someone brutally assaulted Jody Kavanagh and left her and her unborn child to die. I know we're swimming in rarefied waters here, Sergeant, but the law is the law.'

He rubbed his forehead with his fingertips.

Jody put on the radio.

'Oh, good idea, Sergeant,' Elliot said, and moved the dial to Lyric FM. 'Music soothes the soul and helps us think.'

'Hey, I thought the driver gets to pick the music?'

'One moment, Sergeant.' He took his phone out and answered it. 'Macey, yes. Fingerprints, where are we? ... Were there? That is interesting ... No, I'll bear it in mind.'

He hung up.

'What?'

'Macey ran the fingerprints she found in Jody's bedroom. They belong to Bane Russell.'

'He did say he'd he wired up her sound system.'

'He deserves a closer look.'

'Gotcha.'

Elliot rubbed his forehead and closed his eyes. After a while, Nola glanced over and saw that he was asleep. She sighed and left the radio station where it was.

33

When they got back to the station Elliot woke up, pretended he hadn't been asleep at all and went upstairs to talk to Superintendent Connors. Nola returned a call to Sergeant Abby Fencer regarding the Cooper, the dog.

'He's registered to a breeder, Stella Ross, who, believe it or not, we deal with now and then. I should have known – she's an excellent breeder. Do you want me to give her a call?'

'No, I'll talk to her. Cheers for this, Sergeant. How's the brute doing?'

'He's fine, a real sweetheart.'

'If you say so.'

She waited for Elliot to reappear. 'I've got the breeder of the dog – she's in Rathfarnham.'

Elliot nodded. He looked a little pale, distracted.

'How'd it go upstairs?'

'Oh, fine, fine.'

'Really?'

'Well, no, I suspect Diandra Cliff has some powerful friends.'

'What does that mean?'

'It means Superintendent Connors got a call, and now he suggests that we should take extreme care where we dally and whom we dally with.'

'Fuck that!'

'Language, Sergeant.' Elliot frowned. 'There's no need to be coarse. Attend to the dog ... breeder. I have some things to catch up on here.'

The drive to the kennels – which should have taken forty minutes – took one hour and twenty. By the time Nola reached the gates her mood had sunk from angry into seething, so when she got out of the car and stepped directly into a puddle she decided to be as coarse as the moment dictated.

She slammed the car door and stamped towards high wooden gates and looked for a bell.

There wasn't one.

'What the f—' Furious, she dug out her phone and called.

Nobody answered.

It took several more calls before the phone was finally picked up by someone who managed to sound angrier than Nola. A lot of dogs barked in the background.

'*What?*'

'This is Sergeant Kane. We had an appointment scheduled—'

'You're late.'

'I'm at your gate.'

'Now?'

'Yes, now!' Nola could hardly believe it. 'Can you let me in, please?'

'Tsk, stop that ... hold on, I'll be there in a minute.'

She hung up.

Nola waited.

And waited.

Ten minutes went by.

Eleven.

Twelve.

Nola got her phone out.

The gates made a faint pop, and gradually, oh so gradually, opened inwards. Nola faced a short drive and a ramshackle bungalow half-hidden behind overgrown bushes. She left the car where it was and walked towards the house.

She hadn't gone ten feet when two grey and black dogs came rushing towards her, barking furiously. She turned to run but the gates were almost closed. She'd never make it.

'Shit.'

With nowhere to hide, Nola bent down to pick up a handful of small pebbles and then heard a sharp whistle. The dogs slid to a halt, barking furiously, bouncing up and down on their front feet.

Christ, Nola thought, *the size of those teeth.*

A woman appeared from the side of the house carrying a bright-green plastic bucket. She was dressed in several layers of brown, with her hair tied at the nape of her neck in a very loose bun. Her skin was tanned – no, weathered, and she looked about as happy to see Nola as the dogs were.

'Athos, Alecto, ven!'

As one, the dogs turned and raced back to her.

Nola relaxed a fraction. 'Stella Ross?'

'Yes.'

'I've been waiting for you for nearly a quarter of an hour.'

'Now you know what it feels like.'

Nola was astonished. 'The traffic was ... Are you free *now*?' she asked, lacing the question with sarcasm.

'Not really,' Stella said. 'My assistant is off sick, so I'm doing everything myself today.'

'I'll try not to take up a lot of *your* valuable time.'

Stella jerked her head. 'Come on, we can talk and walk.'

'What about those—?'

'They won't touch you.'

Nola eyed the dogs with suspicion. 'You sure about that?'

Stella cracked the smallest of smiles. 'I'd stake my reputation on it.'

Nola walked towards her. The closer she got, the more focused the dogs became, but their owner was right: they didn't touch her.

'They're beautiful dogs,' Nola said. 'What are they, Alsatians?'

Stella winced slightly. 'They're German shepherd dogs – these two are from the DDR line.'

'Huh?'

'East German line, these dogs are not from West German show-line stock.'

'What's the difference?'

'What's the difference between a Toyota and a Maserati?'

'Money?'

Stella grinned. She looked slightly less terrifying when she smiled. 'No, but I take your point.'

Together they walked around to the rear of the bungalow and entered a small kitchen that looked like it doubled as an office. The floor was tiled, the kitchen table swamped in ledgers and paperwork, but it was clean and warm and blissfully free of dogs, as the two shepherds waited outside.

'Coffee?'

'Sure.'

Nola looked around while the kettle boiled. The walls were covered in rosettes, some faded, some bright, calendars, posters of shows, photos of various dogs doing athletic things. Stella was in most of the photos at various ages. Her hair and her clothing changed, but her expression never wavered, even when she stood next to a podium holding a huge gold cup. Another sourpuss.

'Are these all yours?'

'No,' Stella said without turning around. 'Not all of them. From 2000 on, those are my dogs.'

'You started breeding them yourself?'

'I didn't see that I had a choice.'

She finished, shoved some of the paperwork aside, put the coffee on the table in two mugs and fetched a carton of milk from an under-the-counter fridge. After a moment of thought, she went to a press and added an opened packet of Jaffa Cakes.

'There's sugar if you like.'

'Black's fine.'

'So,' Stella said when they sat, 'you said on the phone you have one of my dogs.'

Nola took a biscuit and nibbled the edges. It was a little stale but that had never bothered her. 'That's right, we—'

'Which dog?'

'Cooper, he's a—'

'Belgian Malinois.' Stella got up and left the room. She returned with a set of papers attached to a small clipboard. 'Do you have the chip number?'

Nola retrieved her notebook and read the number aloud.

Stella looked grim. 'Cooper's a personal protection dog. How did he come to be in your care?'

'We took him from a crime scene yesterday.'

'This is related to Jody Kavanagh, yes?'

'Yes.'

'Is she hurt?'

'She's in hospital in a coma.'

Stella's lips thinned. 'I see. Where was Cooper?'

'He was outside, in the back garden.' Nola said. 'Locked out from what we can gather.'

'Stupid.'

'Excuse me?'

'I said stupid – if he'd been with her, she wouldn't be in hospital right now.'

'You can't know that.'

Stella's half-smile appeared and vanished just as quickly. 'Cooper is a highly trained grade-A protection dog. There's no way he'd allow anyone to attack his handler.'

'Well, he can't open doors.'

'Is that so?' She leaned back. 'Athos! A mi!'

Nola turned her head in time to see the door handle snap down. The bigger of the two dogs bounced into the kitchen.

'And he's the daft one,' Stella said, watching her. 'The bitch would buy and sell you.'

'Christ,' Nola said, a little shakily. The dog was right next to her, his amber eyes laser-locked on her face.

Stella sent the dog out and closed the door again. 'What did you need from me, Sergeant?',

'We're trying to get a feel for the last few months of Jody's life. How did she know about you? Where do you advertise?'

Stella snorted. 'I don't *advertise* my dogs; this isn't a commercial operation if that's what you're getting at.'

'I wasn't—'

'People think dogs and the first thing they think of are puppy farms.' Stella scowled. 'Not that I blame them – it's a disgrace what this country allows to happen to dogs. A disgrace. No, I don't sell my dogs to any old Johnny-come-lately. If I did, I'd be a rich woman.' She slapped her hand on the table. 'Do I look like a rich woman to you?'

'Nope.'

Stella flipped a page on the clipboard. 'September third, a client asked me if I could meet with Jody.'

'A client?' Nola opened her notebook. *September*. 'Care to provide a name?'

'Only if I legally have to.'

'All right. Go on.'

'I met with Jody here the following day and she explained what she was looking for. I said I didn't think I could help her.'

'Why not?'

'I didn't think she was a good fit.'

Nola cocked an eyebrow, drank some of her coffee and nearly choked trying to swallow it. Tar would have been an understatement. Molten black lava might have covered it ... at a push. 'What was wrong with her?' Nola managed.

'She'd never owned a dog before, for a start.'

'That's a bad thing?'

Stella gave a look that could only be interpreted one way.

'But you gave her Cooper in the end.'

'She worked for it; she came here and did a week's course on handling – that's how serious she was.' Stella sipped her own coffee and didn't wince once. 'Turns out she was a natural.'

'Did she mention why she wanted the dog?'

'The reasons are none of my business.'

'But did she?'

'She mentioned she lived alone; she mentioned something about a marriage break-up.'

'Was *he* the reason she got the dog?'

'I got the impression the break-up hadn't been his idea, if that's what you mean.'

Nola mulled it over. It didn't make sense. If Jody was scared shitless of Simon Albright to the point that she needed a protection dog, why not get it back in January, and why, for that matter, have him around at her house at all? Why would she have locked the dog outside when he was there? None of it made any sense to her.

'What happens with Cooper now?'

'There is a clause in Jody's contract that, should she no longer want Cooper, I have first right of refusal.'

'He's sort of a witness,' Nola said, giving up on the coffee. She was thinking about the bandage on Simon Albright's arm again.

'I see.'

'He's with the Dog Unit – they'll look after him.' She drummed her fingers. 'If Cooper bit you he'd leave a mark, right?'

That got her an actual full-throated laugh. 'He'd leave more than that, Sergeant – he'd leave plenty of damage, believe me.'

'Do you think he'd recognise the person who attacked Jody?'

'He might, he's a sensitive animal. He'd certainly have a dim view of them.'

'Is there any way we could take teeth prints of Cooper's ... uh, mouth?'

'You mean record his bite?'

'Yeah.'

Stella thought about it for a moment. 'You'd need a sleeve and a mould for his teeth.'

186

Nola took her phone from her pocket. 'Macey, it's ... yes, I know ... Right, but this is different.' She paused, staring at one of the calendars. In it a dog – it might have been one of the beasts outside – was leaping full stretch over bales of hay or straw with ease, jaws bared, fully focused on whatever the hell it was after. 'Cool, we need to take a sample of Cooper's bite ... He's the dog from yesterday ... Yes, I'm serious.' She glanced at Stella, who was watching her, bemused. 'I'll call Sergeant Fencer ... Huh, I doubt it, she knows what she's doing ... All right ... Yes, I owe you one.' She hung up. 'He made quite an impression on our forensics officer yesterday.'

'Good,' Stella said, lifting her coffee cup to her lips. 'That's his job.'

34

Elliot had taken his jacket off and loosened his tie. Nola was munching her way through a bag of Haribo sours while reading some statements from people Jody had either worked with or been acquainted with.

'I don't get it,' she said after a while. 'She's an angel, a lady, a sweetheart, the kindest person they ever met, talented, sweet, good ... oh look, this is new: a pure lamb. Hear that, sir? She was a pure lamb.'

'You disagree?'

'Can you be a lamb and a doxy?' Nola said, stretching. 'Look, whatever, everyone has a skeleton in the cupboard, right? Why would Jody Kavanagh be any different, is all I'm saying?'

Elliot chuckled and raised an eyebrow. 'What's your skeleton?'

'I cheat at cards.'

'Really?'

'Yeah, I do. I learned it from my mam. She has a brass neck when it comes to cards.'

'What do you do?'

She gave him a look. 'If I told you I'd have to kill you.'

'I see,' he said, turning back to the statements. 'Do you

know, I suspect if we talk to Amber Feenah we might get a very different—'

'Hold on there now, chief. I told you my skeleton – what's yours?'

'I don't have any.'

'My arse.'

'Sergeant Kane.'

'What?'

'Decorum, we talked about this, we said we'd work on it.'

'Did we?' She snorted and glanced at her watch. 'I'm going to go get us some coffee. I don't know about you, but I'm wrecked.'

'No coffee for me, Sergeant. I'm afraid my daughter has forbidden it.'

'I won't tell her if you don't.'

He looked disappointed in her. 'I gave her my word, Sergeant.'

Poor sod, she thought, stretching until her back clicked. She left him reviewing notes and went downstairs to the canteen. She took the stairs to give her legs a bit of a workout and was on the upper landing when she heard a familiar voice on the return below.

Paul Deacon.

She stopped and leaned out just enough to catch a glimpse of his back. He was talking to Gracie, jabbing a finger in her face.

Nola jerked her head back in.

Calm down, she warned herself. *They both work in Homicide – it stands to reason they'd have things to talk about. Right?*

She strained her ears. Paul was talking in a low, urgent voice, but she could make out some of the words. It sounded like he was giving her a dressing down.

About what?

'It's not easy,' Gracie said, clear as a bell. Nola could hear anger in her voice, defiance.

What wasn't easy? Nola cursed under her breath. She couldn't stay perched there like an eavesdropping chicken all night – up or down, pick one.

She went down, whistling tunelessly to make her presence known.

'Oh hey,' she said when she saw them.

Deacon was smooth, smooth as grease. 'Two encounters in one day, Kane, that must be a sign.'

'It's a sign, all right,' she said haughtily. 'Hey, Gracie.'

'Oh, hey, Nola.'

Nola kept on walking, still whistling, casual as she possibly could, but she had seen Gracie's face and, unlike Paul bloody Deacon, her friend was not practised in the dark arts of being a total two-faced prick.

Gracie looked scared; she looked guilty; she looked, and here Nola felt a pang of sorrow, like a wild animal caught in a trap.

Troubled, she got her coffee and one for Robbie and went back upstairs, taking the lift. She stopped at his cubicle to drop it off. 'Here, I thought you could do with this.'

'Thanks!' He looked surprised. 'I appreciate it.'

'You're welcome.'

He looked at his watch and groaned. 'I hate typing.'

Nola grinned. 'Nobody likes paperwork, Robbie.'

'At this rate I'll be here all night.'

Nola was sympathetic. 'Tell you what, you know how I got Macey to agree to do a bite test on the dog?'

'Yeah?'

'How about you take that tomorrow? Get you out of here for a while.'

'You serious?'

'Sure, I've got loads of people I need to see.'

'Aces.' He grinned at her. 'You're all right, Kane.'

'High praise, I can never get enough of it.'

She walked back to her cubicle where Elliot was combing over Jody Kavanagh's planer.

He tapped a date with 'Angela G' written in at 3 p.m. 'Who is this person?'

'No idea, sir, none of the friends knew either.'

'But Jody saw her twice a month for ...' He flicked back through the planner. 'Since the start of the year. I have to assume then that she saw this Angela G the previous year too.'

'It's sound like a regular appointment to me, sir.'

'Mm,' Elliot rested his fingers against his stubbly chin. 'We need Jody Kavanagh's bank records. We can check payments made against these dates, see what correlates.'

'Yes sir.'

'Tomorrow, I want you to talk to Fiona Hynes – alone, if possible. I would value your input.'

Nola was pleased. 'I told you there was something off with her story.'

'Perhaps,' Elliot said, looking grave. 'But exercise a little finesse, Sergeant. I suspect, and I could be wrong, but I suspect Fiona Hynes is walking a very fine line right now.'

'What makes you say that?'

'Experience, Sergeant.' He glanced at her, and something in his expression chased the grin right off her face. 'Experience.'

The phone on his desk blipped. Elliot reached for it and listened. 'Of course,' he said after a moment. 'What time? ... Certainly, good evening.' He hung up. 'Fiona Hynes will have to wait.'

'Sir?'

'Morag Kavanagh is coming to see us in the morning.'

The Ice Queen cometh, Nola thought, but somehow managed to not blurt it out.

35

Wednesday

Early the next morning, Nola swung by Elliot's house to collect him. She parked on the road, trotted up the drive to the front door and rang the bell. A young woman around her age answered.

'You must be Sergeant Kane, I'm Shona.'

'Aw, yeah, how's it—?'

Shona stepped out and pulled the door slightly closed behind her. 'How's he doing?'

Nola shrugged. 'You know.'

'I don't, that's the problem – he never tells me anything.' Shona leaned closer and lowered her voice further still. 'You know he's on some pretty strong medication?'

'Yeah, I figured.'

'Do you think someone hit the car from behind yesterday?'

'I think it's possible, don't you?'

'Maybe, but honestly' – she frowned – 'I'm glad you're driving him.'

'I don't think he is.'

The door opened behind Shona and Elliot stood there, looking annoyed and suspicious. 'Are you ready to go?'

'Yes, sir.'

'Do you have your lunch, Dad?'

'Yes.' He gave Shona a perfunctory peck on the top of her head and walked past them and on down the drive. Nola offered Shona an apologetic smile and went after him.

'She seems nice.'

'I won't have this, Sergeant,' he said as Nola pulled away from the house. 'I won't have you and my daughter gossiping behind my back.'

'Sir, we were hardly—'

'I don't bring my business home with me, nor my family to work. I suggest you honour the demarcation.'

'I do, but if you—'

He held up the dreaded finger. 'I've said what I had to say, Sergeant.'

Though the appointment was for eight thirty, Mrs Morag Kavanagh was already waiting for them in the reception area when Nola and Elliot arrived shortly before eight. She sat very still and very upright next to a man Elliot recognised from the courts and knew by reputation: Aldus Crivon.

There was no mistaking Jody's mother; though she was at least sixty years old, she and her daughter could have been clones. Elliot wondered briefly if her surgeon was the same one his sister had on speed dial.

Nola elbowed him in the ribs when she saw them. He winced. She had very pointy elbows.

'Holy shit, that's Aldus Crivon.'

'I'm not blind, Sergeant.'

'I thought he was retired.'

'Apparently not, and will you kindly stop hissing at me?'

'I read about him when I was in was in college,' Nola continued. 'The man's a bloody legend.'

Elliot took umbrage at this. 'He's a defender, Sergeant Kane. They're not our friends.'

'If they can beat us then we need to up our game.'

'All right.' Elliot was annoyed because she was right. 'Put them in interview five and ask them if they want refreshments.'

'Where are you going?'

'I'll be *along*, Sergeant.'

He watched her walk towards them, faintly bemused to see that she approached them in an almost deferential fashion. She had certainly never treated him with that much respect.

While Nola handled the interlopers, he went to the bathroom, took two painkillers, washed his face and hands and mentally geared himself for battle.

They sat waiting for him, having refused all offers of refreshments. Under the bright lights of the interview room, Morag Kavanagh looked older than she had downstairs, albeit icy and determined. Crivon looked close to death. He reminded Elliot of a well-groomed turkey vulture.

Elliot introduced himself and sat down. He placed his notebook closed on the desk before him, then added his silver pen. Crivon unfolded his hands and began, unprompted. 'A terrible business.' His voice was aged, but still carried the gravitas of a seasoned orator.

'Yes,' Elliot said. He turned his attention to Morag Kavanagh. 'You have my deepest sympathy, madam. No parent should have to deal with this horror.'

'Thank you.'

'Have you been to see your daughter?'

'I was there last night,' she replied, her voice steady, her accent cut-glass. 'I will be there later this morning.'

'How is she?'

'She is in an induced coma, Inspector. They removed part of Jody's skull to allow for her brain to swell. Her face was un–unrecognisable.' She tightened her hands on the straps of her handbag. 'Though they say once the swelling goes down she should recover. Look, Inspector, I didn't come here to talk about Jody's injuries. I want to know why *that* man is free to walk the streets.'

'Which man is this?'

'Which man.' She curled her lip. 'Who do you think I'm talking about? I'm talking about that creature she married. It wasn't enough for him to destroy her life, he had to destroy her body too.'

Elliot opened his notebook. 'I have spoken to Simon Albright. Naturally, he denies any wrongdoing of any kind.'

The look on her face could have stopped a charging rhino. Nola would think about it later that evening when she was brushing her teeth. She had seen a lot of reactions on the job, but she had never seen one of such unfettered loathing before. If Morag Kavanagh could have willed death upon Simon Albright using only the power of her mind, he would have crumbled to dust in an instant.

'Wrongdoing?' she said, the words a rasp. 'That man is a stain on humanity!'

Elliot leaned back slightly, hoping to take the heat down a little.

'You're not a fan of your son-in-law?'

'I am not.'

'How did Simon and Jody meet?'

'I don't know, she met him in London somewhere.'

'Did you attend their wedding?'

'No.'

'May I ask why?'

'I ... I wasn't invited.'

Ouch, Nola thought, *that had to sting*.

'Do you and your daughter get along?'

'What business is that of yours?'

'None,' Elliot said mildly. 'But sometimes daughters confess things to their mothers that they might not otherwise say. I wondered if Jody had ever confessed fear or unhappiness regarding Simon to you.' He paused again. 'Was it a good marriage?'

Morag looked at Aldus, who did not appear to be paying attention to what was being said. A ploy, Nola thought, the old boy was listening to every word spoken very carefully indeed.

'I have no idea – how does one put value on such things?'

'Did you always dislike him?'

'No, not *always*.' Her tone chilled further. 'He would not have been my choice for her, but she seemed happy, at least for a while.'

'But things changed?'

'He changed.'

'How so?'

Morag tilted her head back. 'Perhaps it's not that he changed; perhaps it's more accurate to say that he revealed himself. Or was revealed.'

'My dear,' Aldus rattled into life. 'Now is not the time to be circumspect.'

'All right.' She inhaled. 'First and foremost, his name is not Simon Albright. It's Smith, Alan *Smith*.'

Elliot wrote this down. 'When did he change his name?'

'Years before, but we didn't know and neither did Jody. We might never have known if his wife, Veronica, hadn't come looking for her husband.'

'Simon was married before?'

'Not before, he was *still* married.'

'He's a bigamist,' Nola said, shocked.

'That's right,' Morag said. 'As you can imagine, we were horrified and Jody was distraught.'

'When was this?'

'It was the day after St Stephen's Day.' Her mouth thinned so much her lips practically vanished. 'That woman, his wife, came to my house.'

Elliot tried to picture the scene. 'Jody and Simon were staying with you?'

'Yes, they'd come for the holidays and weren't due back to Dublin until the sixth. This woman arrived, as I say, on the twenty-seventh of December. She came knocking on the door bold as brass.' She glared. 'I have no idea how she came to have my address.'

'Can you expound upon what happened a little?'

'There is nothing to expound. She came and delivered her tawdry tale.'

'I imagine it was like a small bomb detonating.'

'It was. Jody slapped him and ordered him from the house and he left.'

'He went and left Jody behind?' Nola asked.

'We thought it best, under the circumstances.'

'Where did this woman—?'

Aldus cleared his throat. 'As you can imagine, this is a private matter. Mrs Kavanagh is a lady of great standing in the community. She has no wish to provide fodder for public titillation.'

'I understand,' Elliot replied. 'But this situation could provide insight into why Simon might harm Jody. If he was humiliated, unmasked, we might understand a great deal about his psychological underpinning.'

Nola snorted. Aldus and Morag glanced at her.

'Sorry,' she said, embarrassed. 'It's just I knew there was something off about him from the—'

Elliot pressed his foot against her foot under the table. She stopped talking.

'Mrs Kavanagh?'

'Well, we were all shocked. At first, he tried to wriggle his way out of it – he stood in the library and tried to deny it to our faces. But that woman, Veronica, she had ample proof.' She glanced at Aldus. 'It was an ugly encounter.'

'I can imagine. What happened then?'

'Like I say, he left. Jody was hysterical.' Her lips thinned again. 'I called Doctor Willis and he came and gave her a sedative.' She gripped the bag again. 'The next day I asked Aldus for assistance.'

Elliot glanced at the old barrister. 'You didn't report him to the guards?'

'I didn't feel it was necessary. Jody was quite unwell from the stress. I did not feel it was my place to add any more upset to the family. My concern was for Jody.'

Elliot considered what he was hearing. 'You had a duty to report it.'

'I have a duty to Mrs Kavanagh, Inspector. I fulfilled it.'

'How so?'

'I made Mr Smith an offer and he accepted it.'

'An offer?'

'He would relinquish the marital home and offer no-contest to divorce, and in turn we would not press charges.'

'How did she find him, this woman – Veronica, was it?'

'She saw his photo in a magazine. I think she was as shocked to find he was alive as we were to discover his dirty secret.'

'Wait,' Nola said. 'She thought he was dead?'

'He led her to believe he was, yes.'

'What a piece of work,' Nola said. 'He let that poor woman believe he was dead for years? That's cruel.'

'He is a cruel man,' Morag said. 'A cruel man and a depraved liar.'

'I have a question,' Elliot said. 'Why would he harm her now?'

'Is it not obvious? He's desperate. And desperate men are dangerous.'

'Diandra Cliff didn't seem to think he was dangerous.'

'Oh, her.' Mrs Kavanagh's expression changed again, disdain replacing anger. 'Diandra Cliff would vouch for a slug if she thought there was money to be made on it.'

'You're not a fan either,' Nola said, nimbly avoiding Elliot's foot.

'I am not.'

'Did Fiona know about the bigamy? She didn't mention it to me when I spoke to her, but perhaps ...'

It was as if Elliot had thrown a bucket of ice over the table.

'Fiona would have no business speaking about such matters, none whatsoever.'

'But she's—'

'Estranged,' Aldus Crivon intoned. 'It has been some years since she chose to remove herself from the family.'

'I'm sorry to hear that,' Elliot said, meaning it.

'She made her bed,' Morag said coldly.

'You don't speak at all?'

'No.'

'Have you never met your grandchildren?'

She straightened her shoulders and looked him straight in the eye. 'Blood is blood, Inspector, I won't deny it, but Fiona made her decisions, and I will abide by them as she must.'

'A difficult situation, it must have been hard on Jody too.'

'If it is, it was not of my making.'

Aldus bent and retrieved his briefcase; he snapped the locks, opened it and removed a brown A4-sized envelope, which he placed on the table.

'What's this?' Elliot asked.

'A history of Mr Albright, aka Alan Smith.'

'Where did you get it?'

'I have connections. As I said, should Simon challenge the divorce, we were more than willing to press charges against him.'

'Does he know you have the goods on him?' Nola asked.

'Yes, I made it quite clear.'

'You have no idea what that man is capable of,' Morag said. 'None. But I do. I am here begging you to please, please, arrest that monster, and remove him from her life once and for all.'

She glanced at Aldus, who tapped the envelope with his index finger. 'Everything within has been checked, validated and is true to the best of my knowledge. The index supplies the names and details of contacts. There is also a sworn written testament from Veronica Smith to which you should pay close attention. My numbers, both home and mobile, are also included should you need to speak with me.'

Elliot drew the envelope towards him. 'Did you know Jody was seeing Jools Byrne recently?'

The news obviously took Morag by surprise, but she recovered quickly. 'Jody said she was seeing someone, but I did not know ... Jools Byrne, really?'

'Yes. I believe Jody was a friend to his ex-wife?'

'Oh, Amber, yes. Pretty, but dull, insipid. A flame to draw the moth but not to keep it.'

'I bet she doesn't feel that way,' Nola said.

'What's she feels is hardly relevant.'

'Mrs Kavanagh, I appreciate you taking the time to come in and speak to us, and on a personal level, I am sorry for what happened to Jody and I hope and pray she makes a full recovery.'

'Thank you, Inspector Ryan.' She got to her feet, as did, after two attempts, Aldus Crivon.

Elliot and Nola shepherded them to the lifts where they said their stilted farewells.

'That poor woman,' Elliot said when they were gone.

'Right?' Nola said. 'Imagine having that as your mother?'

'What?'

'Poor Fiona, all those kids and her own mother won't even give her the time of day.' She took a Twix from her pocket and unwrapped it. She offered Elliot a stick, but he shook his head. 'That's got to be really hard, especially if she favours one daughter over the other. I'd be sick if my mam did that with me and my sister.'

'Well, as she said, Fiona chose—'

'Bollocks,' Nola said. 'You're supposed to love your kids even when they do shit you don't like – it's the natural order.'

'I suspect she isn't happy in Fiona's choice of husband.'

'Yeah?' Nola bit a chunk off one of the sticks and chomped it. 'Simon Albright was no prize by her own account, and she's not holding that over Jody's head, is she?'

'True.'

'You've got a kid – if she got involved with some creep, would you stop loving her?'

No,' Elliot said firmly, the image of Ronan Black looming large suddenly in his mind. 'No, there's nothing on earth that would make me stop loving Shona.'

'Well, there you go,' Nola said. 'Case closed.'

'I really wish it was that easy,' Elliot said glumly. 'I really do. We don't operate using the law of averages, we use the actual law, and so far, we don't have anything concrete to pin on Simon Albright.'

'Did you not hear a word Mrs Kavanagh said? They have a dossier on him; they were going to destroy him.'

'I'm not discounting him as a suspect, Sergeant. I'm saying we need something firm if we want to charge him and make it stick.'

'Like a confession? Sealed with a loving kiss?'

Elliot smiled. 'Sarcasm, Sergeant? You know how I feel about that.'

If Nola was chastised it didn't show. 'He's a liar and he's a shit-heel.'

'I agree with you. I think he's not telling us everything he knows. And he's not the only one.'

'Right.'

'The thing is, Sergeant Kane ...'

'Yes, sir?'

'Not every discussion is a challenge to your authority.'

She took a deep breath, let it out. 'I know that.' Nola glanced at him. 'All right, so we bring Simon Albright/Adam Smith in for questioning, put the squeeze on him until he talks and – Why are you making that face?'

'I still don't think he is our man.'

'Are you serious?' Nola was incredulous. 'The man's a creep and everyone thinks so.'

'Being a creep does not mean you are capable of violence; it means you're capable of being a creep.'

Nola put her hands on her hips. 'In my world, if it looks like a duck, it's a duck.'

Elliot smiled. 'You have a singular intuition and an admirably direct delivery style.'

'I hear a "but".'

'That was a compliment, Sergeant. Butts are for drainpipes. Go speak to Fiona Hynes as we agreed. See if she knew about this complication with Simon Albright.'

'What are you going to do?'

'I will find Mr Jools Byrne and arrange an interview.' He turned. 'Piece by piece, Sergeant, we will build it piece by piece.'

'All right, but while you're building, keep this question in mind.'

'Yes?'

'How did Simon Albright's first wife know where Simon and Jody were staying?'

'You have a theory?'

'Maybe it was all an act. Maybe Simon wanted Jody to find out.'

'Why?'

'The marriage was failing – this way he could put the squeeze on the family for funds. Bigamist, grifter, not too much of a stretch is it?'

'You have a dark mind, Sergeant.'

'You're not the only one with experience, sir.'

36

The Hyneses lived in a ramshackle farmhouse at the end of what might charitably be described as a road if one had never driven on one before. By the time the Hyundai bumped and ground its way across the various craters, Nola feared for its suspension.

She parked under a horse chestnut tree and studied the place through the windscreen. It was grim: a single main house, some converted barns and two ancient mobile homes on breeze blocks, from under which several dogs on chains barked.

Nola gathered her things, got out and walked towards the house. Halfway across the filthy yard, the skin on the back of her neck prickled as she became aware she was being watched.

A woman opened the door before she reached it.

'Mrs Hynes?'

'Yes.'

Nola started. If she had not known her age to be thirty, she would have guessed she was at least a decade older.

'I'm Sergeant Nola Kane – we spoke on the phone earlier?'

Fiona nodded and dried her hands on her apron. 'Come in.'

Nola followed her through the house. It was gloomy inside, chilly and the air felt a little damp. But the kitchen was warm thanks to an ancient Aga which took up most of one wall. A toddler played in a wooden pen under lines of washing stretched from one wall to the other. Four more children sat at the table in the centre of the room, books open before them. They raised their heads when Nola entered.

'Hello.'

They did not respond, but watched her, unsmiling and suspicious.

'Sit down, please.'

Nola sat on a sofa covered in throws.

Fiona clasped her hands before her, unclasped them again. She seemed uneasy. 'Would you like some tea?'

'No, no thank you.' Nola glanced at toddler. It was covered in jam or something equally sticky. She smiled. 'How old?'

'Eighteen months.'

'She looks like you.'

'Yes, I suppose she does. We all take after my mother's side of the family.'

'I can see the resemblance.'

'What do you mean?'

'To your mother.'

'You've met her?'

'Earlier today – she came to the station with her solicitor.'

'Oh, of course she did – shields up.' Fiona sat down on a wooden chair and glared at her. 'Well?'

'Fiona, my boss, Inspector Ryan, said he spoke to you at the hospital and got a feeling you had a view on Simon Albright.'

'What did my mother say – did she ask about me?'

'No.'

'Did she know I was at the hospital?'

'Yes, Inspector Ryan mentioned you were there.'

'Then what did she say?'

Nola thought about Morag's sour face, her brutal words. 'Nothing, really, the conversation was mostly about Jody.'

Fiona glanced towards the toddler, her eyes over bright.

'Fiona, I'm at a loss here,' Nola said. 'Everyone I've spoken to regarding your sister talks about her so highly, but something must have been going on in her personal life. Do you have any clue what it might be? Did she confide in you?'

Fiona turned her head towards the children. 'Go upstairs.'

"S'cold up there,' the boy said. His impudent tone caught Nola's attention. For such a young child, he looked and sounded alarmingly defiant.

'Now.'

With sullen faces they slid from the bench and left the room. Fiona walked to the door, checked to see they were gone and closed it firmly. She stood for a moment, with her head down, thinking.

'How did my mother look?'

'Fine, she's a very elegant woman.'

Fiona snorted. 'She presents herself so, that is true. My sister is the same.'

'What do you mean?'

'You should have seen Jody when she came back from London. With *that* man, all dolled up, going around acting like she was the queen.' She snorted again. 'He took the wind out of her sails all right.'

She sounded bitter and envious, Nola thought, unpleasant in a very unsisterly way.

'You know about his deception.'

'She told me herself, crying over him when anyone with eyes could see he was a fraud. Always looking down his nose at everyone, acting the great I am.'

Definitely a bitter cow, Nola thought, feeling her sympathy for Fiona circle the drain. 'What about the man Jody was seeing?'

'What man?'

'Your sister was seeing someone else lately, Jools Byrne?'

Fiona visibly relaxed. 'I don't know him.'

'She never mentioned his name to you?'

'No.'

'Mrs Hynes, did you know Jody was pregnant?'

What little colour there was drained from Fiona Hynes face. Her jaw clenched and unclenched in rapid succession. 'Get out,' she growled. 'Get out of my house.'

'Mrs Hynes, please, calm down. I not trying to upset you. I only wanted to—'

The kitchen door opened, and two women walked in followed by another much older woman. Nola could see the boy child lurking in the shadows of the hall.

'Are ye right there?' the older woman said.

'She's here about my sister.' Fiona's bottom lip quivered. 'I've said all I needed to say.'

'I had a few more questions, actually.'

'Not today,' the older woman said with unusual authority. Nola glanced between the women and realised a hierarchy was at work here.

'I'm sorry if I upset you,' she said to Fiona. 'It's my job to ask uncomfortable questions.'

'You know the way out,' the older woman said, leaving no doubt Nola should make a swift exit.

Nola did so, closing the front door quietly, and walked back to the car.

A teenage boy stood next to it, looking at it like a wolf would look at raw steak. 'Is it fast?'

'Fast enough.'

'What's the fastest you've ever done?'

'In this car or on the track?'

His head swivelled in her direction for the first time. 'Track?'

'Yup. Me and my sister like to race cars in our spare time.'

'No way.'

'Way.'

He looked impressed and disbelieving in equal measure. 'So what's the fastest you've gone then?'

'Exactly 202 miles per hour.'

'In what?'

'Audi RS 6, it has a 5 litre V10 engine.' Nola smiled. 'Goes like a rocket and you should hear it roar.'

'Monster.'

'It's not complicated – you can ring them up and book a track.'

He didn't say anything but looked past her to the farmhouse. Nola turned her head slightly. One of the women was watching them from the window to the right of the front door.

'I've got to go,' the boy said.

'What's your name?'

'Isaac.'

'What age are you?'

'Sixteen.'

'It won't be long until you're allowed drive.'

'I'm allowed drive now,' he said, and walked off towards the house.

They're like hedgehogs, Nola thought as she drove back towards the city, *so prickly and defensive.*

When she got back to the station, Elliot was, once again, nowhere to be found and had left no message for her. She sat at her desk and buried her head in her hands.

Someone tapped on the door frame. She looked up and saw a man she thought she recognised but did not know. He was carrying an envelope.

'Oh, I'm sorry,' he said. 'I was looking for Elliot?'

'He's stepped out – can I help?'

'No, it's fine. I'll leave this here for him – tell him he can call me when he gets in.'

'Who will I say he needs to call?'

'Special Investigator John Barrow, and you are?'

'Sergeant Nola Kane.'

'Good to meet you.'

'Likewise.'

He put the envelope on Elliot's desk, smiled and left the office. Nola waited ten seconds before she went and fetched it. Barrow, he was one of the cool cats from the fourth floor who bestrode the complicated quagmire that was Internal Affairs and the press office.

She opened it, removed the file within and, keeping her ears cocked, read through it as quickly as she could. It was three pages long and contained an investigative report on a fire that had happened years before, burning a public house to ash. The

Black Top. Nola had never heard of it. She scanned down to the witness statements and read the name of the landlord. Francis Clancy.

Clancy? She wondered if Francis and Paddy were related, and if they were what was Ryan doing looking into this and not, as he should be, paying attention to their case? Was this what Paul Deacon and even Gracie was worried about? A fire in a pub from nearly a decade before?

She put the file back in the envelope and put it back on the desk where Barrow had left it.

Something was going on, that much was clear, and she was being kept outside the loop of both camps.

37

The halfway house was a slightly dilapidated building off the main Navan Road.

Elliot paid the taxi and got out. He stood for a few moments staring, trying to imagine what it must be like to call such a place home. The windows were cheap, single glazed, as was the aluminium front door, though it was the tatty curtains that really gave it an overwhelming sense of despair. At least it wasn't raining. He'd take his gifts where he found them.

Elliot took a deep breath and exhaled slowly. His hands felt clammy, his heartbeat too fast in his chest, but here he was, here he had to be.

No time to be a coward.

Not any more.

Ronan Black had been nineteen years old the first time they'd met. Bad luck for him – if he'd been a year or two younger, things would have been very different. On the day of his arrest, he had been a short, pudgy kid, already an alcoholic and a severe abuser of narcotics. A lifetime of bad nutrition and poor decisions had done a number on his teeth and skin, and like his sister, he had the most remarkable eyes Elliot had ever seen.

Maybe that's what had drawn Natalie to him, those bewilderingly beautiful eyes. Maybe she'd looked past the teeth and the skin, the lack of a central abode. Or maybe at fourteen she had simply been too young to understand that men with brilliant eyes were not the natural friends of young girls who trusted too easily.

Elliot had been hung-over on the day they arrested Ronan and in foul form. Not that it mattered much. His relationship with Clancy, which had started so brightly, was strained. But there was still friendship there, still a sliver of respect, a sense of professional courtesy.

Clancy had been in foul form that day too, full of complaints – marriage issues, a nagging tooth, a non-stop litany of woes that started the second they got into the squad car. Elliot knew his partner was facing a disciplinary hearing owing to a grainy hand-held video taken at a protest on College Green. Unfortunately for Clancy, while his judicious use of his baton to quell civic unrest made him 'one of the boys' in the locker-room, the brass – though sharing the view – understood they had a perfect whipping boy to draw the ire of the 'liberal do-gooders' who, according to Clancy, 'deserved to have their throats cut by undocumented migrants in their sleep'. It was a subject Elliot had heard much of and did not want to hear of again.

But Clancy was no rube, nor willing lightning rod. Within weeks, the dregs, as Clancy called them, had recanted or forgotten which officer swung which bat. Witnesses grew scarce or developed amnesia, left the country. Quiet calls were made, not threats, not exactly, but little by little the case fell apart and was dropped, forgotten about, mostly. Soon after, Clancy applied to Detective branch, and Elliot guessed the speed of his application owed as much to their waning friendship as it did to Clancy's ambitions.

Not that it mattered.

Not that it should have mattered.

Elliot shivered. It was cold and the painkillers were wearing off.

He wilfully resisted taking a top-up.

The front door was opened by a small, stooped elderly man who copped Elliot for a cop the moment he laid eyes on him. 'Which one of them are you seeing?'

'Ronan Black, he's expecting me.' He showed his warrant card and waited while the man took it and studied it carefully before he handed it back. 'Thank you, Mr ...?'

'Beck.'

'Mr Beck.

'Just Beck.'

'Right.'

Beck stepped aside and Elliot entered. The hall was as depressing as the exterior, like an ancient doctor's office from a time when people could neither afford nor wish for adequate healthcare.

'No smoking and no firearms.'

'Right.'

'You can wait in there.' Beck pointed. 'No shutting doors neither.'

'Why not?'

'Policy. I'll go get him.'

Elliot stepped into a narrow living room. It was dual aspect, sharing the concrete to the front with the scrubby lawn out back.

The room had seen better days: the carpet and furniture were old and dated. But it smelled of polish and it was reasonably comfortable. Elliot picked an armchair and sat, glad to be off his feet again.

He did not wait long.

Ronan Black crept into the room, moving silently in ugly purple Crocs. He stared at Elliot, nodded and pulled the sleeves of his jumper down over his hands, a habit Elliot remembered with a jolt, clear as day.

'You came, Sergeant.'

'It's Inspector now, lad.' Elliot said, regretting the 'lad' instantly.

Ronan had changed in the intervening years, lost the baby fat. There was a hardness to him Elliot figured he'd needed to develop. Young, nervous drug addicts needed to grow a stern carapace in order to survive.

'I'm going to assume you have a reason for this visit?'

This too was new, Elliot thought. The Ronan Black of old spoke in a particular vernacular of the inner city, all long vowels and interjected words. This Ronan spoke in full sentences, coherent sentences.

A changed man?

Maybe.

Changed to what, that was the question.

He sat down opposite Elliot and looked at him with open curiosity. 'I'm told you wrote to the parole board.'

'I did.'

'Why?'

Elliot spread his hands. 'I thought it was the right thing to do.'

Ronan laughed. 'A day late and a dollar short, no?'

'Maybe.'

'No maybe about it.'

'You look well.'

'Compliments of Mountjoy – three squares and access to a gym. I'd recommend it to anyone.'

'I think it's fair to say you weren't in great shape the first time we met.'

'That's an understatement. Those first nights in jail ... never experienced anything like the pain. Withdrawal changes a man.'

'I'm sure you were offered medical help – methadone, at least.'

'Never touch the stuff.' Ronan shook his head. 'I've seen what it does to people, they never come off it. Smack, now, smack you can beat if you work at it, but that other shit?' He touched his fingers to his temple. 'That's for life. So come on, Inspector, I know you didn't come see me for the chat. What do you want?'

'I spoke to Carol Joyce. She was Natalie's social worker.'

'Yeah?'

'She confirmed something you said back then about the Black Top pub. You said Natalie went there the night she was killed.'

'For all the good it did.'

'Do you remember what happened that night?'

'Some of it.' Ronan crossed one leg over the other and hugged his knees. His hands were heavily tattooed, his fingers nicotine stained, nails bitten to the quick. The right hand was badly mishappen, fingers and knuckles like a badly-put-together jigsaw.

'What happened to your hand?'

'Someone wanted to teach me a lesson. This was it.'

'Looks painful.'

'It's not,' he said with a flat tone. 'Tell me something. I've always wondered, did you know?'

'Know? Know what?'

'About Clancy, about the knife.'

Elliot sat perfectly still. 'No.'

'See, I think that's why you sent in that letter to the board.' Ronan Black leaned forward slightly, his eyes never left Elliot's face. 'Guilty conscience.'

'You were no innocent, Ronan, now or then. You had no business being with that child – she was too young.'

'I never claimed I was and never claimed to be something I wasn't.'

'Well then.'

'But I'm no killer, that I know.' He tapped his chest with his terrible fingers. 'I know what I am. I know who I am.'

'You were off your head back then.'

'I was wasted, yeah, rolling, but—'

'You had the murder weapon on you.'

'Yeah, see, that's the thing. I never saw that knife before that night, never saw it, never touched it.'

'It was in your pocket when we searched you, your fingerprints on the handle and Nat's blood on the blade.'

'Do you remember what I was wearing when you brought me to the station?'

Elliot concentrated. The arrest had been a lifetime before. Laurie was clinging to life; Shona still thought he walked on water. He was one of the club, one of the boys. A team player.

A fool.

'You were wearing jeans and a T-shirt and a grey quilted jacket.'

'Fair play, man, that's right.'

'What about it?'

'Natalie's throat was cut, blood all over the place. Do you not think if I'd done it and put the knife back in my pocket there'd be a shit ton of blood all over me?'

'Maybe you were careful.'

'Aw, now.' He waggled a finger in reproach. 'You said it yourself, I was wasted. Can't have it both ways.'

'People saw you and her together earlier in the evening. People remembered you arguing. You slapped her.'

'I did and I shouldn't have, but I was a different man then.'

'Did you know Natalie and Rebecca were hanging around the Black Top?'

'Everyone knew.'

'What happened there?'

Ronan grinned. 'Clancy had your number, didn't he? Had you sussed. He used you to nail me and you let him.'

'Tell me about the Black Top.'

'Man, you should see your face right now. I learned a lot during my time inside. I learned about men.'

'Okay.'

'You know I didn't kill Natalie. But I ended up with the knife that killed her in my pocket. Ask yourself how that's possible. Ask yourself how a knife that I never saw before in my life ended up in my pocket when you arrested me.'

'I didn't—'

'Don't sit there and lie, Inspector,' Ronan said. 'Better say nothing at all if that's your truth.' He got up and walked towards the door, where he paused. 'Me, I know. I know who I am. I know what I am. Can you say the same?'

'I can.'

'Yeah, well, we'll see, won't we? Thanks again for the letter.' He left.

Beck was back within seconds. 'Did you get what you want?'

'I don't know that I did,' Elliot said, rising to his feet. 'But maybe I got what I need.'

38

Connors was deeply unhappy. 'I don't understand – why haven't you arrested Simon Albright?'

'On what grounds? The report taken on Friday night indicates he was a guest at his ex-wife's home, and we have no evidence that he had any intention to harm her.'

Connors pinched the bridge of his nose. 'Aldus Crivon called me this morning. He seems to be of the opinion that he handed you all the relevant information required to put this matter to bed.'

'I understand that, sir, but—'

'The man is a bigamist, Ryan.'

'Yes but—'

'He's not even a licensed architect!'

'No, sir, it appears he never finished his degree.'

'What are we waiting for? Bring this boyo in and charge him.'

'The evidence is circumstantial at the moment, though I agree it's building. Sergeant Kane would like us to speak to a woman called Tamara Ford regarding her relationship with Jody.'

'The actress?'

'Yes, sir.'

'Bugger it, Ryan, this case is growing legs. I thought I told you I wanted a neat wrap-up.'

'The fates are busy.'

Connors scowled. 'Don't start with that guff. This is police work, grunt work, DV 101, and this,' he tapped the file, 'is the smoking gun we needed. This guy had a life, married to a hot woman, a top career, wealth. His ex-wife turns up—'

'Wife, sir, they never divorced.'

'All right, his wife turns up out of the blue and pulls the plug on the whole deal, only instead of being pissed with her, he takes it out on the woman who made him.'

'Speculation.'

'Hard facts, Inspector.' Connors leaned back in his chair and stared at the ceiling for a moment. 'I see it, the broader picture. He's a man of a certain age, older than her, a Svengali type. She's young, impressionable, on the outs with her mother and she falls under his spell.'

'I don't know if—'

'Shifting sands, Inspector. His entire life is built on it, then he's found out. She turfs him out on his ear, he's mad as hell, she moves on with her life, he's angry about that, they argue ...' He snapped back upright. 'For God's sake, Elliot, it's practically textbook.'

'Yes, sir, it is, but there are outstanding questions.'

'Like what?'

'Like why did she never change the locks? Why did she ask Albright to come over? Why was her protection dog outside? And then there's Diandra Cliff.'

'What about her?'

'Well, think about it, sir. She made a very big deal to us about how she works at the upper end of the property market. Her company deals in lucrative contracts with the very rich and the very wealthy. Suddenly a man she hired at the behest of her friend turns out not to have the relevant qualifications. Wouldn't that kind of information jeopardise her entire business? Gabriel Frost told Sergeant Kane Jody was thinking of leaving Jolie Laide – maybe there's motive there.'

'What are you saying? You think Diandra Cliff attacked Jody Kavanagh?'

'No, sir, but I think she could do with a closer look.'

Connors glanced at the clock and narrowed his eyes. Elliot guessed they must have gone slightly over time.

'All right,' he said. 'It's Wednesday. Do whatever it is you need today, but tomorrow I want that bigamist in holding and singing like a canary. Are we clear?'

'Crystal.'

'Then I won't keep you.'

Elliot got to his feet and made his way to the door.

'One more thing, Inspector.'

'Sir?'

'I'm told Ronan Black is back on the streets.'

Elliot stood perfectly still, blandly neutral.

'He's a bad egg, that one,' Connors said, reaching for his phone. 'Be advised and make sure you watch your back.'

'Yes, sir,' Elliot said. 'I'll be sure to do exactly that.'

He went downstairs and found Nola hunched over her computer, a pen behind her ear.

'You're back then,' she said.

'Yes.'

'Where were you?'

'I had something to attend to.'

'About our case?'

Elliot eased himself onto his chair and glanced over. She had her back to him, but he could feel her disapproval. 'What is it, Sergeant?'

She turned in her chair and looked him dead in the eye. 'Are you working on something else right now?'

'Why do you ask?'

'That's a yes then. Is it anything to do with Clancy?'

Elliot's mouth went dry. 'Why—?'

'Don't bother if you're going to lie, sir. I can't stand people who lie.'

'I don't lie, Sergeant.'

'Then answer me.'

'I wouldn't like to involve you. I sense you've enough on your plate at the moment as it is.'

'You don't trust me, is that it?'

He shrugged. 'You worked with the man for several years.'

'For him, I worked *for* him, not with him.'

'Semantics.'

She studied his face. 'Do you have a vendetta against him?'

Elliot was genuinely shocked. 'A vendetta? Of course not.' He frowned. 'Is that what they're saying? I have a vendetta?'

'That's what they say.'

'Who? Who says this?'

'I wouldn't like to involve you,' Nola replied sarcastically. 'I sense you've enough on your plate at the moment as it is.'

'All right, Sergeant, be about your business.'

'This case is my business, it should be yours too.'

'Sergeant—'

'I spoke to Jody's bank. Did you know Morag Kavanagh paid off Jody and Simon's mortgage?'

Elliot frowned, trying to keep up with the rapid changes in subject. 'I did not – when was this?'

'January, right after the brouhaha in Sligo.'

'I see.' He thought of Aldus Crivon and his commitment to keeping scandal at bay. 'Well, it was probably to protect Jody.'

'Yeah, except Jody never bought Simon out of it or took his name off the mortgage. Legally he's entitled to half that house.'

'Ah.'

'What do your guts tell you now?'

Nola turned back to her computer. Seconds later the sound of her bashing the keyboard filled the room. Then—

'Holy shit,' Nola said.

Elliot sighed. 'Sergeant—'

'Typical.' Nola clapped her hands together. 'It's always the stuck-up cows.'

'What?'

'It's Diandra Cliff, sir – she's got a record.'

'For?'

'Assault and battery.' Nola turned to him and grinned. 'Let's see Miss Hoity-Toity waffle her way out of this one.'

39

'You don't understand,' Diandra Cliff said. She was sitting behind her desk in her office, looking impossibly groomed and a little bit rattled.

'Try us,' Nola said. 'Go from the top where you broke your ex-girlfriend's nose and put her in the hospital. What are we missing here?'

'I'm not proud of what I did, and for your information I paid Avril full compensation for what happened.'

'Court ordered.'

Diandra closed her eyes, took a breath, opened them again. 'You're being very hostile, Sergeant.'

'Yeah, well, call me old-fashioned but domestic abuse doesn't sit right with me.'

'It was a different time in my life. I was a different woman back then.'

'Abusers always say that.'

'How dare you,' Diandra snarled. 'I am not an abuser. I was under a lot of pressure, the business was struggling, I was drinking too much and things got out of hand.'

'Leopards don't generally change their spots, in my view.'

'I see – you've never made a mistake, is that it?'

An image of Paul Deacon floated across Nola's temporal vision, but she shooed it away. 'Oh, sure, I've made plenty, but I've never brutalised someone I care about.'

'People can surprise you, especially when emotions are involved.'

'Did Jody surprise you? She told you she was leaving, striking out on her own. Is that what happened?'

'Of course not.'

'She didn't buy a protection dog for no reason,' Elliot said mildly. He was quite happy to let Nola run this one. Her natural spikiness was getting under Diandra Cliff's skin.

'That had nothing to do with me. I would never hurt Jody, I … I just wouldn't.'

'Why should we believe you?' Nola asked. 'You've lied to use from the off. We know now that Simon Albright is a bigamist and a fraud – are you really going to sit there and tell us you didn't know? And Jody brought him into your life, into your business. I bet you were pissed when you found out he had no qualifications. How would that look to all your fancy nob clients? How many projects did he work on for you as well as the TV show? If it gets out that he wasn't qualified you could be facing serious financial setbacks.'

Diandra's scarlet nails beat an impatient tattoo on her desk.

'If you know something, Miss Cliff,' Elliot said, 'you need to tell us. The time for lies has long passed.'

'I can't.'

'Miss Cliff, if you're withholding information, you could find yourself in deeper water than you might like to tread.'

Diandra laughed, picked up a pen and twirled it between her fingers. 'You never met Jody before the accident. But I've known Jody Kavanagh for years – well, I should say, I've known a *version* of Jody for years.'

'A version, what do you mean?'

She reached for her phone, tapped for a moment then slid the phone across the table. Elliot and Nola looked at a photo of Jody and Diandra sitting at a café table with the Eiffel Tower visible in the background. They were wrapped in heavy coats and scarves, grinning, two glassed of red raised in salute.

'You see that photo? That was taken the year before Jody moved to London.'

'Okay ...' Elliot didn't really see where this was going, but he motioned to her to continue.

'We were celebrating my thirtieth birthday. That was the day I asked Jody to marry me.'

'You were romantically involved with each other? An item?'

'Yes.'

'So Jody's ...'

'Bisexual,' Nola said, knowing Elliot would never get the word out. 'It's really not that uncommon. What did Jody say to your proposal?'

'She said yes, that's why we're toasting.'

Elliot cleared his throat. 'Right, well ... so you and Jody were seeing each other.'

'I thought she was the one.' Diandra smiled, but there could be no mistaking the sadness in her voice. 'It was a lesson I never forgot.'

'She dumped you,' Nola said.

'She did, quite abruptly.'

'But you were happy to work with her when she came back to Ireland?'

'Yes, as I said, she is very talented and has a *lot* of connections.'

'Did Jody leave you for Simon?'

She laughed. 'Jody left me for London.' She clicked her fingers. 'Just like that it was over and she'd moved on.'

'A complicated woman,' Elliot said.

'She is and she isn't,' Diandra said with a shrug. 'If you understand her true nature, Jody's as uncomplicated as you can get.'

'And what's her true nature?'

'That underneath that glorious façade lies the heart of a predator.'

'A predator? You make her sound sociopathic.'

'She is what she is – she can't help it.'

'Did Jools Byrne understand that, I wonder?'

'I think Jody bit off more than she could chew for once.' Diandra put the pen down and linked her fingers. 'I think if you play with fire, eventually you're going to get burned.'

'So, she deserved it, did she?' Nola asked. 'What happened, she made him do it, is that it?'

Diandra glared. 'Deserve, Sergeant, has nothing to do with it. Would I wish harm on Jody? No, I would not. But make no mistake, she is not the woman you think she is.'

'For the record, where were you Sunday night?'

'Am I a suspect?'

'Sure.'

'I surrender, Sergeant. I suppose it doesn't really matter now.' She smiled again, or managed a grim version of one. 'I was in Cork, with a friend.'

'Does the friend have a name?'

She gave them a name and a phone number. 'She can verify I was with her all weekend; we barely left the hotel room.'

Nola wrote it down.

'It's funny,' Diandra said, no longer looking at either of them, but looking at the photo on her phone. 'I never understood what pain was until I lost her.'

'Try getting your nose broken,' Nola said, rising to her feet. 'I bet it's a lot like that.'

40

Nola and Elliot stood behind the barrier and watched Tamara Ford run across the cobbled streets of Temple Bar, impossibly agile in killer heels and a green silk dress slit to her thigh, her famous dark-red hair bouncing and glossy under the lights.

'Alexander!'

A tall man in a bespoke suit turned at the sound of her voice. Elliot was not much of a film buff, but even he recognised the cleft chin and manly jaw of Tobias Oakenfold, the hottest thing to hit celluloid since Brad Pitt first stuck a hairdryer down his crotch.

'What do you want from me?' Tobias growled as Tamara collapsed into his arms. 'Can't you leave well enough alone?'

'Don't leave me,' Tamara cried, burying her beautiful head in the folds of his arms. 'Not like this, not like this. You can't, you can't.'

'Cut!' the director yelled.

Tamara Ford sprang away from Tobias Oakenfold like he was toxic waste, yanked her shoes off and flung them away. 'Dammit, Harry,' she cried as an assistant rushed in with a robe. 'These stupid cobblestones are lethal! I thought you said you were going to cover them.'

'Darling, I know, but the council were—'

'I don't want to hear it. If I break a leg—'

She allowed the assistant to drape the robe over her shoulders and accepted a pair of Uggs, which she pulled on immediately.

'Did you see the speech she gave in Cannes?' Nola muttered to Elliot out of the side of her mouth. 'She was instrumental in the MeToo movement. That woman doesn't take shit from anyone.'

'I see.'

'And the last producer who tried to force her into a topless scene? She went to straight to the press, said it was gratuitous sexist fodder, created a big stink. The scene was rewritten.'

'Right.'

'She's up for an action role in *Night of the Lady Hawk*, based on the graphic novel—'

'How on earth do you know all of this?'

'I like films.' She looked at her watch. 'Do you think this will take long?'

'Have you somewhere to be?'

'No, but we still need to talk to Jools Byrne and Amber Feenan, the ex. Plus, I want to interview Bane Russell again. See how much heat I can turn up under his arse.'

They drifted across the square to intercept Tamara as she made her way back to her trailer with her assistant in tow.

'Miss Ford?'

'I'm sorry, you can't be here,' the assistant said, forcing her way bodily between them. 'This is a closed set.'

'This is an official visit,' Elliot said, flashing his shield, something he rarely had to do. Most people smelled 'cop' from him at a thousand paces.

Tamara Ford glanced their way, her magnificent green eyes widening. She was tiny in real life, beyond dainty, fairy-on-top-of-the-Christmas-tree small. Her face was, of course, beautiful, haughty with the right amount of cheeky character, her lips rich and full, her famous hair expertly tumbled, but up close, Elliot noticed the heavy make-up, the fine lines around her perfect pout, the subtle signs of work here and there in her jaw-line, things he might not have noticed had it not been for his sister.

All was not as it appeared on screen.

'It's all right, Gina,' she said, her voice husky with a hint of unfiltered cigarettes. 'Drew called – he said you might drop by.'

'Do you have a few minutes to talk?'

'I can take five.' She reached up and grabbed the door of her trailer. 'Gina, go find Lucy and tell her I need replacement shoes for the next shot.'

Elliot and Nola followed her into the trailer. Elliot was surprised at how cramped it was; every available surface was littered with clothes, make-up, magazines, wigs, more make-up and thousands of make-up-stained baby wipes.

'Sit down, if you can find a spot,' Tamara said, waving her hand towards a bench next to a low table covered in bottled water and empty coffee cups.

Elliot managed to squeeze his way through and sat awkwardly amid the chaos. He removed his notebook from his inside pocket. Nola sat beside him.

Tamara opened a door to reveal a full-length mirror. She raised her arms and began to unclip hanks of her famous hair and toss them onto a bureau. She caught them watching. 'What?'

'Oh, I'm sorry, I didn't realise—'

'You thought that was all my own hair?' She threw her head back and laughed. 'Boy oh boy, what shower did you come down in?'

'I'm not au fait with the latest fashions when it comes to hair,' Elliot said, pointing to his own plain cut.

'You're lucky.' She batted her eyelashes. 'Most men your age would kill for a head of hair like that.'

'What age do you think I am?'

'Forty?'

Nola rolled her eyes.

'I'm flattered,' Elliot said, smiling like a dork. 'You can add another ten years to the pot.'

'Yeah?' Tamara closed the door, tightened the belt of the robe, opened a mini fridge and reached for a bottle of wine. 'Drink?'

'No, thank you.'

It wasn't even noon.

'You?'

Nola shook her head, still a little bit starstruck. This was Tamara Ford, and they were sitting in her trailer. Her sister would shit a brick when she heard this.

'Suit yourself.' Tamara poured a hefty glass of white wine, sat down next to Nola and studied Elliot openly. 'Good genes,' she said after a moment. 'Who do you take after, your mother or your father?'

'I have no idea. I was adopted.'

'Oh.' She took a sip of her wine. 'Sorry. Actors are nosy by nature.'

'Miss Ford,' Elliot said. 'We wanted to ask you—'

'About Jody, yeah, I know.'

'What is your relationship with Miss Kavanagh?'

'Relationship?' She laughed and waved her glass. 'There's no *relationship* – we hooked up a few times. A kind of friends-with-benefits gig.'

'I see,' Elliot said. 'But you're married.'

'Don't.' She waggled the glass at him. 'Don't judge, all right – you've no idea about my life.'

'You're right, I apologise,' Elliot said. 'Are you still ... involved?'

'No, all water under the bridge.'

'But you sent her flowers over the weekend?'

'You have been busy!' She tossed her drink back. 'I sent Jody the flowers by way of congratulations. I'd heard she'd bagged Jools Byrne.'

'You sent her flowers for that?'

'It was a little joke between us girls. Look, Jody and I haven't spoken much recently. To be completely honest, we had a slight falling out.'

'Why?'

'A misunderstanding.'

'Would you care to elaborate?'

'Not really.'

'Any insight you can give us into Jody's life might help put whoever hurt her in our sights.'

'I suppose you know about Simon, right? The ex?'

'We've met.'

'Grifter, pure and simple, and believe me, I've met a few of those in my time. A real snake, you know?'

'He seems to have a gift for rubbing people up the wrong way.'

'Right, well, not long after Jody and I had our little fling, I got this ugly text saying – no, *demanding* I pay fifty thousand euros or my relationship with Jody would be front-page news.'

'You were being blackmailed?'

She nodded. 'They had details, details they shouldn't have had. Said they were going to send photos to Mr Ford, like that was supposed to scare me.'

'And did you pay them?'

She laughed, but there was little humour to it. 'Absolutely not.'

'What happened then?'

'I told Jody, "Babe, you've got some bad mojo to sort out."'

'Wait, you think it was someone connected to Jody who tried to put the squeeze on you?'

'I do. I mean, they had my personal phone number and I hardly give *that* to anyone.' She shrugged. 'I assumed it was Simon.'

'Why?'

'Well, who else? The man had lost everything by that stage, he probably thought his ship had come in, but he was dead wrong. I grew up on a council estate – did you know that?'

'No,' Elliot said.

'Yes,' Nola said.

'Yeah, nice enough place, if the truth be told, but the media prefer to spin it like it was some rags-to-riches story. But there's no way I'd let some shitbird blackmail me.'

'Can we go a back a moment? You and Jody, you met her when she was filming *All Buildings Great and Small*, right?'

'She was our interior decorator for the manse.'

'The manse?' Elliot was baffled.

'That pile my husband owns in Longford. Arthur hired Jolie Laide to redo it and Diandra suggested we go with the television show – great idea, production was wild. Seriously, you've never seen it? It was in a ton of magazines.

236

'I've seen it,' Nola said. 'It went wildly over budget, right?'

'Well, shit, that was bound to happen. Those old houses eat money.'

'I saw the argument Jody had with your husband. He was furious about the rising cost.'

'He wasn't really – the row was the production team's idea. Makes great television. Jody was in on it too.'

'It wasn't real?'

'Of course not.'

'It looked real.'

'Down to the creative director – she was good, you know, has a good eye.' Tamara got up and refilled her glass. 'Arthur is a brilliant shouter, very theatrical.'

She leaned back and watched Elliot over the rim of her glass. 'You know, you've got serious bone structure. You ever think of acting?'

'No.' Elliot found he was growing tired of her. 'About the blackmail, did you ever confirm it was Simon Albright who was behind it?'

'Of course not. Look, it was a scam.' She laughed. It was not her screen laugh, which was light and musical, but a totally different animal. 'Fifty grand, are you kidding me? Like Mr Ford gives a shit what I do or don't do.'

'Do you still have the message?'

'I deleted it from my phone, but Gina might know, you should ask her – she remembers these things.'

These things, Elliot thought, like the idea of remembering startling events was alien to her.

'Do you think Jody was involved?' Nola asked, thinking about what Diandra Cliff had told them about Jody being a predator.

Tamara's mouth fell a little. 'I don't know. It did seem weirdly convenient to me, you know? I'm a discreet person, Sergeant. In my line of business I need to be. But, look, I've no intention of leaving my husband. Arthur knew what he was getting when he got me. I never made any secret of what I wanted.'

'And what's that?'

'Security.'

'Security?' Nola couldn't stop herself. 'But you're a famous actress. And a feminist icon.'

'Christ,' Tamara said, disgusted. 'I'm nearly thirty-six, Sergeant. Think of actresses' years like dog years and you'll get it. The work doesn't last forever, and believe me, there are plenty of new faces waiting in the wings.'

'Are you saying you married Arthur Ford for money?'

'What else is there?'

'Love, companionship—'

'Oh, sweetie.' The door opened and Gina returned carrying an almost identical pair of shoes to the ones Tamara had thrown across the street. 'Now, if you'll excuse me, I've got to get ready for my next scene.'

They spoke briefly to Gina, who said she'd have to go through the messages and get back to them. Elliot thanked her, and together he and Nola walked back across the cobblestones.

'It's all bullshit, isn't it?' Nola said.

Elliot glanced at her; she sounded surprisingly sour. 'What is?'

'All of it, it's so fake. People pretend to be cool, pretend to be decent, pretend to be truthful, pretend to argue, but it's bullshit: everyone's out for themselves.'

'Not necessarily,' Elliot said. 'You will find, Sergeant, there are times you draw a line and it's a line you will not cross.'

'Yeah, well, if you ask me I – hey, I know that woman.'

Elliot turned his head and saw a woman with dark-red hair making her way across the square, carrying a black oval box under her left arm. She entered a trailer with a 'Make-Up' sign and slammed the door.

'That's Beverly Russell.'

'The neighbour?'

'Yup, she's a make-up artist. It never occurred to me she worked on sets. Come to think of it, she never mentioned it either.'

'Interesting.' Elliot glanced at his watch. 'Make a note of it and we can revisit it.'

'Man,' Nola muttered. 'This case is like peeling an onion – no matter how much you peel, all you get is onion.'

41

Fiona woke up on the sofa, dazed and a little confused. It was dark out and she had no idea how long she had been asleep.

She stood up, a little unsteadily and looked at the clock over the Aga.

Oh no.

She had been asleep for hours, dead to the absolute world. How was that even possible? Her mouth was bone dry, her legs heavy and cumbersome. What was happening? She thought of the tea her mother-in-law had insisted she drink earlier in the day. It had tasted bitter, but she'd drunk it to be polite. Had—?

Where were the children?

Calling their names, Fiona stumbled through the house. It was empty.

Oh no, no, no, no, no ...

She grabbed her coat from the bottom of the stairs and left the farmhouse. It was raining hard and the yard was dark. Fiona knew even before she reached her mother-in-law's home she was not there. Even so, she hammered on the door with her fist.

'Judith?'

Nothing, no response, the house was in darkness.

With panic rising, she jogged along the rutted lane that ran behind the house, slipping and sliding in the mud and the puddles. She fell once, wiped the mud from her hands on her skirt and ran on towards the mobile homes. They too were empty.

She was alone.

Her children had been taken.

Fiona raced back to the farmhouse, blinded now by a terror so strong she could hardly get the front door open. Inside, she snatched up the phone and called Malcolm.

The phone rang several times before he answered.

'Where are they? Where are my children?'

'What were you planning to do?'

Fear bloomed wild within her. 'Where are my children, Malcolm? I swear, if you harm a hair on their heads—'

'Leave? With my children?'

'Malcom, I beg you, listen to me—'

'It's a curious thing,' he said, as if she had not spoken at all, 'since your sister's return, you have this sudden lapse in memory, wife. I've been thinking about your strange moods and half-truths.'

Fiona moved across the room, stretching the phone line as far as it could extend. She stared at the built-in shelves to the left of the Aga. The bottles and tins had been moved; the secret space behind them was empty. Every penny she had scrimped and saved had been in a small box, hidden behind the stonework.

Gone.

Her only means of escape.

Fiona closed her eyes.

'Did you think I would not know what goes on in my own house?' Malcolm said, his voice low and calm, the worst voice, the voice that made Fiona want to run out onto the road and keep running.

'Malcolm, let me explain.'

'There will be time for truth. There will be time for confession.'

'Malcolm.'

'There will be a time for contrition.'

'Please don't hurt them, Malcolm. I swear I'll do anything you want, anything at all.'

'Sit down with your thoughts, with your soul, and think about your actions.'

He'd hung up.

Fiona threw back her head and screamed. She screamed so hard her voice cracked before she fell to her knees and wept.

He brought them home after midnight. Fiona watched as the convoy of cars travelled along the lane, watched her mother-in-law lay her hand on Malcolm's cheek before she went into her own home. She watched Malcolm cross the yard, the children stumbling along behind him, half-asleep. He carried Rachel asleep against his chest.

Fiona met him at the door. She said nothing, took the baby from his arms and carried her upstairs. The children followed, subdued, exhausted. She helped them into their pyjamas, tucked them in, kissed heads and turned off the lights.

'Mama?' It was Sarah, her voice small and frightened in the darkness.

'Go to sleep.'

'I could not stop him, Joshua – he told Papa about the money. I'm sorry.'

'Go to sleep, my love. All will be well.'

He was waiting in the bedroom, his belt dangling from his left hand. Fiona froze in the doorway, unable to take another step, even though he warned her not to make him wait.

'Confess,' he said. 'Confess and it will go easier on you.'

She confessed.

It didn't matter in the end.

It never did.

42

Thursday

First thing Thursday morning Elliot trudged upstairs to see Superintendent Connors. His boss was buried in paperwork and appeared – for once – happy to be interrupted.

'Bloody budget cuts, Inspector. How are we supposed to run a functional force while we are haemorrhaging money?'

'Rather you than me, sir.'

'Well, sit down, what do you want?'

'You asked to be kept in the loop.'

'Oh, that's right, I did – well?'

Elliot sat and placed his hands on both knees. He took a deep breath and outlined the case, including the paid mortgage and the attempted blackmail of Tamara Ford.

'She thinks it was Albright?'

'That was her impression.'

'This is turning into an ungodly mess, Inspector,' Superintendent Connors said. 'My God, the media would have a field day if any of this got out. First Jools Byrne and now Tamara Ford's involved? I had no idea this woman's life was so tangled.'

'No, we didn't either, but Tamara was very forthcoming. Surprisingly so.'

Connors pinched the bridge of his nose for a moment. 'Elliot,' he said after a long moment, 'this is your first case back after the accident.'

'Yes, sir, I am aware of that.'

'So don't take this the wrong way – under normal circumstances I am sure, more than sure, you could handle it with ease – but perhaps Lupin could—?'

'No, sir.'

Connors sat up. 'It's commendable that you feel that way, Inspector. But I'm concerned. There has been ... talk about you.'

'What kind of talk?'

'Are you on a lot of medication?'

'Prescribed painkillers, sir.'

'That's it?'

'Yes.'

Connors made a face. 'And you're ... you feel well in yourself, do you?'

'I feel fine, sir.'

'Because if at any stage you don't, you only have to say the word.'

'Yes, sir.'

'What is your next step?'

'I'm going to arrest Simon Albright.'

'Ah!' Connors looked relieved. 'The ex-husband, finally ... of course. You've built quite the case against him, I take it.'

'Enough to formally question him.'

'Excellent, excellent. We'll alert the press office.'

'I'd hold off on that, sir.'

'Got to be seen to be doing something, Inspector. The wheel rolls ever forward.' He glanced at his beloved clock. 'Well, Elliot, I won't keep you. Wrap this one up good and tight and put it to bed. Incidentally, how are you faring with young Kane?'

'She works hard, but she has a lot to learn.'

'Indeed, I wonder if I was too hasty propelling her onto you. I could move her to Lupin's squad next week.'

'If you feel that's best, sir.'

Elliot left and walked towards the lift in a daze. Nola was ... well, she was a force of nature and certainly one he had not wanted, but, he realised with a jolt, she was starting to grow on him.

He felt his phone buzz in his pocket, took it out and read the message.

It was from Jools Byrne's PA. He was back in Ireland and willing to talk.

43

Nola stopped at a garage beyond the Spawell roundabout, bought two bottles of Diet Coke and a bag of Haribos and set out for Leitrim.

Even with satnav it took her two hours to find the main gate of Talamh, the imposing eight-bedroomed, five-bathroomed lodge (she'd looked it up before she left the station), and it was with some relief that she drove through a bell-mouthed stone-wall entrance and followed a sweeping drive, flanked by native woodland on either side, until the lodge eventually came into view. Nola, a city girl through and through, who grew twitchier the further she drove from the Pale, was not impressed. On first view, the place gave her the creeps.

She drove under stone arch and parked in a private courtyard. Low-lying clouds rolled down from the hills and it was much colder than in the city. She was glad she had taken her heavy coat.

She trotted up a set of stone steps onto a raised lawn divided by a gravel path that circumnavigated a pond, all this before she reached the front steps of the lodge. As with Tamara Ford, up close things were not exactly as they appeared. The huge house was in a state of disrepair. The steps were crumbling in places, as were several of the windowsills. Two of the windows on the second floor were boarded up and the ornate fanlight over the main door was broken.

She rang the bell, heard a rusty buzz in the distance and waited with her hands wedged deep into her pockets.

Nobody came.

After a minute, during which the searing wind did its best to numb her ears and face, she gave up waiting and made her way around to the side of the house, passing through what had probably been a kitchen garden at one time or another. Beyond the garden, she glimpsed two men standing in a cobbled yard, talking. Neither noticed her approach until she was almost with them. She recognised the taller man as Jools Byrne from his photos, though he was leaner and less sculpted in real life.

'Can I help you?' he asked.

'Sergeant Nola Kane, I thought you were expecting me.'

Jools Byrne held out his hand instantly, all smiles and easy charm. 'I'm so sorry, of course. This is Mack, my estate manager.'

'I'll leave you to it,' Mack said. He nodded to Nola and walked off in the direction of some stone sheds.

'I'm sorry about that.' He gave her an appraising look. 'You don't look like a copper.'

'I'm not,' Nola said. 'Coppers are English.'

Jools smiled. It was a disarming smile, even a little bashful. Nola didn't buy it. From everything she'd read about him, he was quite the party animal, a firm plantation in the society rags. Plus he came from rich stock, and even though she would never admit it in a thousand million years, Nola had a bee in her bonnet about people inheriting huge wealth.

'You found the place okay?'

'Eventually.'

'We're a little out of the way.'

'I appreciate you taking the time to talk to me. I'm sorry about what happened to Jody.'

'Yes, it's horrible. I can't believe it really. I assume you have her ex-husband in custody?'

'It's in hand. Have you been in to see her?'

'No.'

'Really?' Nola raised her eyebrows. 'You know she's in a coma.'

'Yes.'

'If you don't mind my saying, it's weird that you haven't been to the hospital.'

His expression changed. 'I don't have to explain myself to you, surely.'

Nola resisted telling him he did bloody have to explain himself, but she managed to keep her temper in check. 'So, Dubai. It must be nice this time of year.'

'Have you been?'

'Nope.'

'It's a dreadful place, really, absolutely soulless. If I didn't have business interests over there, I'd never set foot in the place again.'

Christ, Nola thought, *first-world problems*. 'When did you leave?'

'Monday. I can provide my flight details, should you need them.'

'I do.'

'Oh?' He looked surprised. 'In that case I'll have them sent to your office.'

Nola looked about her. 'This place is really something.'

'Thank you. As you can see, it's a work in progress.'

'Oh yeah?'

'I'm afraid the estate has been neglected for years.'

'How big is it?'

'Three hundred acres, give or take.' He said. 'I intend to rewild much of it.'

'What, leave it just sitting?'

'Conservation is incredibly important, don't you think?'

'I live in a terraced house,' Nola said, 'with my mam and my sister. There's not much room for rewilding.'

'You're lucky in a way.' Jools said. 'I'm beginning to wonder if I didn't bite off more than I can chew.'

'You inherited it, though, from your mother, right? I'll probably inherit a sofa and an electric toaster from my mother.'

He grew sombre. 'Your mother is still alive, I take it?'

'She is.'

'I'd trade that for a house any day of the year.'

'I'm sorry, that came out the wrong way.'

'It's fine.' He waved an arm, suggesting they walk towards the house, and set off. 'Shall we have a coffee?'

Nola fell into step beside him.

'I should warn you, it's colder in the house.'

'I'm from the Northside, I'll survive.'

What the hell was she doing? Why was she acting like this? The guy was rich, okay, but that was hardly his fault. *God damn, dial it back, Nola*, she warned herself. *Be objective.*

Jools wasn't wrong about the cold, as Nola discovered a few minutes later. The house was freezing and, from what she could see, lacked any form of modernity or comfort one might expect in a country manor. She watched Jools attempt to manipulate a French press with all the dexterity of a drunken chimp for a moment, then, to distract herself from the chill, she looked around the huge kitchen and tried to imagine anyone living there. It was a vast space that took up almost half of the basement area. Stone flagged floor, four arched windows, three overlooking the old garden she had passed through earlier, an ancient Aga wedged into a brick alcove. A long table with a bench on one side and several mismatched kitchen chairs on the other. It was, she suspected, the same now as it had ever been.

A big expensive dump.

'Shit.'

'Are you okay?'

'I'm ... yes, this thing is new. Give me a second. I have a machine in the city – push a button and that's about as complicated as it gets.'

Finally, the one-sided battle with the plunger was won. He poured the coffee into two mugs.

'There you go. I hope you don't mind it black – I'm afraid I don't have any milk.'

'Black's fine.' She took the mug offered and put it on the table. 'But please tell me you have sugar.'

'Ah. No, I don't use it, I'm afraid. Sorry.'

'You don't live here, do you?'

'Oh, no. As I said, I have an apartment back in the city, a rental. I do intend to come back here.'

'And you have a house in Dublin, right?'

'You've done your homework.'

'Yup.'

'I own a house, although I've never lived in it.'

'How come?'

He looked surprised again. Maybe rich people didn't get asked impertinent questions from commoners. 'I'd always lived with my mother.'

'Oh, I didn't realise your parents were separated.'

He leaned against a worktop and folded his arms. 'They were not.' He cleared his throat. 'But they kept separate homes.'

Nola let it drop. After all, he wasn't on trial for his parents' marriage. 'What's the deal between you and Jody.'

'You are direct.'

'I'm on the clock.'

He ran his hands through his hair. 'As I said on the phone, there's not much to tell.'

'But you were seeing each other, right?'

'For a time, but we've broken up.'

'What? When?'

'Friday.'

Nola was stumped. Someone was lying, and she didn't think it was Monica Fell. She sipped her coffee. It was awful. 'Can I ask you a straightforward question?'

He crossed his legs at the ankles and looked at her frankly. 'I doubt I could stop you even if I tried.'

'Did you know Jody was pregnant?'

'Yes, she told me.'

'Is that why you broke up with her?'

'Ah, I see. I'm the cad, is that it? The villain of the play?'

All the warmth and charm vanished in the blink of an eye. Suddenly the room felt a hell of a lot colder.

'I'm not judging you, Mr Byrne.'

'Are you sure?' he said. 'It sounds like you are.'

'I assume it wasn't welcome news.'

'Look, Nola—'

'It's Sergeant Kane, if you don't mind.'

'Of course, Sergeant Kane.' He glowered at her. 'I broke up with Jody because I am not the father of her unborn child.'

'How can you be so sure? You were sleeping together.'

'Because I had a vasectomy the same year I married Amber.'

Nola blinked. 'Before or after you got married?'

'After, when I found out Amber was bipolar.' He raised his chin. 'You can stand there with that look on your face, Sergeant, but you have no right to judge.'

'Who's judging? I'm just wondering what Amber thought about that.'

'She was unhappy with my decision, but I felt it was unethical to bring a child into the world with complications.'

'Complications?'

He scowled. 'What is it women always say? My body, my choice? Well, it cuts both ways.'

'Oh, I see.'

'Do you?'

'What happened when Jody told you she was pregnant? Did you confront her? Tell her about your snip? Were you angry?'

'Yes, I was angry – nobody likes to be duped, lied to, made a fool of. I told her there and then it was over.'

'How did she take it?'

'She made a scene.'

'What kind of scene?'

'Oh Christ, the kind women make – all drama with a distinct lack of accountability.'

'According to our reports the *scene* was so dramatic a neighbour felt it necessary to call it in.'

That rattled him slightly.

'I don't think I like your tone and I don't like the implication.' He tossed the remains of his coffee down the sink. 'There was a row. I left. When I came back her white knight was with her.'

'Simon Albright. Why was he there?'

'She called him, I imagine.' He scowled. 'You're acting like Jody Kavanagh was a victim. Jody's no victim – she's a conniving bitch.'

'She's in hospital missing part of her skull. I'd say she's a victim.'

He shrugged, but the muscle in his jaw bounced furiously. 'I've answered your questions, Sergeant.'

'Okay, but—'

'We're done talking, Sergeant. Have a good trip back to the city. You can show yourself out.'

He stalked out of the kitchen. Moments later Nola heard a door slam.

44

'My God, that's my worst nightmare. Imagine being tricked into raising another man's sprog?'

'Was that comment really necessary, Sergeant Keller?'

'Sorry, sir.'

'You don't have to utter every thought that pops into your head.' Elliot gave Robbie a look and went back to his notes. After a while he put them down and pinched the bridge of his nose. 'What are we looking at here?'

'What do you mean?' Nola asked.

'Who is Jody Kavanagh? Is she a victim? Predator? Funnel-web spider?'

'A what?'

Elliot waved her question away. 'We started this week with a single purpose: find who assaulted Jody Kavanagh and why. Now we're adding arms and legs to this woman's life when we need to start draining the suspect pool. We need to look to motive.'

Without saying a word, Nola got up and left the office, returning a few moments later dragging a whiteboard behind her. She cleaned it, drew two columns and started writing. In the first column she wrote Simon Albright; in the second column she wrote 'ex-husband' and underlined it several times.

'He's still my go-to guy. She ditched him, he's broke as –
broke and she's seeing other people. Plus, there's the pregnancy.
Did he know about it before we told him? What if that's why
he attacked her? And why didn't he mention anything about the
fight when we spoke to him? Why hide something like that?'

'Duly noted.'

Underneath, she wrote 'Jools Byrne'.

'Reasons?'

'He has no actual alibi, since he left Monday afternoon for
Dubai. Plus he was involved in a sexual relationship with Jody,
and he claims she tried to string him along. We don't know if he's
telling the truth about the snip yet. Plus, he's a yuppy shithead
and we only have his word that he broke it off on Friday – maybe
he was jealous at finding Simon at the house. Plus the timing is
convenient, no?'

'Succinctly put, Sergeant.'

'What about Diandra Cliff?' Robbie asked.

'Why would she harm Jody?'

'They had a sexual relationship in the past.'

'That's long over.'

'So she *says*.' Nola tapped the pen against the board. 'And
there is the small business of Simon Albright's fake licence. Jody
put Diandra's company in danger by bringing him in and not
saying anything. Gabe Frost said Jody talked about leaving Jolie
Laide – maybe Diandra wasn't happy about losing her a second
time?'

'A good point,' Elliot conceded. 'Put her down.'

'What about this Amber Keenan chick?' Robbie said. 'I bet she
hated Jody's guts when she learned she was bon–'

'Sergeant.'

'Having sexual relations with her ex-husband.'

'Write her down. Put a star beside her – I want that woman interviewed.'

'Tamara Ford?' Robbie offered.

'Why would she harm Jody?'

'Search me, but maybe Jody was involved in trying to blackmail her and she found out about it.'

'She sent those flowers, though – right?'

'She's an actress – she could be covering her tracks. Just because she says her old man doesn't mind her having extra-curricular lovers doesn't mean she'd be happy with everyone knowing her business,' Nola said.

'On the board, Sergeant.'

Robbie leaned backwards with his hands behind his head. 'We're missing someone.'

'Who?'

'Fiona Hynes.'

'Reasons?'

'She's religious, right? From what Nola said it's clear she doesn't approve of Jody's lifestyle.'

'True.' Nola glanced at Elliot. 'What do you think?'

'Why would Fiona Hynes attack her own sister, though? She's the only family member who stays in touch with her.'

'She's unhappy.'

'Being unhappy does not automatically make you violent. If that were so we'd have our work cut out for us.'

'No, but being unhappy can make you unpredictable,' Nola said.

'All right, put her on the list.'

They stared at it.

'What about the blackmailer, stalker? Who do we think that is?'

'Simon Albright,' Robbie said. 'He's broke and he saw an opportunity to make some money.'

'I sense that he is the key to all of this.'

'Key suspect?' Nola asked. 'Or unlock-the-mystery *Scooby Doo* key?'

Elliot stood up and reached for his jacket. 'It's late. Tomorrow we bring Simon Albright in and get to the bottom of this for once and for all.'

'You think he'll talk?'

'I think he'll talk. I don't think he's got anything left to lose.'

'What time do we go get him?'

'Not you, Sergeant Kane. I need you to—'

'Hold on a second, sir. I was the one who wanted to squeeze that boil from day one.'

'I need you to speak to Amber Feenan.'

'Why can't Robbie—?'

'You're the only one who has met her ex-husband; you are in the best position to judge if she is or is not a suspect. Remember, I want this suspect-pool drained.'

Nola glared at him, livid. 'Yeah, and she's a chick, so there's that, right?'

'If you mean do I think she might find talking to you less problematic, then yes, Sergeant. I think you will better find some common ground.'

'That's super sexist.'

Elliot put his coat on and switched his computer off. 'You're a card player, Sergeant Kane. Why wouldn't you deal the best hand you had? Sergeant Keller, would you mind dropping me home? The Passat is still in the garage.'

45

Just under an hour later, angry and feeling a little hurt, Nola walked up Camden Street and into her favourite pub. The bar was surprisingly busy for midweek, and it took her a moment to realise Gracie was already here, sitting under the bookshelves with Ben Brennan from Narcotics. Nola considered leaving, unsure if she could deal with Gracie right now. She was bone tired and didn't feel like putting on much of a front.

'The usual, Nola?'

She turned her head. 'Oh, sure – thanks, Tony. Busy tonight.'

'Yeah, there's a comedy show upstairs later.'

'Right.'

She got her pint and wandered through the crowd.

Gracie and Ben were so deep in conversation they didn't see her until she was standing right by them. 'Am I interrupting anything of great importance? Solving world peace one pint at a time?'

Gracie scooched over to give her a seat. 'Look what the cat dragged in,' she said. 'Ben, word to the wise, if she offers any you any kind of bet, say no.'

'Oh yeah?'

'Besmirching my good name, Gracie?' Nola said, unable to keep a slight edge from her voice. She grinned to soften it.

'I'm just saying don't hustle the innocent, Kane – it's not sporting.'

Nola put her beer on the table and removed her jacket.

'Good to see you, Nola,' Ben said. 'I haven't seen you around lately.'

'Oh, didn't I tell you?' Gracie said before she had a chance to reply. 'She got transferred to B&T.'

'Burglary and theft?'

'Yeah,' Nola said. 'New squad, you know yourself.'

'She's working for Elliot Ryan.'

'Who?'

'Nola's new boss, he's your man that the fire brigade had to cut free from a garden wall a few months back.'

'Oh yeah, I heard about that. I don't think I know him.'

'You wouldn't,' Nola said quickly and changed the subject. 'Anything new on your end? I saw there was a shooting in Ballyfermot yesterday. Any connection to your current case?'

Gracie and Ben exchanged a look. Nola's curiosity rose.

'What?'

Gracie shrugged. 'Yeah, it was Dean Staunton. He was CHIS.'

Nola understood. CHIS stood for Covert Human Intelligence Source, informants to Joe Public. Grasses or snitches to those who dwelt in the shallow end of the gene pool.

'Shit, how did that happen?'

'Nobody knows,' Ben said. 'He's been on the books for years, no jacket, no bells. Should have been clean, but this? This was brutal. They shot him in front of his kid and his missus.'

'Fuckers.'

'Yeah.' Ben took a long mouthful of his beer.

Nola had worked with him on a case two years before and knew him to be a straight and decent man. This would burn him, leave a mark. 'You ever try a meditation chair, Ben?'

'What's that?'

'It's a weird kind of moving, vibrating chair, supposed to destress you and that. Some kind of sensory mojo, used for hypnosis and accessing restorative memories.'

'Can't say I have.'

'That sounds weird,' Gracie said. 'Why would anyone want to do something like that?'

'You ever see the film *Jacob's Ladder*?' Ben asked.

'Never heard of it.'

'Weird old film about this ex-soldier or something, back from 'Nam.'

'I don't like war films,' Gracie said.

'This isn't a war film – this is about the guy's mind after the war. See, he's all messed up and having weird thoughts and shit, so they treat him using a sensory deprivation tank.'

'What's that?'

'A tank with water – you're supposed to float in it, in the dark. Shuts off all your other senses so you have to rely on your mind to figure shit out.'

Gracie shuddered. 'No thanks, I'm claustrophobic.'

'My dad used one, back in the eighties, after he had a breakdown.'

'You never told me that,' Grace said. 'You never said your dad had a breakdown.'

'It was a long time ago. He got better.'

'I remember your dad,' Nola said. 'He gave us a talk in college about work–life balance.'

'That's him – he's big on mental health issues.'

'You should send him in Nola's direction.'

'Eh?' Nola said, her pint mid-way to her lips. 'What do you mean?'

'Not for you, for your boss.'

Nola put the glass down harder than necessary. 'That's the consensus, is it? The party faithful have decided Ryan's not playing with a full deck?'

'What are you looking at me like that for?' Gracie looked put out. 'It's a joke, Kane.'

'Ha – bloody hilarious.'

'What's this?' Ben asked.

'Nothing,' Nola said quickly. 'Like Gracie says, it's a joke, it's all a fucking joke.'

Nola drank her beer and left them to it, refusing Gracie's offer of a lift. She walked into town, fuming, her head filled with thoughts she could not articulate. A dead CHIS, now that was a turn up for the books. She wondered what the department had on him, what they held over him to make him risk himself and the safety of his family.

On Dame Street she caught a taxi. While it threaded its way slowly towards home, Nola thought of Jody Kavanagh lying with her head open, her baby, if it survived at all, floating inside her in the dark, the ultimate sensory mojo. A little scrap of biological evidence, unreachable.

For now.

46

Friday

Elliot woke up early.

He showered, shaved and dressed slowly and with great attention to detail. That morning, he kissed his wife's photo before he went downstairs, for he knew, deep in his gut, that once something had been loosed into the ether there would be no turning back.

Every spare moment since his accident, he had connected names and numbers from Natalie's diary: first calls, then case files and on to more than one questionable arrest. It was a lot, much of it circumstantial, but enough to open an investigation if that's what was required. Even so, it was Natalie's death that burned his soul, *his* case. And even if he could not undo the past, he would bring everything he had to Connors, lay his soul bare. Let the chips fall where they must.

It was strange that his brush with death had emboldened him. Snapped him from inertia. But now that he was here, tap-dancing at the moral crossroads, he felt lighter than he had in years, stronger.

There was no tabula rasa, but there could be justice.

Downstairs, Shona was standing next to the window in the hall. She was on the phone, talking quietly, with her back to him. As he reached the end of the stairs, he paused to watch her, noticing for the first time the slight bulge at her waist, the messy, tangled topknot, and was struck by something that should have been obvious before now.

Here was a woman who had someone who loved her, someone who cared for her, wanted to spend time with her. And here she was wasting her time, minute by minute, hour by hour, on him. Worse than that, he had allowed it. He had allowed her to shy away from happiness, allowed her to dodge commitment under the guise of nurture.

With that in mind, he entered the kitchen and put the kettle on. She had not yet started to make breakfast, so he went to the fridge, got three eggs and popped them into a saucepan of water and turned on the stove.

Moments later, Shona opened the door, surprised to see him making toast. 'Hey, Dad, I didn't hear you come downstairs. What are you doing? Let me do—'

'Shona, I want you to go home.'

'Excuse me?'

'Today, after breakfast. I want you to go upstairs, pack your things and go home.'

'Dad, listen to me, we talked about this and—'

'You were right,' he said, getting down two cups. He put a teabag into each and added boiling water. 'You were right about me, about needing help. I'm going to get someone in, a housekeeper. I'm going to focus on my health and get to retirement and do my exercise and make a go of it.' He suppressed a shudder. 'I'm going to take up a sporting hobby.'

She peered at him suspiciously. 'What's brought this on?'

'You did.'

'Me?'

'I was lying in bed last night thinking about your mother, may God rest her eternal soul, and I realised something. I realised she was a fool.'

'Dad!'

'No, not in general,' he went on quickly. 'She was certainly the smartest woman I've ever met – present company excluded, of course.' He smiled at her. 'But she was wrong to exclude you when she was ill, wrong to pretend nothing was happening, wrong to ... lie. And that's what I've been doing and ... and I'm sorry. Your mother made a mistake, but she did it because she loved you so much. I promise I won't make the same mistake because ... because I love you more than anything in this world.'

Tears filled Shona's eyes. Elliot felt his own chin wobble slightly. He did not want her to cry: he wanted her to hear him.

'Kiddo, I love the bones of you. I know you love me too. And that's why I need you to go home. I need you to go back to Johann. I need you to believe me when I tell you I will not go gently into the night. I will not climb another ladder while in my cups. I'll leave that to—'

Shona dived on him and wrapped her arms around him so tightly he couldn't complete the sentence. The squeeze was painful, if he was being truthful, but he bore up underneath it and hugged his only child back as hard as he possibly could.

By the time Nola came to collect him, he'd eaten two boiled eggs and a slice of cardboard and was downright giddy. 'Good morning, Sergeant, what a beautiful day.'

Nola narrowed blood-shot eyes. 'You seem ... different.'

'I think we're going to make a difference today, don't you?'

'If you say so.' She walked down the drive towards the car.

After a moment he followed her. 'Are *you* all right?'

She glanced at him. 'How would I know if I was or not?'

'What do you mean?'

'I'm sick of it. I'm sick of people, I'm sick of liars, frauds, people who are supposed to have your back but don't. Sick of it.'

Elliot clucked sympathetically. 'That's life, isn't it, Sergeant? Nothing but one set of difficult circumstances after another.'

Nola got behind the wheel and started the engine. 'If it wasn't for my ma I'd move to a different country.'

'You should move anyway if that's how you feel.' Elliot put his belt on. 'Life isn't a dress rehearsal, Nola. You get one go around – you might as well make the best of it.'

Nola turned her head and stared at him incredulously.

'What?'

'I've never heard you use my name before.'

'Don't worry, Sergeant, I won't make a habit of it.'

47

The atmosphere at the stationhouse was unusually buzzy. Nola left Elliot to his own devices and went to the canteen, where she bumped into Gracie collecting coffee.

'Hey, girl!'

'Hey, yourself,' Nola said, trying to inject the right amount of casual friendliness into her voice.

'Ready for another rip-roaring day with the Fossil?'

Nola felt a flare of pure anger. 'You know you don't have to call him that, right?'

Gracie looked surprised. 'Sorry, I didn't mean anything by it.'

'His name is Ryan, Inspector Ryan, and he's ... he's my boss, okay, so watch what you say about him.'

'Jesus, Nola, I was joking.'

'Yeah, well, that joke has run dry.'

'What is wrong with you? You've been acting weird all week.'

'There's nothing wrong with me, hun, and don't let anyone tell you different.'

'Okay ...' Gracie looked very unsure about that. 'Will I still see you later?'

'Later?'

'Clancy's going-away party – it's gonna be lit! You are coming, right?'

'I've got to run, Gracie. I've a mountain of stuff to organise.'

'Nola—'

'See ya.'

Nola got her coffee, went downstairs and left the station in a foul mood.

Amber Keenan burst into tears. 'Are you fucking serious?'

Nola waited for her to regain her composure. She supposed it was perfectly natural for people to cry when they were angry or in shock, so she kept her impatience under wraps. If Elliot was here, he'd probably be patting hands and making soothing sounds, commiserating and doing that thing he did with his lips, that thing that drove Nola around the bend. Nola wasn't unsympathetic to the plight of others, but in her experience, such as it was, the less you fawned over weepies, the quicker they got a grip of themselves.

And moments later, her theory was proven correct when Amber blew her nose loudly and turned her watery grey eyes towards her.

'I don't understand,' she said. 'What the fuck has any of this got to do with me? You know I came out of a facility yesterday, and, hello, I was there for a month?'

Nola allowed herself one sympathetic cluck. 'I realise this is very hard, but if you could work with me, Miss Keenan, I'd really appreciate it.'

She leaned out of the uncomfortable chair. Amber Keenan's apartment was appallingly modern, all white walls, sharp angles and sleek, uncomfortable furniture. The floor-to-ceiling windows overlooking Hanover Quay might be considered a selling point, if looking over a body of grey water to another block of apartments floated your boat, though the hefty five-figure rent would sink it fast. Nola had no doubt the chair she was currently perched on cost a fortune, but she wouldn't have fished it out of a skip.

'Hold on a minute. Walter? Walter?'

Nola pressed her fingers to her temple. She had a humdinger of a headache that several painkillers had not made a dint in. Maybe she should have asked Elliot for whatever the hell he popped whenever he thought she wasn't paying attention. God, she was sick to the teeth of everything.

'Walter!' A tiny dog ambled into the room and looked at Nola with alarm. Amber snatched it up and held it against her chest. 'I don't want to talk about that low-rent bitch.'

'She's in a coma.'

'So? Am I supposed to give a shit, after what she did to me?'

'Monica Fell said—'

'Oh, fucking Monica, she's so sweet and I love her, but she's a total daisy.'

'A daisy?'

'Turns her face to the sun. Can't cope with conflict.' Amber collapsed onto the sofa with the dog. 'Look, I don't think I can talk about Jody. I'm not able.'

'Your friend or ex-friend or whatever is lying unconscious in a hospital bed with half her face smashed in,' Nola said firmly. 'You need to tell me about her, about Jools. You're not protecting her right now; you are protecting the person who did this.'

If Nola had slapped her the reaction would have been less intense. '*You think I'm covering for Jools?*'

The dog, struggling to escape, yelped and nipped Amber on the hand. Amber yelped too and flung the tiny animal away. It slunk to the end of the sofa and lay there, baring its teeth.

'Shit!' She held her hand up. Tiny as the dog was, its teeth must have been sharper than its brain because her hand was bleeding.

Nola sighed and stood up. 'Do you have any antiseptic? Wipes?'

'Under the sink in the bathroom, down there.'

Nola returned a moment later carrying said items. 'Hold still.'

Amber held her hand out. She was very pale, and up close Nola could smell the alcohol on her breath. Rehab obviously hadn't taken.

'When was the last time you had a tetanus shot?' Nola asked, cleaning the wound carefully, before she put a plaster over it.

'I don't know – before.'

'Ages before or recently before?'

Amber glared at her. 'You think I'm an idiot, don't you?'

Nola put the lid back on the antiseptic cream. 'I don't know what to think of you, to be honest. I don't know what to think of anyone involved in this case. But I can tell you this, the rich person omertà is really starting to get on my nerves. Nobody, and I mean nobody, is levelling with me, and at the end of the day a young woman is in the hospital with part of her skull missing and I'm sick of the bullshit.'

Amber blinked. '*You're* sick of it?'

'Yes, yes, I am.'

'How do you think we feel?'

'I don't know – I'm not a mind-reader.'

Amber laughed and grabbed Nola with her non-injured hand. 'I like you, you're funny.'

'That's a new one on me.'

'People expect so much, don't they? You must be perfect all the time. You start with the right parents, live at the right address, go to the right school, know the right people, stay the right weight, wear the right clothes. Marry the right man.' Amber laughed again. 'You can't be too demanding, oh no, you've got to fuck like a porn star, but be demure around his family. It's exhausting and it's impossible to keep up.'

Nola extracted her hand. 'Tell me about it. Some days I feel like I'm swimming in a pool full of sharks.'

'At least you're swimming.'

Nola looked at her. 'I bet you loved Jools, didn't you?'

She nodded. 'He swept me off my feet. I remember thinking, *This is it, this is the dream.*'

'What happened?'

'I woke up.'

'He told me you were bipolar.'

Amber rested her chin on her bandaged hand. 'Ah yes,' she said, after a long moment of silence. 'The get-out clause.'

'Excuse me?'

'It was the perfect get-out clause – my baggage, my mental health. He weaponised it and used it to silence me. Can you imagine? Using my own brain against me?'

'How so?'

Amber pulled her feet up and hugged her knees. Her smooth face revealed no angst, but her eyes were another story. Nola had never believed the line about the eyes being the window to the soul, but now she could see she had been wrong about that, as she had been wrong about so many other things.

'Jools's father was a bastard – did you know that?'

'I know nothing about him other than he was rich and now he's dead ... Oh, and Jools didn't live with him.'

'Used to beat Jools's mother around the place, broke her nose once. A real prince. Jools hated him and swore he'd never be like him. But you know what? He's worse. In every way possible he has surpassed his father in cruelty.'

'Is he physically abusive?'

'Physically, no. That's not his style. A manipulative gaslighting prick? That's him.'

'So you don't think he hurt Jody?'

'No.'

'Even if she had tried to trick him in some way?'

'What do you mean "trick"?'

'She told him she was pregnant, suggested it was his.'

'Stupid bitch – really?' Amber laughed. 'Well, I can tell you that's unlikely. Jools had a vasectomy when we married.'

'He mentioned that. I didn't know if it was true.'

'Oh, it's true. He couldn't risk tainting the Byrne gene pool with my mad DNA.' Amber tossed her hair. 'Maybe he did me a favour in the long run. You called Jody my friend. But Jody Kavanagh is not my friend – I doubt she's anyone's friend. She's not capable of friendship. She's not capable of anything except opening her legs and—'

'Amber.'

'I don't blame her, not really. We have a session in rehab called "round-table" – have you heard of it?'

Nola shook her head.

'Okay, so, in it, everyone has to speak their truth. Straight truth, no lies. I'd *love* to see Jody do something like that: she'd scorch the earth.'

'What do you mean?'

Amber looked away for a moment. 'You need to talk to Monica.'

'I did talk to Monica. She said she has no idea why anyone would hurt Jody.'

'Ask her about the summer in Brittas, push her a bit.'

'What's this about?'

'I'm exhausted.' Amber got up and went to the kitchen. Nola heard her open the fridge, heard the unmistakable sound of ice hitting the bottom of a glass, the hiss of something poured over it. She looked at the little dog and felt sorry for it.

When Amber returned she seemed surprised to find Jody still there. 'I've said all I want to say.'

'Do you have an alibi for Sunday night, Monday morning?' Nola said. 'I know you said you were in rehab, but I need to be sure.'

'Do I need to provide one?'

'It would be helpful.'

Amber took a long gulp of her drink and sighed; it was the sigh of someone who was done pretending. She walked across the bright, cold room, opened her handbag and returned carrying a wrist ID. It was stamped with the date and time.

'I never thought one of these could be so useful,' she said in the saddest voice as she handed it to Nola. 'Keep it. I'll be sure to have others.'

'You don't have to live like this,' Nola said. 'You can get help. There are other programmes that might—'

'Stop.' Amber held her hand up. 'I've heard it all before.'

Jody rose to leave.

'Was she?' Amber asked in a strange faraway voice. She had drunk two-thirds of the glass and seemed already to be drifting.

'Was she what?'

'Pregnant.'

'Yes.'

'Goodbye, Sergeant Kane. Close the door on your way out.'

48

'I don't think I like the sound of this.' Simon Albright read the warrant. 'What if I decline?'

'You can of course,' Elliot said. 'That is your prerogative.'

Elliot and Robbie were standing on the front step of Simon Albright's grim little flat. Simon looked worse than the previous time Elliot had been there, thinner, more dishevelled, a man unmoored in a stained T-shirt, a stripy dressing-gown and bare feet.

'What happens if I say no?'

'Then we'll arrest you, have you brought to a station, have a doctor take a sample of your blood and your DNA, your fingerprints, of course, and we'll make a note of your resistance in our file for the DPP.'

'My file?'

'Yes, sir. We will prepare a file, then it's up to the DPP how they proceed.' He leaned closer. 'I should tell you, it never looks good when people are difficult. The courts frown upon that kind of thing.'

'I have rights.'

'Indeed. There's no denying you have the right to say no, but it won't supersede a warrant.'

If he thought Simon was pale when they knocked on the door of his flat, he soon learned that a man could go paler still.

'Are you all right, Mr Albright?'

Simon pressed his fingers to his brow. His hand shook. 'How would anyone be all right in this nightmare?'

Elliot moved off the step to give him a moment to compose himself. Simon passed the warrant back.

'You'd better come in. I need to get dressed.'

Robbie and Elliot followed him down the same hall into the same depressing kitchen/living room. They sat on the same leatherette couch while Simon dressed in the bedroom next door. A large portfolio sat on the coffee table. Robbie opened it up and flicked through it.

'Did you design all these?' he called.

'Yes.'

Elliot glanced at what Robbie was studying. In front of one of the buildings stood Simon, Diandra, a man in a hard hat and Jody. 'I didn't know you worked with Malcolm Hynes.'

Simon came back, pulling a pale-blue jumper over his head. 'That was a Norwegian construction, very simple in design but a complex build. Like Tetris, really.'

'Did he do a lot of work for the company?'

'On and off over the years – why?'

'His wife never mentioned it.'

Simon combed his hair with his fingers. 'She wouldn't. Fiona's still sore about it.'

'Sore about what? I'm not sure I follow.'

'Diandra fired him.'

'Why?'

'Jody said she didn't want to work with him.'

'Why was that?'

'He scared her. The man's a complete throwback.' Simon looked away for a moment and swallowed several times.

'Are you all right?' Elliot inquired.

'I admit I don't feel particularly peachy. Something I ate perhaps.'

'You were saying Malcom is a throwback?'

'When I was a lad,' Simon said, 'there were men who came off the boats, men who spent their time at sea, months and months at a time. They all talked about coming ashore, that's all they'd talk about, what they were going to do, who they were going to shag, what they were going to eat – you get the picture. But give them three days and they'd be itching for the sea again. They hated it, you see, hated the solid ground beneath their feet, hated the stale air, the people standing in one spot.' He lifted a bony shoulder. 'Malcolm Hynes is like that. He wants the world to be one way, but it's not and he can't stand it. He used to talk about values and biblical law, but he has no real power and that makes him sick to his stomach.'

'We should head in.' Elliot got to his feet, as did Robbie. 'Simon Albright, I'm placing you under arrest. You are not obliged to say anything unless you wish to do so, but anything you say will be taken down in writing and give in evidence.'

'I need to call my solicitor.'

'We can call him en route.'

'I did not attack my wife. I need you listen to me, Inspector. I need you to believe me on that.' He got to his feet, staggered, and had to sit back down again. 'I'm sorry ... give me a moment.'

'Mr Albright, is something the matter?'

'No.' He pushed himself to his feet and stood. He was as white as a sheet.

'Will you let me see your hand, here, now?'

'I did not hurt my wife,' he said, looking Elliot dead in the eye. 'I need you to believe me.'

'Your hand, sir.'

Slowly, Simon tugged at the edges of the dressing and began to peel it away.

'Oh!' Robbie jerked his head to one side. 'That looks very badly infected.'

'I never liked that dog,' Simon said, removing the last bit of plaster. 'I told Jody it was nothing but trouble. I never wanted any of this. I promised her I'd protect her. I promised her I'd save her.'

'Mr Albright?'

Simon Albright smiled.

Then keeled over in a dead faint.

49

Nola found Monica Fell sitting on a bench in Bushy Park, her little dogs at her feet. She was bundled up inside a padded jacket, her eyes shielded behind massive sunglasses despite the grey skies. She was watching a pair of swans drift serenely across the surface of the lake.

'I don't like swans,' she said, when Nola sat beside her. 'Beautiful to look at, but they can get very violent, you know. I was chased by one once as a child – nasty hissing thing.'

Nola glanced at the birds. 'Least they stay where they're supposed to be. We've got seagulls around our way that would take the food right out of your mouth.'

'Protected species, you know.'

'Really?'

'Um, endangered, I believe.'

'They don't look endangered – there's thousands of them.'

Monica's head dipped a little deeper into her coat. 'How is she? Amber.'

'Hard to say, I don't really know what she's like normally.'

'She sounded drunk when she called me.'

'Yeah.'

'I don't know how to reach her, she's so ... broken.'

'Yeah,' Nola repeated. 'She told me Jools was a proper bastard to her when they were married.'

Monica winced at the bad language, but she nodded. 'A difficult man.'

'But you seemed happy about Jody seeing him.'

'I know, I sort of felt ...' She blew her cheeks out. 'I sort of felt it was kismet.'

'Kismet?'

'Meant to be, two magnets drawn to each other.'

'I thought magnets repelled each other.'

'Oh ... maybe they do, I don't know a lot about magnets. I don't know a lot about anything.'

Nola watched one of the swans arch its neck and flap both wings before settling back on the water. The movement barely made a ripple on the surface.

'Monica, Amber said to ask you about Brittas.'

Monica made a sound, part laugh, part groan. 'Of course she did.'

'She said I should push you about it.'

'There's no need to push, Sergeant Kane. I've thought about nothing else since I heard Jody was in hospital.'

She pulled a tissue from her pocket and blew her nose loudly, and it was only then Nola realised she had been crying before she arrived.

'Are you okay?'

'My husband is so mad with me right now.'

'Why?'

'He's ... he's a different person in many ways from our set, for want of a better word. He's a good man, solid, dependable.'

'Dull as dishwater?'

Monica chuckled half-heartedly. 'Well, I don't call him that, but he likes a quiet life, you know?'

'Sure, who doesn't?'

'Oh, plenty of people, believe you me.'

'Jody?'

Monica said nothing for a moment. 'When we were kids, I thought Jody and Amber were the most amazing people, you know? I was so lucky they were my friends because they were everything I wasn't – cool, confident, beautiful, sporty. They were mythical.' She looked at the swans again. 'At least that's what I thought then.'

'And now?'

'Now ... I can see their feet.'

'Monica, what are you not telling me?'

'I never really understood what it was to love someone until I had my son. The moment they put him in my arms everything changed. I know it's a hormonal thing, a rush of something in the blood, but I can honestly say I knew, I mean really knew, I'd do anything for him. I'd kill for him, you know?'

'Well, I hope it never comes to that,' Nola said.

Monica laughed. 'Me too.'

'Why are you telling me this?'

'Because I still don't understand what happened to Jody, to Fiona. Okay? I don't understand why it happened and I don't understand how it was allowed happen.'

'Why what happened?'

Monica blew her nose again, harder this time. Nola sensed she was stalling so she waited.

'I was thirteen years old. My parents had rented a house in Brittas Bay for August, right opposite the beach. It was great,

I loved it. My brother and I were practically feral. Then I got this call from Jody. Like, a weird call, you know? She asked me if she could come down for a few days. I asked my mom and she said okay and next thing I knew Jody arrived by bus and—'

'And what?'

'She arrived on the Friday, and Morag arrived the next day to bring her home.'

Nola remained quiet; she could see how much this conversation was costing Monica. A daisy, Amber called her, always seeking the sun.

'Morag came in, you know, carrying a hamper for my parents, a great big thing chock-full of expensive bits and bobs, full of chatter, apologising for Jody's arrival. Talking about crossed wires and stuff like that. My mom, bless her, she's a great lady, but she is no match for Morag, and to be honest, I think she was both intimidated and impressed.' She shifted her weight. 'Jody looked at me. We'd been at beach and she was wearing my old swimming togs ... but when Morag snapped her fingers she just got up, walked straight to the car and got in without saying a word. God, I can still see her. Her face ... we were children.' She put her hand to her forehead. 'I should have said something. I should have told my mom.'

'Told her what?'

'That he'd hurt her.'

'Who?'

'Jody's father, he ... Jody told me he'd been hurting both of them, her and Fiona, for ... a while and ... Morag had found out somehow.'

'Hurt them how?'

'You know ... sexually.'

'Jesus.' Nola put her hands on her thighs. 'Wait, her mother found out about it and then what? What did she do?'

'That's just it, she blamed them.'

'She blamed her own daughters for their father's sexual abuse?'

Monica nodded. 'Jody was terrified. She told me Morag hit Fiona so hard she knocked her out cold, and Jody was covered in scratches and bruises.'

'From her mother?'

Monica nodded.

'Fucking bitch. So why did they make up?'

'I don't know, maybe it's just easier this way.'

'Easier for who?' Nola demanded, thinking, *God, Amber was right – she is a total daisy.*

'I don't know. Look, I don't understand what hold Morag had over her daughters, but I know when Jody's dad died Jody came home for the funeral, and after that, she and Morag seemed to make some kind of connection. Fiona was livid about it.'

'I'll bet.' Nola thought of Fiona Hynes face at the farmhouse, her bitterness, her anger. 'I bet she feels betrayed.'

Monica huddled deeper into her coat. 'When we got back to Dublin after that summer I tried to talk to Jody about it, but she insisted I'd got the wrong end of the stick.' Monica closed her eyes. 'We didn't mention it again, but I know what she told me in Brittas and I know she was telling me the truth. I should have said something back then.'

'That's not on you,' Nola said, her voice hard. 'You were a child too; it wasn't your place to protect them.'

'Someone should have,' Monica said quietly. 'They were so young, someone should have saved them.'

Nola turned her head away, sickened. She had not liked Morag Kavanagh when they met, but now ... Jody was unconscious, but would Fiona consider talking to her about what happened back then? Was there any possibility of justice? And then she thought about Aldus Crivon. What was it Fiona had said? Shields up.

'Damn it,' she muttered.

'What?'

'Nothing. Listen, would you be willing to make a statement about—?'

'No, I'm sorry, I can't get involved.'

'You are involved.'

'You don't understand – my husband is already furious about all of this.'

'So?'

'I can't.' Monica got abruptly to her feet. 'I'm sorry. Please, I've told you everything I know. I've got to go.'

She walked off, tugging the little dogs along. Nola watched her until she exited by the river-walk gate and said something aloud that she was glad Elliot Ryan was not around to hear.

50

'He's fine – they'll pump him full of antibiotics and he'll be right as rain,' Robbie told Nola, fanning himself with Elliot's notes.

Elliot scowled and took them from him before he sat down. 'Tell me again, Sergeant, what Monica Fell attests.'

Nola recounted the conversation, including Monica's refusal to give an official statement. Elliot listened, his expression very grave.

'And I checked,' Nola said. 'There is no mention anywhere that the Kavanagh children were ever abused.'

'That just means it wasn't reported,' Robbie said.

'Neither Jody nor Fiona Hynes made any such charge against their father in the intervening years.'

'Right,' Nola said. 'Because one married into a cult and the other married a huckster.'

'Bad choices do not suggest—'

'So Albright still swears he didn't do it, he didn't attack her?' Nola rubbed her forehead. Her headache from earlier had increased massively after her talk with Monica Fell. This bloody case. She felt like she was in a pinball machine – one minute Jody was an angel, the next the devil incarnate, the next a victim. Where did it end? 'What are we missing? If Albright didn't do it and Byrne claims he didn't hurt her and Tamara didn't do it and Amber didn't do it—'

'Nice work, by the way, chasing down an alibi for Miss Feenan. That might have been awkward.'

'It wasn't like I had to go to any great lengths. The clinic confirmed she was there.'

'You know,' Robbie said. 'We never looked at Malcolm Hynes.'

'Why would we look at him now?'

'Well, we didn't know he worked for Jolie Laide, for a start, or that Jody was the reason he got canned. Maybe he deserves a closer view.'

'Who does he work for now?' Elliot asked.

Nola went back through her notes. 'He's a gamekeeper at Grantham Lodge.' She looked up. 'You want me to call them, check to see if he was footloose and fancy-free Sunday or Monday?'

'Yes.' Elliot rubbed his hand over his face. 'Then I think we should go and talk to our cuckold.

'Our what?'

'Have you never read *Othello*?'

Nola shook her head.

'You should. Tragedy, Sergeant, is our bread and butter.'

When he was gone, Robbie leaned in. 'What's he talking about cuckoos for?'

'He wasn't.' Nola turned to her computer and googled 'Othello' and 'cuckold'.

'Oh man,' she said.

'What?'

'This shit is dark. "I will chop her into messes! Cuckold me?"'
She looked at Robbie, who was still a little pale from earlier.

'Maybe he's right, maybe we need to read Shakespeare and shit.'

'I don't like reading old stuff – it gives me a headache.'

'I think there's modern versions, though. Hey, are you okay?'

'I can't get over yer man. Why would you leave your hand like that, like? he must have been in agony.'

'I don't know, Robbie. Simon Albright is not right in the head.' She patted his hand. 'If you ask me, none of this crowd is normal.'

'This case is weird.' Robbie gave himself a shake. 'I don't know, Kane. I think I'm starting to miss the times when we all we had to do was track down stolen bikes.'

51

'You're a lucky man,' Elliot said, coming into the interview room carrying two mugs of tea. Nola trailed in behind him, having won the toss with Robbie, who, it had to be said, made no secret of the fact he was relieved he'd lost.

Simon glanced up quizzically. He still looked as rough as hell, but marginally better. 'Really?'

'With an infection like that, you could easily have suffered gangrene or lockjaw.'

Simon held his newly bandaged hand. 'I don't feel particularly lucky, I must say.'

'I suppose it's all relative.' Elliot slid the mug towards him and sat down. 'Why didn't you go to a doctor?'

Simon shrugged. 'I don't know, maybe I wanted to suffer.'

'Why would you want to suffer?' Nola asked. 'Guilt?'

'If you like.'

'I put some sugar in your tea,' Elliot said. 'I hope you don't mind. You look like you could do with it.'

Simon accepted it gratefully. He drank while Elliot switched on the video recorder, read out the date and time, who was in the room and what the charge was.

'Why don't we go from the beginning?' Elliot said. 'Your name and date of birth, please.'

'Adam Smith, born Hampstead, 7 December 1980.'

'When did you change your name?'

'In 2015, shortly before I met my wife.'

'Which one?' Nola asked.

'Jody.'

'Why don't you tell us about that?'

'What's to tell?' Simon turned his unhappy gaze on her. 'I was unhappily married, working my ass off and getting nowhere. I hated my life, I hated myself, so I left it all behind and became—' He waved his hand down his body. 'I should never have married Veronica in the first place. Our relationship was toxic.'

'How so?'

'She's older than me by a number of years, which, initially, was not that big a deal.' He paused, suddenly self-aware. 'I'm going to sound like a complete twat here, but the truth is the novelty wore off.'

'The novelty?'

'Of being someone's pet.'

Nola shifted in her seat. She had never liked Simon Albright and she didn't want her dislike of him to seep into the atmosphere and taint the interview, but hearing this self-serving, self-pitying drivel was like nails on a blackboard.

'Did you love her?' she asked, a bit too sharply. 'Your original wife?'

'Love,' Simon spoke the word quietly. 'What is love? Really, when it boils down to it?' He looked at her. 'Have you ever been in love?'

'I know what love is, Mr Albright, enough to put a value on it.'

'You're young – of course you think you know what it is. Love is more than a word bandied about, sullied by common usage.'

Nola leaned back in her seat, barely able to keep the contempt from her voice. 'So what you're telling us is you loved your first wife so much you let her think you were dead, and Jody so much you lied to her.'

His face hardened then fell, and in that moment Nola saw something she had not expected to see: genuine grief and shame. It threw her a little.

'I fucked up, okay. I made a complete mess of everything.' Simon leaned over the desk and raised his injured hand. 'A wild animal caught in a snare will chew its own leg off to escape, did you know that?'

'I've heard it said,' Elliot answered, wondering where he was going with it.

'With Jody, I walked into the snare willingly, okay? Eyes wide open.'

'Did Jody ever tell you about her father, about her relationship with him?'

That jolted him. 'What? What do you mean?'

'Did she tell you he abused her and her sister when they were young?'

'She ... not exactly in those words, but I knew there was bad blood between her and her family. I didn't know about the abuse until I moved here.'

'How did you find out?'

'Fiona told me, at our housewarming.'

'Fiona told you?'

'She was angry that Jody had been in touch with their

mother, that she had gone to their father's funeral. Words were exchanged, Malcom became agitated and ... it was unpleasant.'

Despite her misgivings, Nola found she believed him.

'Then what happened?'

'They left, and later that evening Jody told me the truth. And so, I ... suggested there might be a way to ... capitalise on the ... um ...'

'Abuse?' Nola was back to dislike. 'You thought she and you could make a few quid off it, am I right?'

'It was a mistake. Morag does not like to be threatened. Next thing I know, there's a private investigator crawling all over my history and he found Victoria. You know the rest.'

'Wait,' Elliot said. 'Are you saying it was Morag who found your ex-wife? She didn't see a photo of you in a magazine?'

'Of course not, I rarely allowed my photo to be taken. No, it was Morag who found Veronica and Morag who dropped that particular bombshell into Jody's lap.'

'Divide and conquer,' Elliot said. 'She's very astute.'

'I should have been honest with Jody from day one. She would have understood, but once the confrontation in Sligo happened' – he shrugged – 'everything was destroyed.'

'Not everything, Morag coughed up and paid Jody's mortgage.'

'A paltry sum for Jody's continued silence.'

'You'd rather blackmail her, is that it?'

'I wanted her to pay for what she had done to Jody.'

'What happened last Friday night?'

He took a shaky breath before he spoke. 'Jody called, hysterical. That man was there—'

'Jools Byrne.'

Elliot stepped on Nola's foot. Let the man talk.

'I drove straight there. Jody opened the door, distraught. I managed to calm her down. Byrne had gone, but he came back.' He balled his hands into fists. 'I'm not much of a fighter, but the things he said to her, to me ... We fought, and he did this.' He pointed to the fading bruises. 'I thought he was going to kill me but then Jody let that dog into the house and the stupid thing attacked me.'

Nola thought about how angry Jools Byrne had been when she'd interviewed him. Now it made sense. He probably thought Jody and Simon were in it together. Hell, it was still possible.

Or maybe ... the thought hit her hard. Maybe Ryan had been right all along. Maybe Simon Albright, odious as he seemed, was an innocent man.'

'Oh God, I know how this sounds,' Simon said. 'But it's true, all of it. You have to believe me – I would never hurt her.'

'Are you the father of Jody's baby?' Nola demanded.

'No.' He shook his head vehemently. 'Jody and I haven't been ... intimate in a very long time.'

Elliot scribbled something in his notebook. 'So,' he said after a moment, 'if you're not the father, who is?'

Simon swallowed, cleared his throat, cleared it again. He looked like a man facing a firing squad. 'I don't know.'

'I don't believe you,' Nola said. 'I think you do know; I think Jody told you. I think you agreed to keep her secret. I think you and she are very much aligned.'

Simon Albright put his head in his hands. 'I don't care what you think.'

'Of course you don't, because without her, what are you?'

'Nothing,' Simon Albright mumbled. I'm nothing at all.'

52

Nola called Angela Golden and made an appointment to see her while they were waiting for Simon Albright's solicitor to arrive – his brand spanking new solicitor since the solicitor they called at his behest declined to take his case, leaving Simon high and dry. The new solicitor, picked hastily from a phonebook, was already twenty minutes late, so they said to hell with it and went and had lunch.

'Coffee?'

'No,' Elliot said morosely. He had opened his mail and found a handwritten letter from Ronan Black sent the day before. In it, Ronan, once again, spoke of his innocence, his sadness over Natalie, his time inside, and named the man he thought killed Natalie as Francis Clancy and Paddy Clancy as the man who planted the murder weapon on him. Elliot should have been ecstatic, but something darker was threaded throughout Ronan's words, something unsettling, a finality that made him call the halfway house only to find Ronan Black was missing.

Nola got her usual order of a double espresso with three sugars and drank it in two gulps.

Elliot watched her enviously. 'It must be great to be young.'

'Oh, it's a laugh a minute,' Nola said. 'Our wages are shit;

everything we do is expensive; there's nowhere to live unless you want to share five or six people to a three-bedroomed shitbox; no one will insure us to drive a car and the government hates us. You're right, it's great.'

'I didn't mean—'

'Yeah, I know.' She cut him off abruptly. 'Look, my ma is great and I love her to bits, but I'm twenty-six and I share a bedroom with my sister. I'd like a place of my own – doesn't have to be pricey, just somewhere I can bang a nail in a wall or paint a room without asking for permission.'

Elliot nodded. 'I understand.'

'Do you?' She looked unconvinced. 'Anyway, come on, let's go see if Albright's bird has landed.'

And land she had, albeit on one wing, a mousy little woman with an old briefcase and a ladder in her tights.

'Yvonne Duggan,' she said, shaking hands. 'I'm sorry I'm late. I was in court and you know how it is.'

'Certainly.'

'Now, eh ... Albright, is it, Simon?'

'Yes, he's in interview room one.'

'Have you spoken to him?'

'Yes, he was quite forthcoming for a while.'

Yvonne winced. Nola grinned. A Chatty Cathy client was never good news for solicitors.

'I see.'

'Do you have the particulars of the case?' Elliot asked.

'I read them on the way here. Has he been charged?'

'Yes.'

'I'd like to see him, please.'

'Of course. Sergeant?'

Nola led the solicitor to the interview room. Elliot walked back towards his cubicle, mulling Simon Albright's admission over in his head. He believed the man, even if he did not hold him to any moral standard. Human nature was complex, and there was always room for—

The phone on his desk rang. He reached for it.

'Inspector Elliot Ryan?'

It was Barbara Pine from the parole board. She sounded very old and very tired. 'I'm sorry,' she said. 'I thought you should hear it from me.'

'Hear what?'

'Ronan Black was found dead in a flophouse in Smithfield in the early hours of this morning. Heroin overdose.'

Elliot was afraid to breathe let alone speak. 'I thought he was clean.'

'He was. It's always the way. They think their bodies can handle what they could before. Anyway. Like I say, I wanted you to hear it from me.'

'I appreciate the call.' Elliot hung up and sat staring into the middle distance. He was still there when Nola arrived back.

'I don't think that's going to be a match made in heaven,' she said. 'She gave him a right earful about talking to us.' She glanced at him. 'You okay, sir?'

'Yes.' Elliot refastened the top button of his shirt and straightened his tie.

'Only we should probably get a move on.'

'Where?'

'Angela G, sir, remember?' Nola frowned. 'We have an appointment to see her.'

'Right,' Elliot said. 'Then let us proceed, Sergeant.'

Downstairs, they exited the lift and were walking across the reception to the side entrance when Paul Deacon, Gracie and Paddy Clancy entered through the main doors.

Clancy whistled when he saw them. 'Just the couple I wanted to see.'

Nola turned her head and gave Gracie a look.

'You're coming tonight, aren't you, Sergeant? Free bar from eight, plenty of grub. You look like you could do with a good feed. How about it, Elliot, you can bring Shona if you—?'

Elliot let him come into range. He'd be in the dog-house over this, no question, but if there was something he could do, he *had* to do it.

Here and now.

Life and death.

Piece by piece.

No longer a coward.

For the rest of her life, Nola would remember the punch. It felt as though it came from the previous decade, travelled over time, swung upwards and caught Clancy under the chin with a dull meaty smack that lifted the dapper cop off his feet, sending him sailing in an arc back towards the door from which he'd entered. It was so fast, so powerful, so sudden, that no one reacted, not a single officer, until Clancy's head bounced off the tiles and he skidded across them until he lay, motionless, spark out.

'What the fuck —?'Deacon managed after a shocked second and rushed to his boss's side.

'Sir!' Nola cried, stunned.

Elliot shook his hand out and kept walking towards the side exit. After a moment's hesitation, she rushed after him.

Outside, he staggered and fell onto one knee. He was white as a sheet and looked like he was going to be sick.

'Sir, what have you done?'

Elliot fumbled in his jacket pocket and found his painkillers. 'Please,' he said. 'Open them and give me two.'

She did as he asked and watched him toss them down, grimacing as he swallowed.

'You knocked Clancy right out.'

'Come on.' He got to his feet and shook his head to clear it. 'I think you should drive, Sergeant.'

'Sir, please listen to me, there's going to be trouble over this –'

'Then stay here.' He turned his face to hers. 'I'll understand if you do.'

Nola glanced back at the station. No one was coming after them but people were beginning to congregate around the prone Clancy.

'Sergeant.'

She opened the passenger door, helped him in and got in the driver's side.

'Please—'

She took the end of his seat belt and clicked it into place. 'He's going to have your badge for that.'

'Please drive, Sergeant, but if I ask you to pull over, do so.'

Nola started the engine and drove them away from the station, feeling sick in the pit of her stomach. 'Why did you do it? In front of everyone?'

'Because it needed to be done, Sergeant. It needed to be done.'

53

Angela G answered the door of her cottage dressed in denim dungarees, a beige cardigan, wellies, gloves and a large floppy straw hat. She did not appear at all happy to find Elliot and Nola there.

'Mrs Golden?' Elliot asked

'Ms,' she replied, removing one of the gloves to shake hands. 'I never married.'

'Ms Golden, my name is Inspector Elliot Ryan, this is Sergeant Kane. Thank you for agreeing to see us.'

'I don't feel you left me with much choice, Inspector.'

'I'm sorry you feel that way,' Elliot said, sounding contrite. 'I dislike making people feel they've been backed into a corner.'

'Yet here you are.'

Nola shifted her weight from one leg to the other. 'Lovely garden,' she said. 'I've never seen one like it before. Must take a ton of work.'

Angela's expression softened a fraction. 'Thank you, Sergeant, you should see it in the summer.'

'I'd like that.'

'Do you garden?'

'Not really, I live in a terraced house with more of a yard than a garden.'

'Size is not always an impediment; you can do the most wonderful things in a small space.'

'I'll have to take your word for it.'

'Well, come in, I was about to put the kettle on.'

They followed her into a small but bright kitchen leading onto a plant-filled conservatory where a large marmalade cat lay curled in a wicker chair fast asleep.

'Will you have tea?' she asked.

'Lovely,' Elliot replied.

'Please sit.'

They sat beside each other on a pine bench at the table.

'I must tell you,' Angela Golden began when the tea was served with a plate of gingersnap biscuits, 'I am not at liberty to discuss anything about my patient's sessions.'

'Nor would I want you to,' Elliot said. 'I'm hoping you might help me paint a picture. Jody Kavanagh has met with you twice a month for almost two years. You must have gotten to know her very well, better than most.'

'I knew her before that. Before she left for London.'

'She was a client then?'

'For a while.'

'Almost everyone we've spoken to says she's the nicest person, sweet, kind, butter wouldn't melt in her mouth, that sort of thing. But someone wanted to harm her, and someone did. I think it's possible Jody knew she was in danger months ago. I think that's why she got a protection dog. I think someone very close to her did not, in fact, love her or think her sweet and kind. I think someone close to her hated Jody and wanted to do her harm.' He sipped his tea. 'How's that picture looking?'

'I would say you're using broad strokes.'

'That's the only brush I have right now.'

'Hate.' Angela shook her head a little. 'It's such a toxic energy, it consumes people.'

'Was Jody consumed by it?'

'Jody Kavanagh is a chimera.'

'A what?'

'A hybrid, Sergeant, two beasts in one.'

'Her boss called her a raptor.'

'Diandra?' Angela smiled. 'A little rich – I think Jody is slightly more complex.'

'We know about the abuse, from when she was a child.'

'Do you?'

'Jody's friend Monica Fell told me,' Nola said. 'She said Morag Kavanagh knew her husband was abusing both her children and did nothing about it.'

'Oh, she did something about it: she silenced them.'

'Why?'

'To avert scandal, I imagine. Morag is part of the Hamilton-Ray family, old money and plenty of it. This would have been huge.'

'Monster.'

'All too human, I'm afraid. I've never treated Morag Kavanagh, but I imagine she's an interesting subject. You've spoken to Fiona, I assume?'

'Yes, she's a bit ... angry.'

'She's more than that, Sergeant.'

Nola took a second biscuit.

'Do you know what detachment is, Sergeant?'

'Feeling alone?'

'Not quite. In a psychological sense, detachment can often be deployed as a coping mechanism. Being emotionally unavailable reduces the chance of having to deal with unwanted feelings. It's a carapace of sorts, but self-defeating. A person might be so detached they never get to experience pain, but neither will they experience joy or love. It is not a comfortable existence, but neither is the alternative.'

'Sounds awful,' Nola said. 'Like being stuck in limbo.'

Angela smiled. 'Very astute, Sergeant. I like to think of it as being set in aspic.'

'Is Jody set in aspic?'

'Jody Kavanagh is a complex woman with complex needs. Her sense of self was developed as a child, and she has never moved past it. Her views are like that of a twelve-year-old.' Angela was no longer smiling; instead she looked wary, cautious. 'I cannot share details with you,' she said again. 'But you say you want to get into Jody's shoes, Sergeant. I suggest you consider what you were like as a twelve-year-old, what Jody was like as a twelve-year-old and work from there. What broke the camel's back, so to speak?'

'The abuse, the—'

'She endured that.'

'Her mother covering for her father?'

'She endured that too, in a fashion.'

'Was it because Fiona left?' Nola asked. 'Monica Fell said Morag physically attacked Fiona, knocked her out, and we know Fiona left home very early.'

Angela gave her a nod of approval. 'As sisters they had some solidarity, protection, a shared truth. When Fiona left, she left a child behind.'

'Fiona was a kid too.'

'Not to Jody. To Jody, Fiona's leaving was the biggest betrayal of all.'

'And to Fiona, Jody reconnecting with her mother is as bad?'

'Yes, I imagine so. Those poor girls, pitted against each other, when the real villain sits alive and well in Sligo.'

The cat in the conservatory woke, stretched, turned around and went back to sleep.

'Now,' Angela said. 'I really must get back to work. It's going to rain shortly.'

'How can you tell?'

'When you get to my age you feel it in your bones.'

'Would you mind if I took another one of these?' Nola asked.

'Please, help yourself, take as many as you like.'

'Ta.' Nola took the remaining four.

Angela laughed. 'Sergeant, you are a tonic. And if you're in the neighbourhood over the summer, please stop by and I'll show you the garden.'

'I'd like that a lot. Maybe you could give me some tips.'

'Gladly.'

They left, with Nola waving furiously.

'What the hell was that?' Elliot asked when they got back to the car. 'I thought you lived with your mother?'

'I do, and she's got a pretty decent garden for a terraced house.'

'Then what was all that palaver about?'

'I dunno,' Nola said, wrapping the biscuits in tissue before she put them in her bag. 'She reminded me of Nana, and that's how I'd handle Nana. Lots of compliments, act dumb and let her do the talking.'

Elliot smiled.

'What?'

'Nothing, I'm ... well, I'm impressed.'

'Thanks.' Nola's phone bleeped. She answered it and listened with the widest grin stretching across her face. 'Oh, you absolute beauty. I owe you one – no, I owe you a million ones! Pints are on me.'

She hung up.

'Good news?'

'Yes, sir, if I'm right we're about to engage in some serious cancel culture.'

'Cancel culture?'

'A fate worse than death if you're a so-called content creator. We need to find a judge.'

'Now? Why?'

'We're going to need a warrant.'

Elliot glanced at his watch. 'We could try Judge Foyle, but his office closes in twenty-five minutes.'

Nola grinned and put on the blue lights. 'Don't worry, sir, we'll catch him.'

'I was afraid you were going to say that,' Elliot said and put his belt on.

They made it with three minutes to spare, and Elliot kept his eyes open for most of the way.

Progress.

54

While Nola and Elliot were high-tailing it back across town, news of Clancy's broken jaw had reached upstairs. Connors pressed the phone to his ear and his eyes grew so wide they looked like they might pop clean out of his head.

'He what?' He listened incredulously. 'When was this?'

He listened some more. 'By ambulance?'

Lights were flashing on his phone. He ignored them. 'No, of course not ... I don't give a shit, Herring, that's your job, man – tie it down, smooth it out, whatever you need to do, do it. Were there witnesses? ... Oh, that many? ... Well, yes, I want them all ... No ... No ... Damn it, Herring, don't keep firing solutions at me when we don't know what the bloody problem is! Where is he now? ... What? ... What do you mean he left?'

He hung up and sat staring at the clock. After a moment he pressed his intercom. 'Olivia?'

'Sir?'

'Get Philip Redmond. Tell him I want to see him ASAP.'

'Yes, sir.'

He got up and walked to his window.

What the hell was going on? Elliot Ryan involved in a fracas? Ryan? Good Lord, if it had been Kane ... but Ryan? He'd hoped she'd gain some manners from him, not the other way around. Redmond would know what to do. He was the union rep, and if anyone could sift gold from shit it would be him.

His intercom beeped.

'Well?'

'He's at St Margaret's, sir, on the back nine.' Olivia paused for a moment, predicting his reaction to what she had to say next. 'He wonders if the situation could wait.'

Daragh Connors was a good man, a decent man, a man both feared and revered in fairly equal distribution among his fellow officers. But Superintendent Connors had always had something of a hair-trigger temper, something he worked extremely hard to rein in.

Usually.

Mostly.

Olivia listened to his view on the matter and called Phillip Redmond back and relayed the superintendent's answer, leaving out many of the words he'd used for brevity and because she was a good Christian woman and wanted to stay that way.

Redmond arrived within the hour, and he was not happy. 'I have one day off a week, Daragh, one, and it's sunny, so this better be good.'

'I think we have a situation.'

'Let's hear it.'

'Inspector Elliot Ryan assaulted Inspector Clancy in the reception, in full view of several officers and two civilians.'

'He did what?'

'You heard me.'

'Fuck me. Where is he now?'

'Your guess is as good as mine.'

'And Clancy?'

'Gone to the hospital with a broken jaw.'

'But ... isn't he retiring?'

'End of the month, but tonight's his big party.'

'Unlikely to happen now, is it?'

'No.'

'Shit.'

'Quite.'

'What brought this on,' Redmond scratched his chin. 'Isn't he leaving anyway?'

'I have no idea.' Connors leaned back in his chair and crossed his ankles. 'You're the rep – what do we do in this situation?'

'Full view of everyone, you say?'

'Hammer blow, apparently.'

'I suppose we wait and see what Clancy wants to do, but at the very least we need to rein Ryan in before he does a number on anyone else.'

'He's been under a great deal of stress lately, you know, after the accident.'

'Mitigating factors won't cut it if Clancy decides he wants retribution.'

Both men sighed. Difficult days were not unusual, but they were always unwelcome.

55

Bane looked up when Nola and Elliot entered the room. 'This is, like, a violation of my civil rights.'

'I read you your rights when we arrested you.' Nola turned on the video recorder and pressed record. She gave the date and time, her name, Elliot's and 'Interviewing Dean Russell'.

'My name is Bane,' he said, scowling.

'Not according to your birth cert it isn't, Lee.'

'I don't have to talk to you.'

'That's correct,' Elliot said. 'Of course, if you do talk, you can give us your version of events. If not, we'll come up with our own.'

'I think,' Nola said, 'it might be easier if we lay out what we have. We searched your mother's house, your room, of course—'

'You can't do that – that's private property.'

'Yes,' Elliot said. 'We know, that's why we had a warrant.'

'It's like time,' Nola said. 'On this side of the table, time and the law are both real.'

Bane's right leg started jimmying up and down.

'I had a friend look into your online activity. You're very popular on YouTube and Twitch,' Nola said. 'Wolfsbane20XXX.'

'So?'

Nola grinned. 'I've been reading through some of your online chat. You like to harass women—'

'Look, I—'

'Don't interrupt me, Lee. Now, I can't pretend I know everything about the platforms you trawl, but I imagine shit-talking is fine. What I can't imagine is how your personal training clients would feel. I wonder would they be comfortable knowing what you really feel about women.'

'You can't do this—'

'I'm curious, too – when did you find out Jody and Tamara Ford were seeing each other?'

His face fell. 'What?'

'Your mother works on film and television sets, did she—?'

'Leave my mother out of this.'

'Why did Jody get a protection dog?'

'I don't know.'

'It wasn't for Simon at all, was it? She needed protection closer to home – she needed protection from you.'

'What happened?' Elliot asked. 'Did she find out it was you who tried to blackmail Tamara?'

Bane glared. 'I'm saying nothing.'

'Sexism, homophobia, racism, blackmail.' Nola laughed. 'I mean, you've been really busy, Bane. Can't imagine your Instagram followers will understand why you feel the need to be so hateful, but I suppose we'll leave it up to them to decide if you need to be cancelled or not.'

The word 'cancelled' struck home hard and fast. 'What do you want?'

'Why are your fingerprints in Jody's bedroom?'

'I told you, I did some wiring for her.'

'When?'

'I don't know, ages ago.'

'Did you sleep with Jody Kavanagh?'

'Do I need a solicitor?'

'Why?' Elliot asked. 'Have you done something wrong?'

'No, but ... like, am I in trouble?'

'I don't know,' Elliot said and glanced at Nola. 'Is he?'

'Are you the father of Jody Kavanagh's unborn child?'

'What?'

'Jody was pregnant – did you know that?'

'No, she never told me.'

'But you have slept with her?'

'Once, before.' A hank of dark hair fell over his brow. 'Look, she was at a post-production party, drinking a lot. I think she was upset about something. I offered to take her home.'

'And did you?'

'What?'

'Take her home?'

'Well, like I said, she was upset. We talked and ... one thing led to another.'

'You slept with her?'

'Yeah.' He looked down. Nola scowled, picturing the scene: Jody, drunk and vulnerable, and Bane ready to pounce.

'And then what?'

'Then she acted like nothing happened.' He sneered. 'Wouldn't ever talk about it.'

'You mean she wasn't interested in a relationship with a content creator?'

He scowled. 'Hey, you know, in a way, she took advantage of me.'

'How's that?' Elliot asked.

'She's older.'

'What happened on Monday?'

'Look, do I need, like, a solicitor or not?'

'Fine, have it your way.' Jody closed her file and stood up. 'Maybe your mam knows a good one.'

'I said don't bring my mom into this.'

Like a child, Nola thought. 'Again, this isn't on me: this is on you.'

'Wait! I'll talk.'

Nola sat back down.

'I was in bed, okay, I heard someone yelling—'

'Who?'

'A woman. I went back to sleep and then the stupid dog woke me up, barking. So ... I got up, went to see what was going on and Jody's front door was open.'

'What did you do?'

He looked down at his hands. 'You need to understand something, okay. Like, I have a public profile – if this got out it would ruin me.'

'True, attacking women isn't generally a good look.'

'Stop saying that! No, okay! I never touched her, I swear.'

'What did you do?'

If a man could have died from squirming, Bane would have popped his clogs there and then.

'What happened?' Elliot asked. 'Young man, you are in a lot of trouble right now. The best thing you can do is talk to us and help us understand why you attacked your neighbour.'

'I didn't,' he said vehemently. 'Jody was on the floor when I went in – there was blood everywhere.'

Nola smiled. He had put himself right in the crime scene, stupid muppet. 'Go on.'

'I ... I didn't know what to do.'

'Did you call for an ambulance?'

'No.'

'Why not? That would be a normal thing to do if you innocently found your neighbour lying injured, right?'

He nodded.

'So why didn't you call for an ambulance?'

'I didn't ... I didn't want to be involved.'

'You *were* involved. You were involved the moment you set foot in her house,' Elliot said.

'Nah,' Nola said, 'He had a better idea.'

Bane glared.

'You took her phone, didn't you?'

'She had, you know ... messages and shit.'

'Stuff you didn't want us to read, right? Stuff about Tamara Ford, about the night you brought Jody home from the party? That kind of thing?'

'Aw, man, this shit is so messed up.' Bane put his head in his hands and groaned.

Nola glanced at Elliot, who shrugged.

'You took her phone and you went back to your own house and left her there, on the floor, badly injured. What did you do then? Go back to bed?'

'No ... I had a shower and I waited.'

'For what?'

'I dunno, I just waited. Then an ambulance came so I figured she'd been found.'

'Where is Jody's phone now?'

'Look, I didn't hurt her, okay. I swear on my life.'

'No, you left her to bleed to death,' Nola said. 'A simple solution to your simple idiot problem. Where is the phone?'

'It's under the gnome in the back garden.' His shoulders slumped. 'Are you going to tell my mom about this? She'll kick me out.'

Nola stood up. 'Sir, I'll be right back.'

She left and called Robbie. 'You still at the house?'

'Yup.'

'Is there a gnome in the back garden?'

'Yeah, why?'

'The phone's under it.'

'Hold on.'

Moments later she heard Robbie laugh. 'Got it – he'd buried it in a plastic bag.'

'Nice work, Sergeant, now we're cooking.'

She went back into the interview room.

Bane was still slumped forward, his head in his arms. 'I can't get a record,' he cried. 'I'm going to Vegas next year for the World Gaming series.'

56

As soon as Robbie got back to the station, Nola found a charger and waited impatiently for the phone to hit 50 per cent, then drove directly to the hospital. She met with Dr McCann, agreed to be quick and went into Jody Kavanagh's room.

It was the first time she'd laid eyes on Jody in person. Standing, looking down at the intubated woman shocked her. She was so small in person, so vulnerable. Nothing like the person Nola had been building up in her head.

Nola pulled on her gloves and removed the phone from the evidence bag.

She leaned across Jody's body and took her right hand. 'I'm sorry about this,' she said softly. 'I'm sorry I have to touch you without your permission, but my name is Nola Kane and I am going to find the person who did this to you and you're going to help me.'

Carefully, she pressed Jody's index finger against the fingerprint ID and the phone flashed on.

Working fast, Nola scrolled. She took screenshots of all the messages from the last fifteen days before she went into Jody's security app. She ran through the short time-framed videos until she reached Monday morning.

She watched what Jody's camera had recorded. Watched Fiona Hynes enter the house. Watched the argument develop. Watched Jody waving her arms, watched them struggle, watched Fiona pick up the statue and smash her sister in the back of the head with it twice. Big swings with a lot of weight behind them. Watched her drop it. Watched her send a text from a mobile phone and replace it in the charger on the counter. Watched Bane/Lee Russell creeping around like the louse he was. Watched him take Jody's phone and skulk out the way he came. Watched Simon Albright arrive, watched him turn Jody, watched him fold over her inert body, clearly hysterical. Watched the ambulance come, watched it all unfold with a sad and heavy heart.

'I'm sorry,' she said to Jody. 'I don't think we'd be best pals if we met, but you didn't deserve what happened to you. I hope you and your baby pull through.'

She patted Jody's still hand awkwardly, sent everything to Robbie and turned off the phone.

57

They drove to the farmhouse in silence. Nola helped Elliot from the passenger seat, but backed off when he refused her offer of help to walk to the front door.

'I'm all right, Sergeant. I can manage.'

'You don't look all right. You look to me like you're in a lot of pain.'

'Looks can be deceiving.'

Nola let it go. This was his moment, and she wasn't about to trample all over it.

He raised his hand and gave the official copper's knock.

After a moment, a sullen-faced boy came to the door and peered out. 'What?'

'Now then, young man, you should say "hello" and "can I help you",' Elliot said, frowning. 'That's what you should say. It's always polite to say hello.'

The boy blinked. His face was filthy, covered in peanut butter and jam.

'Do you remember me?' Nola asked, figuring they'd be waiting a while for this particular child to go formal. 'It's Joshua, right?'

The boy nodded.

'Okay then, can we come in? We're looking for your mammy.'

The boy shook his head.

'No?'

'No, s'not allowed.'

'That's good,' Nola said. 'That's good that you listen to what your mammy tells you. Where's your sister?'

'S'inside.'

'Can we talk to her?'

He thought it over and came to a decision. Clearly talking to Sarah was not off-limits.

'Sarah!'

Sarah came to the door, carrying the toddler on her hip. Nola's heart did a little dip when she saw her. She looked tired and grubby. No child should carry so much weight in her eyes, or on her shoulders, or on her hips. It wasn't right and it wasn't fair.

'Sarah, it's me, Sergeant Kane, Nola – remember me?'

'You were here the other day. You made my mammy cry.'

'Yes, well, I'm sorry about that. I didn't mean to upset her.' Nola leaned down so she was at the girl's eye level. The toddler stared with her eyes wide, like a little owl. 'Sarah, is your mammy here?'

Sarah shook her head.

'What about your daddy?'

Another shake.

'Who's taking care of you?'

'I am.'

'Where is Mammy?'

'She went out.'

'On her own?'

Another nod.

'To the shops?'

'I don't know.'

'Did she say when she'd be back?'

'No.'

'Sarah, honey, can we come in?'

'Okay.'

They followed the child down the flagstone hall and into the long, cold kitchen. The fire was out, the air frigid. Two of the younger girls were on the sofa, one sucking her thumb; the boy was nowhere to be seen.

Nola felt a queer shivery feeling. Something was wrong in this house; something was very wrong.

Sarah set the toddler beside her sister and watched as she immediately climbed down.

'Is that your daddy's truck outside?'

Sarah nodded.

'Did he not go to work today?'

A quick head shake. Why, Nola wondered, did this child look so terrified?

'Sir,' Nola said, wearing a fake smile, 'I'm going to nip outside and call Robbie.'

'Good idea, Sergeant.' Elliot turned to Sarah. 'Did Mammy say when she'd be back?'

'No ... but she was sad. She was crying.'

'Okay, Sarah, I want you to stay here with ...' He waved at the children. 'I'm just going to check upstairs very quickly, and I'll be right back.'

He left the kitchen, checked the living room, backed out and took the stairs several steps at a time, ignoring the agony in his back. The landing was dark and wide, five doors leading off it, three open. He poked his head in, saw they were children's rooms and backed out again. The fourth door was a bathroom, dominated by a clawfoot bathtub; two lines of damp clothes were stretched across it, waiting to be dried off downstairs. He tried the fifth door. It was locked.

He jiggled the handle. It was old and felt loose in the frame. Elliot gave it a soft shoulder and almost fainted from the pain.

'What are you doing?'

He turned. Joshua was at the top of the stairs staring at him. 'I'm trying to get this door open.'

'You'll break it.'

'I don't have a key.'

The boy went across the landing to the bathroom, opened the mirrored cabinet over the sink and returned with a set of keys on a heavy keyring. 'It's this one.'

'I think you should go back downstairs.'

'Why?'

'Because Sarah is scared, and she needs you.'

He waited until the child had gone then unlocked the door. What he saw in the darkened bedroom made perfect sense, perfect monstrous, horrible sense. Malcolm Hynes lay sprawled naked on the bed, his eyes open, his throat slit. The bed was covered in blood, gallons of it. Elliot took a closer look and turned his head away.

He hoped that particular injury had been made post-mortem. He sincerely hoped that was the case.

58

The wind was fierce and cold and wild. It whipped the tide into a rolling, foaming mess, sending spray high enough that Fiona felt it on her face.

She stood small in Malcolm's coat, felt the weight of it. It smelled of him and this brought tears to her eyes. He had never seen it coming, never thought for a moment she could do what she did.

She closed her eyes. Monday seemed like a lifetime ago. She had gone to Jody's house, cap in hand, to ask – no, plead for help as she had done before, but this time there was no help, no understanding, nothing but Jody's cold vicious tongue. Oh god, why did she have to be so cruel? Why had she humiliated her like that?

'What do you mean she paid your mortgage?'

Jody's face, so full of smug surety. 'She owed me.'

'You'd take her money? After what she did to us?'

'To me you mean,' Jody replied, her upper lip curling in open disdain. 'You left, remember?'

'What are you talking about?'

'You left me Fiona, you left me in that house alone, *with him*. God, you make me sick – look at you, look at the state of you, standing there so high and mighty. I don't care, okay? I don't care what you think. Yes, I'll take Morag's money and whatever else she wants to give me.'

'It's blood money.'

Jody's expression grew hard. 'Doesn't stop you coming here with your paw out, now, does it? What do you need this time? More abortion tablets? Christ, you bloody hypocrite. I can't help you – you won't even help yourself.'

The anger, where had it come from? Had it always been there buried under the surface? Too late to take it back, too late to stop what was coming.

Too late.

Sacrifice, she thought, watching the birds wheel through the air, screaming and squawking, alarmed or angered by her presence. Did she blame them?

No, they were within their rights to protect what they had.

Mothers protected their young.

Some mothers.

A sudden gust made her wobble and sent stones skittering over the edge to the roiling sea below. The rocks had been breached and were filled with pools of calmer water. When she and Malcolm has been first married, they'd come here after high tide to search those pools for crabs, snatching them from the water into a plastic bucket. In those days, Malcolm talked endlessly of sustainability, of taking the noble path; she'd listened rapt as he described his vision of a better world, a purer world, one where their children would grow strong and independent, free from the hellish shackles of modern society. Their children would understand the world did not owe them favours; they would be free-thinkers, bright, able to challenge and debate. They would know their own worth.

God, she wiped the tears from her face angrily. What a fool she had been. She had swallowed every single one of his lies hook, line and sinker.

She had allowed him to take control, believing it to be love. So desperate for someone to love her, she had overlooked all the red flags and drowned out the faint but insistent inner voice pleading with her to look closer, to question, to think.

In many respects, she had surrendered. Surrendered her identity, her self-respect, her family. She'd thrown all her eggs into a Malcolm-shaped basket.

Shame washed over her. Shame and rage and fear.

She had nothing; she had no one. She had gambled and she had lost.

The sea, though, the sea would cleanse her, take her, deliver her from her pain.

A car came up the coast road, engine high. She turned to watch its progress and was not at all surprised to see it was driven by Nola Kane, with Elliot Ryan sitting as pale as milk in the passenger seat. It pulled in and Nola got out.

'Fiona, whatever you're thinking of right now, please don't do it.'

Elliot opened the door and got out too, moving slowly and in obvious pain. He shut the door and stood swaying slightly in the wind.

'Don't,' Fiona said. 'It's too late.'

'Fiona.'

'No. I don't want to hear what you have to say.'

'That's okay, I don't want to say it.'

'Then why did you come here?'

'To stop you from making a mistake. Another one.'

'I'm not making a mistake.'

'You have five little children who might feel differently.'

Fiona swallowed, tried to speak and felt her throat constrict. She put her hands in the pockets of her husband's coat and took a step backwards.

Nola held her hands out, fingers splayed. 'Stop!'

'It's too late.'

'Your children need their mother,' Elliot said. 'Now more than ever.'

'I can't ... I can't do this any more. Please, just leave me alone.'

'Fiona, listen to me, listen. You've made some mistakes, I get it, but the one you're planning is the worst one, and it's a mistake you can't come back from. Okay? Please, I am begging you, think of your children, think of yourself. You are worth thinking about, you have value.'

'No! You're wrong. I ... stop saying that.'

'You've been dealt a bad hand your entire life, but you're still here – because you're strong, because you won't be beaten. Not by your mother, not by your father, not by your husband, not by Jody, not by anyone.'

'It's too late.'

'It's only too late if you step off the ledge. You are in control, Fiona, you and only you.'

She began to weep openly, a small broken woman in a man's coat. Nola felt a lump form in her own throat. She had never seen a more devastated person in all her life.

'I can't live like this.'

'You can!' He took another step. 'Fiona, listen to me. Don't do this, don't give up.' Elliot moved away from the car, shuffling a little. 'You have a chance to turn things around. You can show your children how strong you are, teach them. They need you now more than ever.' He reached for her. 'Don't you care for them? Don't you love them?'

She flinched, an actual physical reaction to his words. 'I love them more than anything in the world.'

'Then shield them! Protect them from this pain. Don't let them suffer like you suffered.'

Fiona screamed and collapsed, weeping. Nola didn't hesitate. She covered the ground like cheetah. Dropped to her knees and wrapped her arms around the sobbing woman, making sure to keep her weight as far from the cliff edge as possible. 'It's all right,' she said. 'It's going to be all right.' She looked over her shoulder.

Elliot nodded once then slumped against the car, close to passing out.

59

Elliot took a taxi home, showered and returned to work in a different taxi. He took a single painkiller and swallowed it with a scoop of water. He gazed at his appearance in the bathroom mirror, trying to come to terms with his decision.

The punch had been unwise, he knew. Apart from causing him physical harm, it had undermined his standing and possibly his case. Nevertheless, what was done was done and could not be undone.

So be it.

He straightened his tie, picked up his briefcase and exited the bathroom. Word had obviously gone around the station like wildfire: everyone fell quiet as he walked to the lift and all eyes were on him.

Dead man walking.

It was almost amusing.

He got in the lift and rode it up. Olivia was still there when he entered the outer office, though she was putting on her coat, ready to call it a day.

'Oh, Inspector,' she said when she saw him. 'What did you go and do that for?'

'It was a long time coming, Olivia.'

She gave him the saddest smile. 'I hope they go easy on you.' She walked towards him and gave him a kiss on the cheek. 'Take care.'

She left.

Elliot cleared his throat, rolled his shoulders and knocked on the door.

Showtime.

'Enter!'

He did so.

The pack were waiting. Connors, Herring, Stall and, in the corner, Philip Redmond, his union rep.

'Hello, Philip, I'm sorry you got hauled in.'

'Yes, you and me both. Sit down, please.'

Elliot sat on the remaining single chair.

'Do you mind telling me what the living fuck you're playing at?' Stall demanded. 'You put Paddy Clancy in the hospital – they've had to wire his jaw shut!'

Elliot looked down at his right hand. His knuckles were a little puffy, but they no longer ached.

'Elliot,' Connors said. 'What did you do?'

'I got him with an uppercut, sir.'

'Is he trying to be funny? Do you think this is funny?'

'Not especially.'

'Hold on, Andrew,' Conor said. 'Elliot, what were you thinking?'

'Thinking?'

'I feel this is on me. I knew you weren't well, I think you came back too soon and ... well, this is the result of, of ... eh, too much stress.'

'Stress?' Stall nearly shrieked. 'He put the man in the hospital.'

'Yes, we know,' Connors snapped. 'Elliot, Philip has spoken to Clancy within the last half hour. He's groggy, but from what we can gather he does not want to press charges.'

Elliot smiled.

'What?' Stall demanded. 'What are you smiling at? My God, man, are you on drugs?'

'There's no need for that kind of accusation,' Redmond said quickly.

'Then what's he smiling at?'

'What *are* you smiling at?' Connors asked, narrowing his eyes, a shark sensing blood somewhere in the water.

Elliot reached down and lifted his briefcase to his lap. He snapped the locks, opened it, removed a salmon-pink cardboard file and closed it again. 'I'm smiling because Clancy played his hand.'

'What are you talking about?'

'Nola Kane would enjoy a hand like this,' he said, more to himself than the others. 'She'd enjoy it.'

'Are you quite all right?'

'Yes,' Elliot said. 'Doesn't it strike any of you august fellows as odd that Clancy, Paddy Clancy, doesn't want to press charges against me? Even though I cold-cocked him in public, with a wealth of eyewitnesses?'

Stall and Redmond exchanged glances. *Ah*, Elliot thought, *it had occurred to them and had likely been discussed.*

'Well?'

'All right,' Connors said. 'Why is that?'

Elliot stood up and put the file on his desk. Before he sat back, he added the red diary from his inside pocket.

'What is this?'

'This is a project I've been working on. I started it before my accident and completed it late last night. I think there are some gaps, but for the most part, it is all self-explanatory.'

Connors reached for the diary and opened it. His eyes scanned the pages, and as they did, he lost some of his tan.

Elliot got to his feet. 'If you need me, sir, I will be at home.'

'Wait, what? What's going on here?' Stall shouted, getting to his feet. 'Where do you think you're going? Ryan? Ryan?'

Elliot left the office and closed the door gently. He was never a man for a dramatic exit, and besides, he had had all the excitement he could take for one day.

60

My name is Jody Kavanagh. I am twenty-eight years old. I am an interior designer. I live in Kilmainham, Dublin.

I have a sister called Fiona who is older than me by a year and two months and we could pass as twins. I know this because a woman came in and told me. She told me I was married but separated. My ex-husband is called Simon. He comes to see me every day. He smiles a lot, but his eyes are sad. The woman says my sister is in a different hospital, awaiting evaluation.

I am not to worry about Simon, the woman says, because he has made his bed and now he can lie in it.

I cannot remember Simon's face when he is not here. The woman says he looks a bit like an old-fashioned dork. She tells me this while she eats chocolate. She talks a lot. I don't remember her from the before time.

I do not recognise my mother when she comes to the hospital room. She looks out the window and clears her throat a lot. Different people come and stay for a while, talking about things I am supposed to know, people, places, until my head begins to ache and I feel exhausted. A woman called Monica brought me a huge bunch of flowers. She talked a lot and cried and hugged me. I wish I could remember what the flowers were called.

I am alone when I wake up. I feel upset, frightened, agitated. A nurse gives me an injection and I sleep.

When I open my eyes again the room is much darker and I am alone again. I try to remember where I am and what I am doing here. I see pictures, fragments, scenes. None of them are connected and none of them make sense.

I try to concentrate.

I sleep.

I dream of a dog barking.

When I wake up, a man in a white coat is standing at the end of the bed, reading a chart. He smiles and says good morning. I try to say good morning, but my throat hurts and my tongue is too big for my mouth.

When I open my eyes the sky beyond the glass is full of grey clouds.

Time passes.

I can see better.

My feet and hands tingle.

Monica visits and bursts into tears. 'You're breathing on your own!'

She is so happy. I want to say something but cannot. My throat hurts.

I sleep.

Days pass. The woman comes back. When I try to tell her I don't know what happened she says I am not to worry about it. She says it will come back. She says it's normal 'under the circumstances'.

I do not understand what she means by this.

I stay awake for longer and longer periods. I start to make words, whole sentences.

I understand I am in a hospital for the first time.

I want to know why.

The woman comes back with an older man. She introduces him as Inspector Elliot Ryan. I understand for the first time that the woman is a cop. I am wary, but I don't know why.

I try to speak, but it's very hard.

The woman says I was attacked in my home. She says my heart stopped twice.

She says I was in a medically induced coma for several weeks.

She says I was lucky because Simon found me in time.

She asks what I remember.

I don't remember anything.

She says not to worry about that, it will come back when I am myself again.

I have no idea who 'myself' is and this frightens me and makes me upset, but I am too exhausted to cry.

This morning a priest came to see me. He was old and looked tired. He sat on the plastic chair by my bed and told me he has prayed for me since I came in. Every day.

I asked him how many days that was, but he said he didn't know. A woman came in and asked him to 'please excuse us'. The priest looked annoyed, but he left. The woman said her name is Dr McGann and she is a consultant in the hospital. She asked me a lot of questions and wrote things on a clipboard. She said I would need physiotherapy. She said I would recover, in time. I asked how long. She said this depends on me. She asked how I am feeling. I said I'm tired. She did not write this down.

My mother came in after lunch. She sat in the plastic chair and read a book. I tried to stay awake, but when I opened my eyes I was alone and it was dark outside my window.

The hospital is nice at night, quiet. The nurse who checks on me has a soft voice, strong hands and smells of soap. She says her name is Joan and she has been looking after me since my surgery.

I don't remember her face, but her voice is familiar, soothing. I feel safe with her. She asks me if I am feeling a little better and I tell her I am. She says I will be back on my feet in no time. She leans down and whispers that my baby is doing fine.

When she leaves, I stare at the ceiling and concentrate.

My baby?

My name is Jody Kavanagh, I whisper. I am twenty-eight years old. I live in Kilmainham, Dublin. I have a sister called Fiona. I have a husband soon-to-be-ex called Simon. I have a mother. I have friends.

Somebody tried to kill me.

But I am not dead.

I am not dead.

I am not dead.

My baby?

My baby.

Mine.

61

They waited.

As predicted, the tabloids had a field day, especially when they twigged that Fiona Hynes was a member of the Hamilton-Ray family and the mutilated dead man was the son of a so-called cult leader who himself had disappeared in 'mysterious circumstances' back in the eighties.

'Dead, I reckon,' Robbie said, offering Nola a semi-glazed doughnut. She took it gratefully and took a huge bite. 'Dead and buried – you know how that lot operate.'

'What lot?'

'Religious cults and that.'

'We've made a couple of blunders, Robbie. I don't want to do any more speculating.'

'Part of the job, if we didn't speculate we wouldn't figure things out.'

Nola nodded and went back to her paperwork. There was so much still to process, but they were making headway. Fiona Hynes admitted to everything, to assaulting her sister, to texting Simon Albright from her sister's phone, to murdering her own husband. Not even her own solicitor could stop her from talking. She was, she told him, free to speak her mind at last, and by God did she have a lot to say. No wonder Aldus Crivon was on the phone day and night, issuing all manner of legal threats.

It was Thursday, almost a week after the arrest of Fiona Hynes, and so far they'd heard not a sausage about Elliot other than he was on gardening leave. Inspector Lupin got snippy if they asked too many questions, so they kept their conversations to themselves.

But it was clear something was rumbling in the ether and Nola was worried.

Still, she kept her head down and worked hard. Bike thefts, oh lordy, there were a lot of bikes stolen across the city. She and Robbie tracked containers heading abroad, checked serial numbers, checked lost-and-founds and generally did whatever the hell Lupin asked them to do.

Her phone rang.

'Sergeant Kane?'

'Yes?'

'Superintendent Connors wants to see you, right now if you could.'

Nola stood up. She glanced over to see if Robbie had heard, but he was typing furiously.

Superintendent Connors glanced up when she entered. 'Sit,' he said.

She sat, noticed there was jam on her sleeve and rolled it up to her elbow to hide it.

'Sergeant, I want to commend you on your handling of the Hynes case.'

'Thank you, sir.'

'Difficult circumstances, I think we can agree.'

'Yes, sir.'

He gazed at her for so long she had to fight not to squirm. 'You worked with Paul Deacon for two years.'

Nola tensed. *Here be danger*, her senses said. 'That's right.'

'How did you find him to be?'

She leaned backwards slightly. 'In what regard?'

'In any regard. How would you speak to his character?'

'His character, sir?'

'Is he trustworthy?'

She smiled and shook her head. 'I had a personal relationship with him, sir, and in *that* regard he was most certainly not a man to be trusted.' She thought about it for a moment. 'But as Inspector Ryan often says, a man can be many things, but that doesn't make him a bad person.'

'Oh God, you're not quoting Ryan at me, are you? So how did you find working with the inspector?'

She looked down and thought about her answer before she delivered it. 'He is a complicated person, but fair, and I would say a man of great integrity.'

'Did you know what he was working on?'

'I knew he was greatly troubled by some old cases, not that he disclosed information to me, sir, but I could tell he had a lot on his plate.'

Connors linked his fingers. 'Going forward, Sergeant, where do you see yourself – with Lupin?'

'I ...' She hesitated and thought, *I need to choose my words carefully.* 'Inspector Lupin is a fine man, but if I was given another option, I might take it.'

'Is that so?'

'Yes, sir.'

'Have you ever given any consideration to IA?'

Nola was genuinely surprised. 'Me? No, sir, never.'

'We have many fine men and women working on this force, decent, committed, upright.' He looked at his walls for a moment. 'And then we have another type, operating with impunity, or so it seems.'

'Sir, if you're asking me if I know of any bent officers, I don't.'

'And if you did?'

She spread her hands. 'I don't know what I'd do in that position. I like to do the right thing, but you know how it is, sir. If you get tagged as a grass, the tag stays forever.'

'Yes, I know how the world works, Sergeant. Privy to it, one might say.' He leaned back. 'All right, you may go.'

She stood up and was about to leave when she decided to press her luck.

'Inspector Elliot, sir.'

'What about him?'

'If I was offered a unique position, I would happily work him.'

'You like him, do you?'

'That's the thing about fossils, sir. They put up with a lot, but they weather the storms, they endure.'

'All right, Sergeant.' Connors smiled. 'Please, don't let me keep you.'

She skedaddled.

62

'Christ, this is worse than I thought.' Assistant Commissioner Andrew Stall, looking more like a vulture than ever before, was incensed. He turned to the third page of Elliot's report and winced as he read down the page. 'A fifteen-year-old.'

'Deceased,' Detective Herring, fresh from the press-office oven, said, unable to keep the relief from his voice. 'Death by misadventure.'

'That is not what Inspector Ryan believes,' Superintendent Connors said. 'And, frankly, there are questions to be asked. What happened at the Black Top? Was the girl there or not? Ronan Black's statement is fire, pure fire.'

'We can't say, sir. The witness statements appear to have been misplaced.'

'Misplaced?' Stall snapped. 'Gentlemen, this is a laundry list of gross misconduct. If the press gets so much as a whiff of missing statements and a dead child we're facing a firestorm that will burn the department to the ground.'

Detective Herring was bearing up under his blazing gaze with surprising tenacity. Connors had always considered the man spineless as a jellyfish, but he was, on this occasion at least, holding his own. 'We're in a position of strength.'

'Strength?' Stall looked like he wanted to claw his eyes out. 'You think a long-time serving officer up to his neck in corruption and murder is strength, do you?'

'No, of course not. But consider this. If Ryan plays ball we can alter the narrative.'

'The "if" is doing a lot of heavy lifting in that scenario.'

'Yes, but I think—'

'I'm not interested in what you think. What say you, Connors, you know the man better than anyone?'

'I thought I did,' Connors responded drily. 'Turns out none of us can lay claim to that.'

'Will he play ball?'

'I don't know – he might, given the right incentive.'

'And what might that be?'

'He doesn't want Clancy to profit from his service.'

The three men sat silently for a moment while Stall digested this. 'Losing a pension at this stage is a big blow.'

'Clancy cannot be seen to profit from his actions.'

'The rank and file won't see it like that.'

'They'll see it however we sell it, sir, and that's on us.'

'You think they'll accept the take-down of a fellow officer, a popular officer about to retire?' Stall shook his head. 'It stinks to high heaven.'

'You'd rather we open an investigation into events going back over a decade?'

'What about Paul Deacon? He's been with Clancy for a long time – do you think he sparkles? Dammit, how much deadwood are we talking about here?

'That's a lot of sawing.' Connors sat forward. 'Under the circumstances, and considering we don't have anything on him,

I suggest he keeps his rank as it is until we can be sure of his ... fealty.'

'He won't be happy. I know he has his eye on an inspector's badge.'

'Cut off the head and the limbs will thrash about until dead.'

'Do you always talk in riddles?'

'No,' Connors said. 'But I want you to see it in technicolour. Elliot Ryan,' he nodded to the file in his hand, 'has done us a favour. I intend to see to it that his wishes are met, in as much as the department can meet them.'

'Is he still going to take his twenty-five?'

'I believe so.'

'You believe?'

Stall looked so sour Connors almost laughed but did not. In truth, he could understand the man's position. It's never a good feeling to have a situation bubbling outside of one's control, relying, as they were, on the chips to fall exactly as Elliot Ryan had planned them to. For a man like Andrew Stall, used to controlling the game, this must have been a very unpleasant experience.

'I think if we kept to our word, he would keep to his.'

'All right,' Stall said after a moment. 'I will talk to the commissioner and Minister Dell.' He closed the file and waved it. 'I take it this is the only copy?'

'That I am aware of.'

'And you.' Stall turned to Herring. 'I better not get a sniff of this across the media, nada. I know you're friendly with the Stork creature. If she gets wind of anything you are to stamp it down to dust.'

'Yes, sir, I will attend to it personally.'

'See that you do.' Stall rose to his feet, nodded, turned on his heel and left the office.

Herring visibly deflated. 'My God,' he said shakily. 'I thought his head was going to explode when you gave him the file.'

Connors frowned. 'He is correct, Herring. I've kept up my end of the arrangement. IA will have their hands full and you can be certain Clancy won't go gently into the night. The dying wasp has the most painful sting. It's up to you and the team to make sure none of this, and I mean none of it, ends up as tabloid fodder. We cannot be accused of a cover-up.'

'I'll do my best, boss.'

'This place is like a colander, Herring, remember that.'

'Yes, sir.' He put his hands on the arms of the chair as though to rise and paused. 'What about Inspector Ryan, sir? Do you think he will be happy with this decision? He wanted Clancy arrested.'

'Inspector Ryan is a pragmatist, Herring. He'll come around – I'm sure of it.'

'But won't he want—?'

'Don't let me keep you, Herring.'

Herring got the not-so-subtle hint. 'Yes, sir.' He left, closing the door quietly behind him, as was his way.

Connors sighed, leaned back in his chair and closed his eyes. Dear Lord, what a kerfuffle, with plenty to play for over the coming days. Ryan, he shook his head in wonder. He had underestimated the old codger: he would not do so again. And Kane, she had surprised him. He wondered idly how effective they might be in IA. Certainly it would suit Ryan, a man of his experience, and with Kane as his leg-woman ... It would take both of them off his hands too, which was no bad thing.

He sat up and sniffed the air.

Superintendent Connors opened the window behind his desk a crack and let the cold fresh air rush in. The unpleasant stench of Stall's aftershave thinned and eventually there was no trace of it at all.

63

Elliot woke up and stared at the ceiling. It was warm in the room, the sunlight streaming across his bed. He got up carefully and went to the bathroom, noticing that the pain that morning was not as bad as it had been, tolerable at least.

He'd take it.

He had a pee, washed his face and hands, found his robe on the back of the door and put it on, went downstairs and opened the kitchen door.

Ah, blissful silence.

He put the kettle on, made a cup of tea and a slice of toast – white, covered in butter, real butter. The phone rang as he was putting the last piece into his mouth.

'Hello?' Nobody spoke, but he could hear breathing on the line. 'Who is this?'

'You're a dead man, Ryan. You won't know the minute, you won't know the hour, but you're a dead man.'

They hung up.

Elliot replaced the handset and opened the fridge. Shona had done a little shop, nothing too fancy, but there were eggs. Humming under his breath, he made himself scrambled eggs on another slice of toast and relaxed.

If they were ringing him at home, they were suffering, and if they were suffering, all was right with the world.

He finished his breakfast, solved Wordle in three lines and went back upstairs to shower.

The call he had been expecting came through at eleven.

'All right,' Connors said. 'I will go to bat for you.'

'Thank you, sir.'

'Don't make me regret this, Inspector.'

'I will do my best.'

'Aye, that's what scares me. Monday, Inspector, report back for duty.' Connors hung up.

Elliot gave a little whoop and clenched his fist.

Let them threaten him, let them try to intimidate him all they liked. He knew who he was, he knew what he was.

He wasn't a coward.

And on that note, he called Margaret and agreed to meet her in the Phoenix Park for a walk. It wasn't ideal, but he had made promises and he intended to keep them.

64

Nola was waiting in the car for Elliot to finish paying for their petrol. She took a bite of Yorkie and chewed it while her thumb scrolled through Twitter. Something caught her eye, a name she recognised. She sat up straighter, pressed connect and read the first of several announcements.

'Socialite and model Amber Feenan was found dead in her apartment by her maid earlier this morning. Gardaí are not looking for a suspect. Miss Feenan, ex-wife to Investor Jools Byrne, was twenty-nine. She is survived by her mother, Irina, and her brother, Taddy.'

Elliot shuffled back towards the car. He sat in and handed her a bag of Haribo. 'Here,' he said. 'I got you the sour ones – I know you like them.'

'Thanks.' She tossed them on the dash.

Elliot frowned. 'Are you okay, Sergeant?'

'Amber Feenan died.'

'Ah.'

'That bastard broke her.'

'You refer to Jools Byrne?'

She nodded. 'She loved him more than anything in the world and he tossed her aside like rubbish.'

Elliot put on his seat belt. Nola started the engine and drove out of the garage. After a while she put the radio on.

'When you're driving, Sergeant,' Elliot reminded her gently, 'you get to pick the station.'

Nola did not reply, but she turned the music up. Elliot relaxed his head against his seat and allowed the 'Flower Duet' from *Lakmé* to fill the space.

It seemed fitting.

Acknowledgements

While She Sleeps is a culmination of shared work. From agent to editor, to author friends who, despite being hugely busy, took time to help and offer words of encouragement. To this end, thank you to Faith O'Grady, Ciara Considine and the team at Hachette Books Ireland. Special thanks to Emma Dunne for her wisdom and tireless creativity, she's a rare peach and this novel would not exist in its current form without her. Thank you to Liz Nugent, Adrian McKinty, John Connolly and Patricia Gibney for answering the call, from a professional and personal standpoint, your generosity warms the cockles of my heart. Thank you to the booksellers for all you do (especially Bob, because, just because). Thank you to the readers who I hope enjoy this novel and take pity on some of the characters.

I dedicate this novel to Jennie Ridyard, my darling friend, walker of dogs, drinker of wine, listening ear and kindest soul. You don't know what you mean to me, but trust me, whatever it is, it's to the moon and back.

And finally, as always, thank you to my family and friends, for everything and forever. I love you all dearly.

Arlene Hunt
June 2022